CHARMED TO DEATH

Sonoma Witches #4

GRETCHEN GALWAY

Eton Field

CHARMED TO DEATH

Eton Field, Publisher
www.gretchengalway.com

Cover design by Gretchen Galway
Stock art images: Depositphotos and Shutterstock

eBook ISBN: 978-1-939872-27-2
Paperback ISBN: 978-1-939872-28-9

v.20210205

Not for the first time, screaming fairies drew me out of my house in the middle of the night.

Who's dead now? I wondered, pulling up my hood to shield me from Northern California's first big storm of the season. After months of summer drought, the sky had finally opened—just in time for the winter solstice. Wishing I was wearing a bra, I jogged down the hilly street that led from my bungalow to the river. I was still in my pajamas, having only paused to pull on a raincoat and garden clogs.

The fairies' cries were coming from the Silverpool Bridge. A few voices were angry, but most were simply afraid. They didn't know my name, but the locals had learned there was one young, female witch nearby who could hear them, and I was flattered, though unhappy with the time and weather, to be summoned again.

My rubber shoes kept slipping out from under me on the wet road. Only my magic—a gravity spell enhanced with the redwood bead necklace I wore—kept me on my feet.

I paused at the stop sign on Main Street to catch my breath. Just across from me was the bridge over the Vago

River, already swelling with the sudden runoff. And right in the middle of the bridge, forming a Circle marked with glowing lanterns, was a group of people.

Witches. I took a moment to count them.

Nine.

No wonder the fae were alarmed. It looked like a Circle of Summoning, which at this time of year could only mean one thing.

I used my magic to amplify my voice. "What in Brightness are you doing?" I shouted. The rain was falling in diagonal sheets now. Not a drop for six months, then a flood.

The huddled figures on the bridge didn't reply, but one or two looked over at me, their worried faces lit from below by the lanterns. Worried, not angry or triumphant.

They weren't a serious threat.

I wiped the rain off my face with both hands and sighed. Something about the solstice made otherwise decent, law-abiding witches want to explore Shadow. Unfortunately, the fae didn't know these particular witches didn't have the heart or the skill to summon anything more dangerous than an extra gordo burrito at the taqueria down the street. The fairies were screaming as if a mob of demons was about to appear any second to consume them.

The loudest voice was coming from beneath the bridge where the river fairy hung out. I sent out a calming spell, hoping he'd quiet down. He'd spoken to me in the past— maybe my magic could touch him. His piercing cries were certainly touching my ears. Most people couldn't hear fairies; I didn't always appreciate my gift.

"Hey, you're scaring the fae," I told the witches.

"Who are you?" a voice shouted in challenge.

I paused. Some witches might use my name against me, but this crowd was too pitiful. "Alma Bellrose. I live here."

Maybe it was because of my nightgown-and-clogs getup, but they didn't seem intimidated by my presence.

I wiped the rain off my face again, tempted to go home and crawl back into bed. Where was Raynor? A high-profile Emerald witch and famous demon hunter, he'd arrived last week to take over the job as Protector. Keeping out witches like these tourists, as well as supernatural beings, was his job, not mine.

It was the most dangerous week of the year. With only six days until the solstice, fae from all over California had come to our remote village in the redwoods to celebrate at the magical Silverpool Wellspring. Right behind them, hungry for their spirit energy, were the demons. From the heaviness of the rain soaking my shirt, I expected the magical pool of water, triggered by floods, to appear any day now.

The witches began dancing around the blazing ring of candles. Humans weren't supposed to know there was a wellspring here, but obviously the word had gotten out. Events of the past few months must have led to rumors, and rumors led to silence spells being broken.

I gave up on home just yet and stepped out into the street to approach the bridge.

As I got closer, I saw the lanterns didn't even contain real flames. LEDs. With a weak show like that, the fae had nothing to worry about. Snorting to myself, I moved some of my power away from a defensive boundary spell to a rain-deflection spell.

A tall man stepped back from the Circle and pointed at me. "Stay away." His jacket was better than mine, with nonmagical brand markings that suggested he was a well-compensated, traditionally employed individual when he wasn't standing in a Sonoma County rural backwater in a rainstorm at midnight, trying to summon a demon.

I didn't slow down. "Evening," I said, stepping up on the

walkway that ran beside the road across the bridge. I was about ten feet away from the edge of the Circle. "Who are you?"

"Did you not hear me, foolish stranger?" the tall witch asked. "I told you to stay away."

"I feel the same," I said. My rain-deflection spell was working, and I appreciated how it kept the rain out of my eyes. I looked down at the LED lanterns, some still marked with price stickers getting soggy in the downpour. "Did you get those at Cypress Hardware?" I expressed my scorn in my tone of voice.

"Begone," another witch said. She was about my age, midtwenties, with a face heavily pierced with steel—lip, nose, eyebrows. Metal gave power, but from what I could feel from a scan, she hadn't had much to begin with.

They weren't going to do any real harm, but the fairies didn't deserve to be terrorized. I was pretty sure I had the power to overwhelm a few of them, but there were nine in total, and they had the passion of their stupidity to fuel them. I'd need help.

Rather than waste my time arguing, I touched my redwood bead necklace, drew from the power in the old tree, and cast a spell that hid me in darkness. It wouldn't have worked in daylight, but in the midnight rainstorm, it bought me a few minutes of cover, long enough to walk past them to the other side of the river.

From there it was a short walk on the shoulder to the driveway that led up the bluff to the Silverpool Vineyards. Raynor, the new Protector, had moved in last week. He must not have set up enough spells to alert him of strange activity in town or he'd be down here already. He hadn't arrived with any apprentices or assistants, either. He'd been demoted from his big job in San Francisco. Maybe he was sleeping because he was bitter about his reduced circumstances.

The private house next to the tasting-room building was at the top of the hill. I rang the doorbell, then sent a spell through the warded threshold to give him a more effective alarm. Sizzling light flashed, and I jumped back with a yelp at the sting.

Good boundary spell. I'd been at the house many times before, but that was a new one. I decided to give him time to come to the door before risking another jolt. He finally arrived a few minutes later, opening the door with a bleary bark of annoyance.

"Alma!" he said.

"Hi, Raynor." The rain continued to pour down. "Can I come in?"

"Demon's balls." He did not invite me inside. "What time is it?"

I huddled under the eaves and looked behind me, down toward the bridge. "Strange witches are in town. Freaking out the fae. Don't you hear them?"

Raynor was the only other witch I'd ever met who could also see and hear the fae, even when they didn't want us to. We'd learned it was because we'd had demon interlopers in our family trees. Mine was recent; his was a mystery, at least to me.

He stepped out onto the landing with me, his eyes widening as the sound of the piercing cries reached him. Rain pelted his bald head. He was an impressively large, muscular man, built like a Hollywood action hero, but that didn't stop his blue-and-white-checked pajamas from getting wet.

"What's the matter with them?" he asked, swiping the rain off his forehead.

"Some witches are trying to make a Summoning Circle."

"Demon's balls," he cursed, shaking his head. He stepped back into the house. "Hold on. I'll be right there."

"Wait! Don't leave me out here. Your boundary spell zapped me."

He called out over his shoulder, "Alma Bellrose, I invite you to enter" as he ran away into the house, his bare feet slipping on the tile. It was a rich man's ranch home, all modern lines, monochrome palette, hard surfaces. It was perfect for a metal witch who eschewed messy, earthy things. Quite in contrast to my woodsy cottage.

He reappeared a moment later in all black, denim and fleece, and strode past me to the closet. As I watched him pull on his boots, I thought about how strange it was to see Raynor, the former Director in San Francisco, live like a normal person.

"Let's go," he said, gesturing at the door. Polite witches usually didn't touch each other unless they were intimate friends or more.

I ducked back out into the rain and strode ahead, fantasizing about my warm bed. I'd left Random, my dog, snoozing on the quilt. Somehow he'd known this wasn't a walk he'd wanted to join.

With his long legs, Raynor walked faster than me, and I had to jog to keep up with him. We hit the bottom of the hill, then turned toward the bridge. I knew immediately something was wrong.

There was nobody there.

2

"Where did you say they were?" Raynor was striding faster, his head swiveling around as he cast scanning spells.

I cast a spell of my own, but felt no sign of them. Running alongside him, I peered through the dark at the bridge to see if they'd just turned off the lanterns, but no—it was empty. "They're gone."

He spun around to face me. "They're what?" Rain fell on his lips, making him spit.

"There were a bunch of them," I said. "Nine."

He pulled out a flashlight—nonmagical items had many benefits—and swept its beam across the bridge, road, and walkway. Then he aimed it at me. "Are you hexed?"

Recoiling from the light, I threw up a spell to extinguish the bulb. "Hey! You're blinding me."

"You're sure you saw—" he began.

"You heard the fae." I paused, realizing the unpleasant whine had stopped. "They're calm now."

"What did you do?"

"I didn't think it did anything," I said. "I sent a calming spell to the river fairy and told the witches to cut it out."

He walked to the center of the bridge, in the middle of the roadway, and squatted down with his hand extended, searching for magic fingerprints. "They were here."

"Of course they were," I said. "I didn't come to your house in the middle of the night for fun. The fairies were making it impossible to sleep. You should've been alerted too. Maybe your boundary spells are too strong."

He grunted and stood up. "Maybe," he said. "So where in Shadow did they go?"

I went over to the railing and looked down into the river, which was rushing from the new rain. Had they fallen in? Enough fae, when united in a common cause, could do unpredictable things.

"Well, that's your job, isn't it?" Turning, I smiled at him, proud my magic was keeping my face dry while his was shiny with pelting rain. "Good night, Protector."

"How many did you say there were?"

"Nine, I think. They had the elements of a Circle set up." I started walking toward my side of the river. "Other than the LED flames, it was textbook."

"LED? Seriously?"

"I know, right? Maybe somebody at Cypress Hardware store could tell you who bought them. I'm sure you'll see them around town."

He made a frustrated sound. "I don't want to see them. I want to block them. They're stirring up trouble, asking for demons to come here right when the wellspring is about to show up."

I stopped and turned to him. "That's the idea."

"I need your help. Tomorrow. And don't bother arguing —I've got a budget now. I can pay you."

"*Now* you have a budget? Didn't you have one before?"

"It was watched too carefully," he said. "But now I have a discretionary fund. I can pay fired Flint witches with Incurable Inabilities such as yourself whenever I want. And I want you now."

In spite of myself, a warm flush spread through me, which I ignored. My brain knew he didn't mean it romantically, but my body was stupid. And lonely.

More relevantly, however, my bank account was short on funds, and I was excited at the thought of remedying that situation. Selling magic beads wasn't a direct route to financial security.

"I'll tell you my rates," I said. "If you can afford me, I'll help you."

He nodded. "I knew the money would hook you." He turned away, casting a belated spell to shield himself from the rain. "I'll text you in the morning."

I watched him walk away for a moment, then turned and hurried back home. Although my face was dry, the rest of me was soaked, and garden clogs made terrible running shoes. I was cold and miserable when I reached the top of the hill where my house and two others perched on a bluff, surrounded by redwoods.

Just as I was passing the second house, my feet making squishy sounds in my shoes, the changeling Seth Dumont appeared in front of me, as dry as a cotton ball in a sauna.

"Did he believe you?" he asked.

I glanced at Seth, a handsome, dark-haired guy around thirty. Knowing he'd flirt if I showed how happy I was to see him, I kept walking. The house next door to mine was his, but just last week he'd said he was leaving town, and it had been dark all week. He and I had a long history but were now friends, or something in the neighborhood of friendship. The witches at the Protectorate, however, especially the ones guarding this town, wouldn't want him to be here. They'd kill him if they could.

"Yes, he believed me," I said. "I'm a very credible witch."

Seth fell in step beside me. "He probably felt their clumsy magic on the bridge."

"He would've believed me anyway," I said.

"I made sure I left some of it, just so he wouldn't think you were crazy."

Annoyance shot through me. He was the one who had done something to the witches instead of letting Raynor do it.

He was always teasing, testing, taunting me, but it was better not to show he'd gotten under my skin. Especially when it was cold and clammy, and I really, really wanted a hot shower. "Thanks," I said tightly.

"Aren't you going to ask if they're OK?"

My annoyance faded, and I couldn't help but smile. I'd learned to trust him with my life. For a supernatural villain, he had a heart of gold—even if he'd stolen it from a baby in Minnesota. "I'm sure they're fine," I said.

"You don't know that. I'm no better than a demon." He leaned close. "A monster."

I reached over and patted him on the arm. He wore an old-fashioned cable-knit sweater, perfectly dry. "Sure you are."

"My mother was a lake fae. I unlawfully possess the body of a human being whose spirit has now departed. Who knows what I'm capable of?"

This past summer, he'd been permanently severed from his original lake fae form when he was forced to kill his twin. Now he was a creature of mystery, neither human nor fairy, with unpredictable powers—and irresistible charm.

We'd reached the edge of my driveway. My protective boundary spells felt unpleasant to him, so I stopped. "I am glad you're back, Seth," I said, risking another pat, which made his eyes widen. "Whatever you did with them was probably better than they deserved." Then I turned and went back into my house, where my shower and dry, smart dog waited. I wasn't feeling quite so lonely anymore.

3

"There's a full-on campground forming out on the west side of town," Raynor said.

It was the next morning—not even nine, which meant I'd had far too little sleep—and he'd asked to meet me near the catering truck in the parking lot of Cypress Hardware. He was wearing a black leather jacket studded with silver, which gave him tremendous magical power and political authority.

Quite in contrast, I wore normal clothes, and only one of my redwood beaded necklaces was visible—not intimidating to anyone. Hidden in my pockets as usual however were a velvet bag, an extra strand of wood beads, a pair of empty glass vials, a sachet of healing herbs, and a tiny folding knife. My hearth witch kit couldn't compare with a Protectorate silver-studded jacket, but it worked for me.

The guy inside the truck waved at Raynor to pick up his order, and I was grateful to see the Protector return with two cups.

"They set up tents there last year, too," I said, taking one of the cups from him. "About four or five."

"There are ten times that many this year. We'll go check it out, walk around, and you can see if you recognize any of the witches from last ni—" He scowled at my arm. "Hey— did you always have those?"

Because my right hand had been on my necklace as I scanned the people around us, I'd taken the cup from him with my left. That had accidentally exposed the four thin, black tattooed arcs that went around my wrist. I'd been wearing bracelets to cover them, but that morning I'd gotten careless.

I pulled my jacket sleeve down. "They're nothing."

The most ineffective excuse ever made, but it was early in the morning and my brain hadn't gotten started.

"There didn't use to be so many," he said. "You had one or two. Why did you get more?"

I tested the tea, disappointed it was too hot to sip. "They started appearing this summer. I've learned they might be the marks of survival."

"You didn't put them there?" he asked.

I shook my head. "Have you heard of survival marks before?"

"In the old days, witches used to cast them on babies after they'd passed their first birthday," he said. "They'd get new ones every year after that."

"Right," I said. "That's what they are. I guess."

"Survival marks are spells cast by witches on their own offspring. They don't just appear randomly on adults."

I sipped the tea, risking a burn on my tongue. "It was transferred to me from another witch when he died."

Raynor, a ruthless demon hunter with a string of deaths behind him, grinned with pleasure. "You triumphed over a weaker witch and gained his mark," he said. "It's a battle trophy."

"I believe it's a near-death mark," I said. That's what another witch had told me recently.

"That makes sense. You've got"—he counted—"four? Have you killed four beings this year?"

"I haven't killed anyone."

"Yet a surprising number have died when they cross your path," he said, grinning again.

Unlike Raynor, I abhorred violence and didn't like to joke about it. "How many are camping on the outskirts of town?" I asked. From the line growing at the coffee truck, the population of the town had tripled since last week.

"Dozens. I can't believe how many witches have set up tents," he said. "Cooking pits. A latrine. It wasn't this bad before?"

"Every year attracted a few strangers, but they had the sense to lay low." I looked down the street at the newest shop in town: Silverpool Books. My friend Birdie, new to her witch powers and a recent inheritance, had just opened her doors, although she only had a few shelves so far. I could see her inside, setting out the few books she had in the window. I waved, but she didn't see me.

"Seems unlikely she could make a go of a bookstore in this town," Raynor said, following my gaze. "How many people live here—ten? Fifteen?"

He was only exaggerating because he was still sore about being assigned here. "There are at least five times that many. Maybe ten times."

"And it never sleeps," he muttered. "It's practically New York City."

"If you don't want to be here," I said, "why not quit? You could go freelance. Famous demon hunter like yourself could get lots of clients. Travel, set your own hours, choose your own adventure."

"I don't want to give those New York Emeralds and

Sapphires the satisfaction." He adjusted the silver buckles over his broad chest. "Let's get going. We'll take my wheels." He started walking toward a black sports car that would have trouble navigating some of the rural mountain roads in town, especially once the flooding started.

I got into the passenger seat, sank into the leather, and sipped my tea without telling him he'd buy something beefier with more road clearance and all-wheel drive within a month. It was best he enjoyed the process of discovery for himself.

"The Protectorate has had excellent wards around the wellspring for years, so I'm going to focus my boundary spells on the highway." The wellspring was on the west side of town, which was probably why the invading witches had set up camp nearby. They wouldn't know exactly where it was, but they would feel a concentration of magic. As for the wards being excellent—well, they weren't nothing, but I'd always been able to break through them.

"You might want to, uh, give those wellspring wards a boost," I said. He shot me a look, and I added, not about to confess anything, "Just in case."

He snorted, guessing my meaning. Unlike most Protectorate witches, he had a high opinion of my magical talents. "If only the stupid fairies didn't insist on coming here and causing so much trouble," he said. "If only we could block *them* out."

"Human beings are the problem. The fae just want to drink springwater and enjoy their existence under the stars."

He sighed and slapped the wheel. "It's bad enough having all these fae congregating in large numbers and attracting demons, but now we've got the stupid witches casting summoning spells." He stopped at the stop sign in the middle of town, scanned the sidewalk for menace—I could feel him draw on his magic, enhanced by the silver—and then hit the gas.

"What's the matter with people these days? They're so bored they think getting possessed by a demon would help them make great social media content?"

I studied him, his clear brown skin, smooth scalp, and relatively unlined face. I'd thought he was in his forties, but witches could hide their age pretty easily. "How old are you, Raynor?"

He laughed. "I sound like an old man, don't I? Get off my lawn."

Instead of laughing with him, I thought about his question: Why *would* witches want to be possessed by a demon? We were taught they would be more powerful than we could imagine, taking over our minds and souls, committing unspeakable acts of Shadow, shaming our families.

But there was another rumor: that a demon in human society could achieve unlimited wealth and power. Organized crime was littered with possessed humans. Fashion and politics, too. And most of all, corporate America. Seth had hinted once that if I wanted to find a demon in hiding, I should investigate the billionaires.

"Witches are just like other people," I said. "They get unhappy and look for cures outside themselves."

"Being tired makes me unhappy." He looked over at me. "I didn't get enough sleep last night, thanks to your nocturnal visit."

"You owe me," I said. "Those witches should never have been able to set up that Circle in the middle of town. You've got to be ready to act at any moment. You're the Protector. Protect."

We passed the small commercial section of town and drove along the river where a few weatherworn, wood-framed cottages were perched on stilts. "I'm better at killing."

"Maybe you'll get lucky and have the chance to do both at the same time."

"That's what the Sapphires in New York told me last week," he said. "But they're always making promises they can't keep."

I smiled. He wasn't as bloodthirsty as he wanted people to think. Like Seth, he had a Bright heart.

When we passed a turnoff for a narrow, private lane, we both held our breath and looked around, casting scanning spells for trouble. The wellspring was just off to our right in a seasonal ravine. Up the road was the house of a former friend of mine, now a vacation rental.

Several minutes later, we reached the outskirts of town. Raynor pulled the car over on the shoulder and peered up at the dark sky. The cloud cover was thick, but there wasn't any wind, suggesting the worst of the storm had passed for now.

"If we're lucky," he said, "it won't rain while we walk around the campground."

I got out of the car and sank up to my ankles in mud. My boots were waterproof, but the laces were going to be a mess when it dried. When I'd tromped over to the asphalt, I put my hand on the redwood pendant I'd chosen for the day and used a dry-water cleaning spell on both feet.

Raynor strode over and got between me and the road. "What in Shadow are you doing?"

I pointed at my now-clean boots. "You parked in a lake. I had to wash off the mud."

"They'll notice your magic," he said, gesturing at the open field up ahead where people congregated around tents, RVs, and other vehicles. "Not everybody can just casually throw spells around like that. We don't want them to know what you're capable of."

"Why not? Besides, they'll think it was you," I said. "The

Protector of Silverpool." I waved my fingers in the air for mock emphasis.

"We don't want them to know we're coming. We want them out of their tents where we can see them."

I saw his point. "Your silver jacket doesn't exactly blend in," I said.

He patted the rows of silver buckles, zippers, buttons, and studs. "I'll be under a cloaking spell. You're just a regular girl having a good time on a solstice vacation like all the other witches."

I sighed, wishing it were true. "Got it."

A few minutes later, we were walking through the field, but only I was visible to a casual viewer. Grateful somebody with enough magic had protected the ground from rain, leaving it relatively mud-free, I stepped through the grass and approached the rise where most of the tents had been set up. Smoke rose from several campfires, and somebody was playing a flute. I smelled bacon—most witches, who'd had an ancient history using animal parts for magic, had no interest in vegetarianism—and my stomach growled.

Right away, I spotted the witches from the night before. The white-haired woman with all the piercings was the one playing the flute. I wondered if all her face hardware, especially the lip stud, ever caused magical conflict with her sterling silver instrument.

Her audience was made up of—I counted—eight other witches, including the tall man I'd spoken to. He wore a red raincoat, unbuttoned, slung over his shoulders like a cape. Superwitchman.

I stopped and turned away, hiding my face from the group, and spoke to the invisible Raynor beside me.

"Flute girl and her friends," I said. "The tall one with the red jacket is their leader, I think. He acted like it last night."

"You're sure?"

"They kind of stand out," I said.

"OK, head back to the car. I don't want the others to know you work for me. It'll open at your touch."

Given the amount of money he'd promised to give me for my assistance, I didn't argue about him saying I worked for him, an arrangement I'd resisted passionately in the past. "Brightness be upon you," I whispered, walking away.

I didn't look back until I was in the car (I climbed in through the driver's seat) and picked up my tea, which had gone cold. Given his previous freak-out, I didn't use a quick warming spell, but drank it as it was. From a distance, I saw a bright flash, a second, weaker one, then nothing.

It was about fifteen minutes later when he returned to the car, his cloaking spell gone and amused disgust on his face.

"They had the nerve to argue," he said, leaning back in his seat with a sigh.

"What was the light?"

"Just a show of strength. They got the picture." He started the car and pulled a U-turn onto the road. "They drove up from the Bay Area. I'll tell the Diamond Street office to follow up."

As we drove back into Silverpool, I asked, "Did they mention what happened to them last night? How they... departed the bridge?" I was curious to know what Seth had done to them.

He gave me a wary glance. "What aren't you telling me?"

I shrugged and looked away at the river, which was bulging with rushing brown water. Just a few more feet until it overflowed its banks. "Just curious," I said lightly.

He snorted. "So he's back, is he? Tell him I'm under orders to execute him."

My stomach tightened. It had been months since Seth had come to Silverpool; I thought Raynor would let him be.

I closed my eyes. Many times before, I'd told Seth to leave Silverpool for his own safety, but he'd ignored me. Even when I told him what Raynor had just said, he'd brush it off and do whatever he liked, just as before.

Raynor cleared his throat. "Don't get upset. I won't do it unless I have to."

"That's comforting," I said, my voice wavering.

"He can leave. If he's got the power to apparate nine resistant, albeit pathetic witches several miles, he's got the power to exist elsewhere."

But he wouldn't. "You'd think," I said.

"Listen…"

I braced myself for more threats on Seth's life, but Raynor said, "I've got another job for you."

4

"There's going to be a meeting in Berkeley tomorrow night." He tapped the wheel with the many rings on his fingers. "I want you to go."

My stomach fell. Leaving Silverpool meant losing some of my power, which was increasingly amplified by my house. "What kind of meeting?" Though with Berkeley witches, I could guess. Something alternative, earth-based, and slightly nuts.

"It's a Shadow gathering of the demon-curious," he said.

"In Berkeley? But they're usually more interested in hearth magic," I said. Then admitted, "Like me."

"There's a long history of kitchen witches seeking possession by demons," he said. "This group has been meeting for years. The Protectorate knows about it but doesn't take them seriously."

"So why send—"

"I want you to memorize the faces, come back home, and let me know if any of the witches from that meeting show up here," he said. "Just like you did today. It worked beautifully."

The thought of leaving Silverpool now made me extra uncomfortable because it meant leaving Seth alone with Raynor. "Berkeley's at least two hours from here," I said. "It's too far to go there and back at night. I won't drive through the forest in the dark, not this time of year." The fae went crazy, trying to lure drivers off cliffs, into trees, down into ravines.

"Stay over. Come back in the morning," he said.

We drove past Birdie's bookstore. Inside, several people were already looking at the books she'd set in the window. With all the wellspring tourists in town, maybe she'd actually make some money.

"They'll see I'm not one of them," I said. "I can hide for a few minutes, but not for an entire meeting full of old, clever, suspicious witches like those types."

"They won't notice if you go in your other form," he said.

Oh no. My nose began to itch just at the thought of turning into a cat. It would've been an amazingly useful gift —if I wasn't allergic. Every time I shifted into cat shape, I spent hours in upper respiratory distress, all-body itching, and violent sneezing. I even lost the use of my brain for a while.

"I'm useless in cat shape," I said. "I don't know my own name for several hours after I shift."

"So if you shift early in the day, you'll have time to adjust," he said.

He had an answer for everything. "It makes me sneeze."

"I'll pay you twice what I paid you today," he said.

I closed my eyes. That would buy a lot of Benadryl. "I'll think about it."

He turned left at the bridge to go up the hill to my house. Belatedly I thought of telling him to just drop me off there and I would walk, preventing any chance of him running into Seth, but I missed my chance to look casual about it.

"When you go," he continued, "make sure you wear the copper ring. If any witches have an amulet that can read demonprint, it'll be one of those people. That's what they want for themselves, after all."

Sinking in my seat, I casually—uselessly—covered my left hand with my right. He'd given me a copper ring to hide my demon ancestry—a precious gift. Unfortunately, the copper ring was no longer in my possession. I'd used it to pay for a wish from the genie at Cypress Hardware. A heroic act, one that saved lives and property, but... he might be annoyed about it. Furious, even. My stomach clenched into a fist.

"Where is it, by the way?" he asked, pulling off the road before he reached my driveway. Like Seth, he found the boundary spells around my property line to be unpleasant, especially since the time Willy, my resident gnome friend, had expelled him by force.

I popped open the door and said lightly, as light as a fairy's wings, "Somewhere safe." What could be safer than a genie? He'd know if I lied to him, so I had to tread a careful line. "I haven't said I'll take the job."

He took out his phone and tapped it a few times. "I'm sending you what I owe you for today with an advance for tomorrow. It'll help you make up your mind."

"Raynor, I'm not a total mercenary. I've got a code I have to follow. You can't just throw money—"

He leaned over the seat and gave me a rare smile. "Alma, my dear, if there's one thing I know it's that you have a moral code." His brown eyes met mine, and I softened, suddenly aware of the deep connection we shared. Both of us had lost favor with the Protectorate; both of us shared the dangerous gift of demonprint. And when there was a choice between breaking the rules and doing what was right, I trusted him to make the right one.

I didn't tend to get close to people. It had taken a supernatural emergency to help me open my heart to Birdie's friendship. Because I'd moved so much as a kid, had a criminal father, and had attended a string of boarding schools, I'd learned to keep to myself.

And the last man I'd slept with had turned up dead on the Silverpool Bridge just down the street, which hadn't made me eager to rejoin the dating scene.

But Raynor was unique…

The roar of an engine broke the moment. We both spun around to look at an approaching white motorcycle. The rider was a woman in tight leathers, generously adorned with rhinestones, and a helmet that alternated between all colors of the rainbow.

She pulled up beside the car, dismounted, and strode over to the driver's side door. The color-changing spell she'd used on her helmet continued even after she pulled it off her beautiful, raven-locked head and set it on the roof of Raynor's car, which meant it was a strong one to persist after losing contact with her body.

"Found you, darling," she said, leaning down to Raynor and kissing him through the open window.

It went on for a while.

My face felt hot, and I hoped both of them were too busy with each other to notice the telltale flush on my skin. I told myself to be grateful; her arrival had snapped me out of a moment of temporary insanity.

Well, no reason to dawdle. I slammed the door, called out, "Talk to you later, Raynor," and turned to go inside.

They kissed another few seconds before Raynor said, finally getting out of the car, "Hold on, Alma. I want you to meet Kelly. She's moved into the winery with me." He turned to her. "Haven't changed your mind now that you've seen the place, have you?" His voice held a tone I'd never heard from him before. It was magical, but not the witch kind.

"It's just what I need, Ray. Perfect." She kissed his cheek and turned to regard me. "I'm sorry, what was your name again?"

I smiled, clenching my teeth. It wasn't jealousy. I just didn't like her. "It's not important," I said. Giving my name was a courtesy, and I didn't think she'd asked me respectfully.

"Alma Bellrose," Raynor said. "Alma, this is Kelly Tucker. She's a writer." We didn't shake hands, which was always safer with witches. Too easy to give something away about yourself.

The name did sound familiar. I looked at her jewelry more closely. Her necklace was amethyst, her rings an assortment of precious stones—turquoise, obsidian, garnet, topaz. "You wrote the book on North American rocks, isn't that right?" I asked.

For the first time, she gave me a genuine smile. "That's right. *American Superstones.*" She gave Raynor a suspicious look. "Did you tell—?"

"Nope. She's just full of surprises." He smirked at me. "Aren't you, Alma?"

"I'm really quite ordinary, as you can see." I scratched my neck. "Nice to meet you, Kelly. I've got to—"

"Oh, what musical wood sprites you have here," she said suddenly, looking up into the trees. "They sound nothing like the fae in Golden Gate Park. And they're tinier. Almost like butterflies. The ones in San Francisco are so big. Ugly, really."

The air went out of my lungs. She had the sight? That meant...

"Kelly has traced her demonprint to a great-great-grand-father," Raynor said.

"And I think my great-grandmother on my paternal line

as well," she said proudly. "I remember now. Raynor told me about your gift. It's such a relief, isn't it? To be able to talk freely with your own kind?"

I didn't feel particularly relieved. In fact, I felt sweaty and tense. Why had Raynor told her about me? Who else had he told? Just because we shared the trait didn't mean he had the right to tell others. It could mean exile, imprisonment, or death for witches to be associated with demon possession. That was one reason it was so shocking for the visiting witches in Silverpool to be summoning them. But for some people, the thrill of power, even evil power, was always tempting.

"I really do need to go," I said. "Excuse me."

Before Raynor could mention the job again, I hurried away, so eager to be inside that I used the front door instead of walking down the driveway to the back the way I usually did. I shut the door and leaned against it, drinking in the strength of my home's walls.

When the motorcycle rumbled back to life, I didn't even risk peeking out the window to watch her go. My pulse was racing, unhappy with the new development. No—unhappy with Raynor. The more people who knew my secret, the less safe I was.

My dog Random ran through the house from the kitchen to greet me, surprised I'd used a different door than usual. I stroked his black fur, mumbling affectionate things and drinking in the comfort of his presence.

My phone vibrated in my pocket; I took it out and saw a text from Raynor.

"*You can trust her,*" he wrote.

I didn't reply. I peeked out the window and saw his car still sitting out front.

"*You had no right,*" I typed.

"*I didn't mean to tell her. She's*"—the words stopped, then began a moment later—"*stronger than I thought. All those rocks I guess.*"

That was supposed to make me feel better? If she was strong enough to get secrets out of an Emerald witch, a former Director and current Protector, she was strong enough to trick him into trusting her.

The loss of my copper ring was suddenly more dangerous than I'd realized. It was the only magic I knew that would hide my demonprint from other witches. I couldn't afford anyone else discovering the truth of my family tree.

I'd have to see if I could get it back from the genie.

Today.

❧ 5 ❧

The genie lived at Cypress Hardware, which she owned and managed. To get my ring back from her, I'd have to find something of equal or greater value to trade.

My most precious objects were stored in my living room, so after I'd watched Raynor drive out of sight, I walked over to my massive, twentieth-century steel file cabinet. Putting my hand on my redwood necklace, I sent a key of power into the canister lock, then spoke the password.

"Peach pie with vanilla ice cream," I whispered. Every week I changed the words, but it was always something delicious.

The bottom drawer began to shake, and I felt my knees weaken as my power drained out of me to open the most powerful lock. Finally the drawer slid forward, and icy-cold smoke wafted up from the opening.

Sinking to the floor, I took a deep breath, nuzzling Random, who had come over to hang out, until I felt strong enough to continue.

Inside the bottom drawer were a few pieces of metal

jewelry I'd saved from my years at the Protectorate, several velvet pouches with organic items that a stickler might call illegal, my old baby blanket, a black-market book of spells I'd bought in high school, and a few vials of wellspring water.

It wasn't safe to store the springwater in large quantities, which was why the fresh source attracted so much trouble, but I'd begun to make sure I always had some on hand. It was valuable for trades, although it wouldn't be useful with the genie this time of year, given the solstice was only days away and the river already on the verge of overflowing.

I rifled through my other treasures to find something else the genie might value. The baby blanket wasn't for sale. The metal was too insignificant for her. The spells, useless; I wasn't even convinced they worked. And the velvet pouches of organic material seemed unlikely to be of interest for anyone but a hearth witch, or maybe a serial killer. (I hadn't ever hurt anyone, but some items, disgusting but preserved, were a powerful backup magic source for a witch on her own.)

I closed the cabinet drawer and reset the spells. Unfortunately, I was going to have to ask the genie her price. She'd been fair in the past; maybe she'd be reasonable. Terrifying, but reasonable.

My phone rang again, and I took it out to see Helen Mendoza's name on my screen.

Now *she* was a creature who was not reasonable. She was a woman old enough to be my grandmother—and with her white hair and cluttered Victorian house in San Francisco, she certainly looked like one—but Helen was a crafty hearth witch who collected secrets, manipulated others, and struck hard bargains.

And I owed her. Worse, she was growing impatient with my failure to pay up. Two weeks ago, in exchange for her help, I'd promised her my magic staff made from a redwood beam in my house. It was my most powerful magic object, and I'd been desperate to offer it to her.

But then the Protectorate took it as evidence after a deadly battle with another witch, and they hadn't given it back. Raynor had been kicked out of his job before returning it to me, and now it was locked up in the office on Diamond Street—which happened to be next door to where Helen lived, very annoying to all parties—and they weren't taking my calls.

"Hello, Helen!" I said cheerfully.

"Where's my staff?"

"I told you. The Protectorate has it. They confiscated it after that little trouble we had here a week or two ago. Maybe you remember it." I paused for emphasis. "I almost *died*?"

"All I care about is you're not dead and you owe me," she said.

"I'll call again," I said. The Flint-level trainee agents at the Diamond Street office hung up as soon as they heard my voice, but I'd keep trying.

"If you don't settle your debt, your life will be forfeit," she said.

I laughed—perhaps a little nervously. Even Helen wasn't that greedy. "The solstice is days away. How about I bring you fresh wellspring water, as much as you like?"

"Too dangerous. I don't want any demons here sniffing around. The vials I have are enough."

"I'll come down to the city and ask the new Director personally."

"He's a pencil-pushing bore," she said. "He'll find a reason to keep it for himself."

I rubbed my eyes, starting to panic. There had to be something. Jewelry? She'd be unimpressed. Home-baked cookies? Even more unimpressed.

"What do you want me to do?" I asked finally.

Her tone brightened. "Now we're talking," she said. "I want you to go to a witch meeting tomorrow night. It's in Berkeley."

❧❦❧

A SHIVER RAN down my neck. "Berkeley," I repeated.

"I want an account of the magic they talk about," she said. "The headliner is supposed to reveal some new secret and what have you. It's probably bunk, but I need to make sure. I can't have Nellie trying to hold anything over me, and she's going to be there."

"Who's Nellie?" I asked, distracted by the sensation tingling through my body. First Raynor, now Helen. It couldn't be a coincidence. Either I had to go to this meeting in Berkeley or I'd really, really better not.

"Don't worry who Nellie is. She's just one of many witches who think they can know more than me," Helen said. "They never succeed, of course."

I put my hand on my stomach, feeling the hole opening up there. Was it telling me that something important was going to happen tomorrow night or that I'd had a stressful year, and one more adventure just might break me for good?

"I need to think about it," I said softly.

"No, you need to decide right n—"

I hung up on her and turned off the phone. Then I stretched out on the floor against Random, who had fallen asleep next to me, and tried to get a handle on the message in my gut. Fear? Fate?

After a few minutes, the strongest message was hunger, so I had lunch. I would need my strength to face the genie.

I set out for Cypress Hardware on foot. Although the rain had begun again, it was only a light drizzle, and I'd decided it was bad for me and the environment to be using my Jeep for short trips. There was also the danger Jen Bardak, the genie, might take it as payment, and I didn't want to tempt her. I couldn't afford a new car right now.

I did bring some jewelry, however, just in case she might value it. Genies were unpredictable. When I got to the store, I paused just inside the sliding doors and made a silent wish for her company. Then I draped a cedar-beaded bracelet over the antler of an animatronic reindeer. Christmas was next week, and the store had the usual displays of holy lawn herbivores, inflatable cartoon characters, next to colorful lights, gift supplies, and candy.

The figure that came to greet me near the reindeer, however, was a man I'd never seen before. He wore the dark green vest of a Cypress employee and came at me with an aggressive stride, as if he'd seen me pocket a bag of chocolates.

"Can I help you?" he asked, a tight smile on his lips. His name tag said, to my surprise, NICO, STORE MANAGER.

Store manager? I'd thought the genie did everything herself. "Hi, are you new?" I asked.

His expression was frozen in the false smile. "What brings you to Cypress today?"

"I'd like to talk to Jen," I said. "She knows me."

His scan struck me like a bucket of ice water, cold and unwelcome. I sucked in my breath and took a step back while his magic picked over and through me. I defended myself lightly, letting him see enough of my nature to realize I wasn't a threat. Maybe with all the strange witches in town, buying up all the LED lanterns and whatnot, she'd instructed Nico to play defense.

"She's very busy today," he said. "Why don't we see what I can help you with?"

Other customers, witch and nonmag, were coming in through the doors and having to maneuver around us to get their shopping carts. I tried to move deeper into the store to get out of the way, but Nico blocked me. I regretted dropping my offering near the door instead of near the summer clearance section, which was farther from the exit.

Although it would force me to spend everything I'd brought with me before even getting a chance to negotiate for the copper ring, I took out my newest necklace, with redwood needles dipped in springwater, and flung it into the gift bag of a giant, inflatable Santa. Then, ignoring Nico, I said aloud, "Please, Jen. I wish we could talk in person."

Nico closed his eyes for a long moment, then looked at me and jerked his head to the side. "Garden center."

As I walked past him, I resisted the urge to gloat, though I did give him an ice-water scan of my own. I marked him as a witch, of course, but not a metal one. Potions would be my guess. His clothing, even the vest, had been soaked in materials I didn't recognize. Liquids made from interesting things in interesting ways. Strange.

My spirits lifted as I walked through the store to the outdoor nursery at the far end. The genie's choice of location for meeting me was a hopeful sign. She knew I was an earthy type and that all the plants would make me happy. Nico's hostility wasn't coming from her.

"Hello, Alma!" Jen called out from my left. She was unpacking boxes of spring daffodil bulbs, setting them on a side shelf. "Lovely touch with the springwater." She put a hand on the necklace that I'd just given to Santa; it was now around her throat.

Jen Bardak was a tall, strongly built woman who appeared to be forty or fifty, with short black hair and heavy eye makeup. She wore jeans under a red poncho, and large, glittering snowflake earrings dangled from her ears.

Because she appreciated direct speech, I came right out with my request. "I have been thinking about getting my copper ring back," I said, careful not to use the *w* word. Sometimes she came up with her own price for a wish and took it without asking.

"You mean this one?" she asked, holding out her hand. The ring, just a simple band, was on her index finger, invisible if you weren't looking for it.

"Yes, that's the one I was thinking about."

"You've already emptied your pockets," she said.

"Your guardian saw to that."

She smiled, and her red poncho turned into a green vest just like Nico's. Then I saw the store manager's name tag—it was his actual vest. "Isn't he great? Only a few days and he's already proving himself quite useful."

"Is that his role? To raise your prices? Make your services out of reach?"

She wagged a finger at me. I watched the copper ring sway back and forth. "Every item between these walls is a service. You think a town this size could support a retail establishment of this magnitude without my help?"

I bowed my head, regretting my accusation, which had only made negotiating more tense. "Sorry. He surprised me. I hope we can do business."

She kicked aside the box of bulbs and strode over to a velvet divan that had suddenly appeared next to a display of poinsettias. She sat, reclining into gold-tasseled cushions, then patted the puffy seat next to her.

I paused, then walked over slowly and perched on the opposite end. "I was hoping we could negotiate in an abstract way at first so I don't find myself living on a pallet behind the grocery store. If you don't mind."

Her eyes narrowed. "I'd hoped your understanding had evolved beyond those nasty stereotypes, Alma."

"Yes, yes. Of course, of course." I wiped my sweaty palms on my knees, afraid again I'd offended her. Like me, her powers were enhanced by her dwelling. Unlike me, those powers seemed godlike. "Theoretically, what could I offer you in exchange for the ring?"

"Theoretically," she repeated.

I nodded, swallowing over my dry throat.

She stared at me, her hair now in a severe updo. The vest and jeans had been replaced with a tailored black pantsuit. My redwood-and-springwater necklace rested on an off-white silk blouse. Her aura of unwavering power made me feel half her size—and then I realized I was, in fact, half her size. Ten feet tall, she towered over me.

I gave up pretending to be chill and jumped to my feet, ready to run out the emergency exit behind the dormant fruit trees. It was no use trying spells against her; she was in another league.

And then, in a blink, she was just a normal-sized middle-aged lady in a green polyester vest with a badge that read "ASK ME ABOUT OUR PAYMENT PLANS."

She said, "Sorry, kiddo, please have a seat."

Holding my hands together to stop them from shaking, I took a deep breath, swallowed, and sank back down on the divan. My heart was beating against my ribs the way I would've been beating against the emergency doors to get out if she hadn't backed down.

"It just so happens there is one thing you could do for me," she said warmly, patting my knee. "You see, there's this meeting in Berkeley tomorrow night..."

❧ 6 ❧

The next day I was on the road to Berkeley.

Once I'd heard the third request to attend the meeting, I'd known it was fate. Whether or not it was going to kill me, I had no choice but to walk into it willingly. At least that way I could prepare.

"What do you want me to do there?" I'd asked the genie.

"That will be obvious when you're there," she'd replied. "When you feel an urge to do something, listen to it."

As a human being, my entire existence was made up of urges. I hoped I would recognize the particular urge when it struck.

I'd agreed to try, and she'd given me the ring. I wore it now on a short chain around my neck.

Raynor had been smug when I told him I'd accept the job, but that couldn't be helped. Helen, in San Francisco, would give me a place to stay the night after the meeting as long as I swore to share every scrap of information I gathered. And as she'd done before, my friend Birdie took in Random, who was happy to make new friends at the blossoming bookstore.

The rain in western Sonoma County was replaced by a light mist when I drove over the Richmond Bridge, and even though it was a Friday morning in December, the San Francisco Bay held a few sailboats. Sea fairies trailed behind, leaping like dolphins in their wake and shooting glistening patterns of light into the sky. I had to grip the steering wheel and mutter a concentration spell to keep my attention on the road. Someday, I told myself, I'd come back and enjoy the show properly.

The traffic along the bayshore to Berkeley was a slog, and when I finally found a quiet, semi-industrial street in the flats, about a half mile from the meeting where I could park the Jeep, I was in a bad mood.

Mostly I was dreading the next six hours. When I was in an emergency, such as being chased by hostile fae or humans, my survival instincts kept my human thoughts somewhat functional. But just casually turning into a cat on a quiet morning? I had no idea what would happen. I did know, however, that come sundown, I would need to be in cat-walking distance from the meeting. Which meant I was going to have to lock myself inside my own car to prevent my cat body from going anywhere.

And *that* meant I had to set up—nose wrinkling—a litter box in the back. I'd placed an enchanted, potted sword fern on the passenger seat to keep the cabin cool and oxygenated, but if there was a spell to prevent a cat from discharging waste for six hours, I hadn't discovered it.

With a sigh, I sat behind the steering wheel, gave it an affectionate pat, locked the doors, cracked the window an inch, made sure the potted fern was working its magic, and then, reminding myself of the fate that called me, shifted into a cat.

I immediately forgot everything. Who in Shadow had locked me in here? I found a few treats, which made me feel better, but I really hated the grainy sand in the box—garden soil was much better—and the fern tasted terrible.

It was four o'clock when I finally had the wits to read the clock on the dash. I stopped clawing at the seat—my poor seat—and jumped into the back to get a clear look of the street behind me. The meeting was around the corner, six blocks toward the hills. Other witches might be parking here, just like me, to avoid being seen. I watched the few passersby until it was time to go.

With my human consciousness, I remembered the spell to open the window long enough for me to jump out. After it snapped back into place behind me, I sauntered up the sidewalk to the meeting house.

The sun was just setting, and cold, damp wind blew off the bay, ruffling my fur. I trotted eagerly to the warmth of a witch's house, even if the people gathered there were dangerous. I was a cat. They were beneath me.

The house was an old two-story Craftsman with a weedy front yard behind an arbor. As I got closer, more witches appeared on the sidewalk, striding in mixed disguises alongside me: college student, homeless man, businesswoman, mom with stroller, another homeless man, a delivery driver, woman walking a gray pit bull.

I avoided the last. The dog knew what I was and pulled at the leash to—I wasn't sure what it would do. Love me? Eat me? I didn't want to find out.

I crept into the yard and through the garden to the back where a door was open for the gathering. There I paused, listening to my human and cat senses—was it safe to enter? Other witches were tapping their noses at the threshold, and I felt a surge of delicate magic as each passed inside. I watched several more come and enter until I decided it was an invitation boundary, not a filter. They wanted witches to come to the meeting; they wanted their life choices to attract others, to spread. They were evangelical about their possession-seeking.

I slipped inside and found myself rubbing up against the legs of the people lining up to take a seat. Witch bodies felt good, all tingly and warm from the magic. More than one person bent down to pet me, which was even better. Later I would be ashamed of myself for being so promiscuous, but it had been so long since I'd been petted. I thought of Raynor and Seth, then jumped up into the lap of a blond man with a short beard. *Pet me, Blondie.* He obliged.

"Hello, chonky kitty," he said. Though his fingers felt good, I didn't appreciate the editorializing. I jumped off to find somebody else.

Remembering my duties, I turned back to get a good look at his face and then around at the other witches who greeted, ignored, or avoided me. Some were old, some young. Even though the crowd had gathered for an illicit topic, they were still traditionalists when it came to their magic amulets—mostly metals like silver and gold, some copper. Very few with jute, leather, bone, and wood like me.

I never would've expected so many ordinary-looking people to be interested in having their bodies taken over by an evil Shadow spirit. What was the matter with them? I'd had a terrible childhood, but even I didn't want to be possessed by a demon.

The meeting space took up the entire ground floor, probably created by knocking out the old walls and using magic to keep the upstairs from caving in. The ceiling bulged slightly, and I eyed it warily. A kitchen was on one side, open to the room, with bubbling pots on the stove. That might have been for atmosphere; I didn't smell meat cooking. Couches and chairs were arranged in a circle around a wide, square coffee table. It was the speaking platform.

As I wandered around, I counted three dozen people.

There were also four dogs, three birds (a parrot, a cockatiel, and a raven), an iguana, too many cats to count, a white rat, and a tank of freshwater fish.

If any of the animals were humans in disguise, I wouldn't be able to recognize them later. But remembering the human faces would be easy; I'd put a memory charm in my catnip.

The meeting began, and I walked to the front of the seats and sat to watch. Now I'd work on paying my debt to Helen. Every foolish, dangerous, or interesting word that was spoken, I would have to absorb and memorize for sharing in a few hours when I went to her house to spend the night.

A fortysomething woman in purple leggings and a T-shirt, carrying a candle as big as a bottle of cabernet sauvignon, climbed up on the coffee table in the middle of the circle. The crowd, chatting and eyeing each other, ignored her until she tapped the candle with her finger and it burst into sparkling flames. As all eyes turned to her, she lofted it over her head and began to chant.

Around me, the other witches joined in, some loudly and some softly, but in unison. There were no words, just *ah* and *oh-ra* repeated over and over.

Creeped out, I licked my paw to soothe myself. The woman on the table stopped with a final *ah!* and then lowered the candle. Closing her eyes, she blew out the flame —but instead of being extinguished, the flame raced up the current of her breath and disappeared into her mouth.

I stopped licking and watched, my paw frozen in midair, as she clamped her lips together over what was obviously painful, just as one would expect a mouthful of fire to be. Smoke puffing out her nostrils, her eyes wept agonizing tears.

Uncomfortable with her suffering, I dropped my gaze to her shirt. The basic white tee held a black, circular image I'd never seen before, some kind of distorted yin-yang symbol. Instead of the balance of black inside white and vice versa, there was mostly black with a small teardrop of white. And inside the white teardrop was a large black circle, disproportionate to the original design.

My interpretation was that the Shadow had expunged the Bright, and inside the Bright was even more Shadow. I looked around the room and saw the symbol repeated on other shirts, even a baseball cap.

Is this what they thought demon possession would be like? Fun enough to get its own logo? They acted as if it was a sport, with hats and shirts showing what team they were on.

They had the wrong idea. The black-or-white depiction was false. Demons weren't all Shadow—in fact, like my friend Seth, not all creatures the Protectorate called demons were actually demons. Supernatural spirits who possessed the human mind were a diverse, complex group of individuals.

But I couldn't blame these witches for not knowing that;

it was what they'd been taught. My nuanced perspective had formed over the past year from personal experience, and I was still finding it hard to accept.

The witch with the mouthful of flames suddenly gasped. A little cloud of fire about the length of a banana sputtered out her mouth, then vanished. There was no smoke, just a blur in the air where the fire had been.

She smiled—I studied her lips, a little disappointed they weren't blistered—spinning around to wave at the gathered witches, who clapped politely. Perhaps they'd seen her trick before. I resumed paw-licking but made sure I'd memorized the witch's face. If she came to Silverpool, I'd recognize her.

She began speaking about how stupid it was the group had to meet in secret. How stupid the Protectorate was to restrict knowledge, which was the birthright of every witch. How stupid it was that witches feared possession by an immortal spirit when such a union would be the ultimate experience available to human consciousness.

The attention of the crowd wandered. To try to bring them back in, she raised her voice and began repeating herself—"Birthright! It's our birthright!"—until an older woman standing next to the table swatted her legs with an umbrella. The speaker jumped and spun around, then saw who had hit her and fell silent. With a sigh, she reached out a hand and helped the old lady up on the table with her.

The older woman pushed the fire-eating witch off the table, took out a phone, and began to read aloud from its screen. By the third sentence, I recognized the *Book of Herbes and Remedies for Young and Olde*, which I had in hardback on my own shelf at home. It was a great resource but not exactly theatrical.

The audience around me groaned, and a murmur of voices grew into full-out rebellion of the program on offer.

The woman on the table didn't seem to mind if anyone listened to her or not.

"Can't anyone stop her from doing that every time?" a woman behind me asked, barely trying to lower her voice.

"It's her house," a man replied. "She does what she likes."

Eventually the house owner stopped reading about ceanothus sachets, pointed her umbrella toward the kitchen, and a gong rang out. Most of the witches got to their feet, some clapping politely, and walked over to get a drink and a snack. My cat nose smelled springwater punch, which was extravagant, but explained the large turnout. And as for it being too dangerous to serve such a large quantity of springwater—well, these witches actually wanted demons to come calling.

The couple behind me didn't get up for the refreshments.

"I wish they'd get to the point," the woman said, scratching my ears. "Nobody needs to convince *us*."

"Randy's going to talk next," the man said. They were young for the crowd, looking college-aged. I was enjoying the petting too much to turn my head and study their faces, but I'd seen them when I'd walked around. "He knows a witch who knows another guy's sister who saw an old book on possession. The Protectorate would never admit it exists, of course."

"If it's the one with all the doom and gloom, I've already read it." Her delicious fingernails found a great spot on my left cheek. "Lionel makes sure everyone cracks it open if they use his library."

The man lowered his voice. "Careful. He's here tonight. See? In the back."

"I didn't say anything to be afraid of," she muttered.

"The book you saw isn't the one Randy's talking about," he said. "Everyone knows Lionel has that one. It's a different book. They're a set."

"I've heard about that one too," the woman said. "It's

43

called *Temptations*. It's a rundown of all the bennies of possession. Historical human awareness, apparition, psychological influence—even things we can't imagine."

"No, it's not that one either."

"I'm pretty sure that's the other book in the set," the woman said. "One warns you, one tempts you."

"No, no. There's a *third* one." The man's voice lowered. "The one that tells you *how*."

"Randy saw it?"

"No, somebody he knows."

She scoffed. "Right. His sister's cousin's friend or whatever."

"Relax. I'm just telling you what I heard."

The gong was sounded again, and everyone returned to their seats. The couple behind me fell silent and leaned back in their chairs. Sadly the scratching came to an end, but it allowed me the willpower to turn and look for a guy who might be named Lionel. There were dozens of people, half male, and I had no idea who they were talking about.

Randy, however, was probably the man who next jumped up on the coffee table. If his red hair hadn't been cut so short and his face clean-shaven, he would've looked exactly like an actor in a historical Viking drama. Almost as big as Raynor, but with a ginger's coloring. And bright blue eyes.

To my shame, I began to purr.

"I'm here to announce the book *Instructions* has been spotted!" he shouted, lifting his arms.

The gathering perked up. I heard a woman whoop. The man behind me clapped. A dozen voices asked *What? Where? Who?*

"The tome is in California, that I can swear to you," Randy said, pointing at one of the witches who'd spoken up. "I was unable to acquire it myself, but there are those I trust who say it's nearby."

There was a long silence. Randy's smile wavered.

After the pause stretched on, the woman behind me shouted, "That's it? How's that supposed to help *us*?"

Randy frowned at her, massaging his hands together, fiddling with the rings on his fingers. He wore a lot of metal, mostly platinum. A wealthy witch. "Nobody knew if the stories were true," he said. "Now we do."

A man from the other side of the circle called out, "All we know is you're standing up there and you don't have any book in your hand."

A chorus of voices shouted their agreement. Randy spun around, scowling at the people gathered all around him. "Do you need everything spoon-fed to you? Who do you think demons will choose—witches too lazy to solve problems for themselves or those who show initiative?"

That seemed to hit home. The crowd quieted, and Randy continued.

"I didn't have to share this knowledge with you, but I made the oath to do so," he said. "Did all of *you* take the oath? Or are you just parasites on the body of knowledge we collect here?"

The witches looked around the room, some sheepishly. One middle-aged guy said, "Thank you, Randy," and stood to clap. A few others joined in.

"Demon's eyebrows," the woman behind me muttered. It was a sanitized version of the curse. I'd only ever heard it used around children.

"Thank you, Randy!" the guy behind me shouted. He stood and joined the others who were clapping.

Helen would definitely be interested in hearing about a magic book on possession. One of three. The entire topic made me want to vomit—my own mother had been possessed, and me born during the horrible time—but I'd promised to acquire every secret that was shared. It was probably nothing, because rumors were always going around about magic that turned out to be nothing, but it could be Helen's problem to figure it out.

Randy got off the table, and the owner of the house got back up, took out her phone, and resumed her recital of the magical properties of salvias grown on western-facing hillsides versus southern.

I rolled onto my back and listened to the plant lady. Botanical magics was a much better topic than demon possession. Maybe there was a secret code embedded in the particular topics the old witch chose to read. The couple who'd been talking about the books didn't wait for the botanical lecture to finish and got up to leave while the witch was still speaking.

For Helen's sake, I listened until the end, then stood with the remaining witches. With my feline grace, I snaked around the crowd, jumping on chairs and sofas, and got a last look at all the faces again, noting their head fur, pointy noses, distorted paws, and hairless limbs.

Then I decided it was time to go. As I joined the cluster of bodies shuffling toward the back door, I found myself preoccupied with so many bottoms without tails.

Near the back door, a man reached down and stopped me with a well-placed scratch. He was sitting on a stool, a cane in his fist. Behind the thick lenses of his glasses, his amber eyes were watery and bloodshot, but alert.

"Hello, kitty," he said, his voice rough with age.

I purred.

"I bet you'd like a saucer of milk, wouldn't you, kitty?"

I was *totally* wanting a saucer of milk. He was very smart.

"Come with me," he said, grunting to his feet. "It's not far."

I felt a powerful urge to rub against his legs, but I didn't want to knock him over; he was very unsteady on his feet, even with the cane. As soon as he took a step toward the door, the crowd parted.

"Nice to see you, Doctor," said a woman with silver wire threaded into her braids. "Have a good evening."

"Watch your step there, old friend," a man in a suit said, holding open the door. "Take my arm if you like. I'm not casting any spells tonight."

A raven, perched on a small woman's shoulder, directed a ragged croak at him, then bowed its beak.

The old man nodded and smiled, acknowledging the tributes quickly before returning his attention to me. "Come along, kitty. That cream is waiting. Not far. It's not far at all."

We stepped outside, and I inhaled the fresh night air. The city lights shrouded the stars. More of my human brain took charge for a moment. Unlike my cat self, a saucer of cream offered by a strange witch who was clearly luring me to his house did not seem like a great idea.

But then I remembered what the genie had told me about following an urge.

"This way, kitty," the man said softly, ambling down the driveway.

The genie wanted me to follow him. The urge was stronger than any other desire I'd had that evening, and since the meeting was over, with my duty to Raynor and Helen accomplished, I trotted after the old man and hoped he wasn't lying about the cream.

🐾 8 🐾

As we walked at a banana-slug's pace down the sidewalk, I decided the elderly witch was even older than he looked. Hobbled and unsteady, with gnarled hands gripping the head of his aluminum cane, he had trouble lifting his feet over cracks in the sidewalk. I trotted around him, mewing and doubling back, and that seemed to amuse him.

"White house, kitty," he gasped. "White fence."

I saw his property just ahead and trotted up to it, enjoying the way his smell grew stronger when I wriggled under the gate. Other cats lived there—many—but they let me walk through the overgrown garden and up the steps to the front door without any fuss.

In spite of his difficulty walking down the sidewalk, once he'd reached his own steps, the years dropped away and he climbed them easily. Holding the cane lightly now, he used his free hand to stroke my back before opening the door.

The overwhelming sense of his magic wafted out of the house and struck me in the whiskers.

"Go on in," he said.

By that point, I couldn't have resisted even if I'd wanted to. His power had become far stronger than mine as soon as I'd crossed over the property line.

His house was the most powerful focal point for witch magic I'd ever experienced. How many years had he lived there? Fifty? Seventy-five? I scanned it with my talent for woodcraft and identified the framing of his house as being from a Douglas fir tree that had lived a century ago. Then I sensed a splinter of the same tree hanging on a gold chain around his neck.

Intrigued by the way he used magic similar to my own and powerless to change my mind anyway, I slinked over the threshold and paraded into his living room.

He closed the door. "Please take your true form," he said. "If you'd be so kind."

Although he was asking politely, his magic gave me no room to refuse. Flicking my tail at him, I walked behind the sofa below the window. If his magic was life-threatening, I might be able to jump out.

Shifting back into my human form was always a relief, and I changed instantly. Naked, I sat cross-legged on the floor behind the sofa, in no hurry to stand up and expose myself.

"Could I have a robe, please?" I called out. "Or a blanket?"

A tracksuit from decades ago—1970s?—appeared in my lap. Avocado green with orange and yellow stripes. It could've fetched a high price at a vintage clothing store in San Francisco, but I valued it even higher. Being naked with a strong witch was scary.

I put it on—like magic, of course, it fit perfectly—and stood up.

We looked at each other across the room. I could feel a wish coming true—a snapping into place of magic and urges and payment—for him. He'd requested this. He'd requested *me*.

I sneezed. Then again. My nose began to swell and itch.

"Thirsty?" he asked.

I nodded, unable to speak just yet. My mouth was dry, tasting of bugs.

He walked away and came back a minute later with a bottle of beer. "I'd pour, but this way you can scan it more easily," he said.

The cap was still tight, and after checking for dangerous spells, I snapped it open and brought it to my lips. Cold, wet perfection, the best beer I'd ever tasted. The best liquid of any kind, better than cream, far better than springwater. My head swam, but I didn't care. This was my destiny; might as well enjoy it.

I sank into an oversized easy chair and took another swig. All around the room, covering each wall and the hallways to either side, were floor-to-ceiling bookshelves, tidily filled with books. Small labels marked each shelf at the ends. Stools and stepladders were arranged nearby. It was more than a man's living room; it was a library.

"Well? What brings me here?" I asked, then sneezed again. To my left, a cat was perched on a rocking chair. A second and third cat were sleeping together on the sofa. The lingering effects of my own cat shape plus the many cats in the house were going to make me unable to breathe soon. Whatever the old man wanted—or the genie required—I hoped it was satisfied quickly.

He walked over and removed a small box from a shelf, removed something from it, then dropped a white, bean-like object in my palm.

"Eat it," he said. "You'll feel better."

I wasn't in the habit of imbibing weird beans from a strange witch. The lack of an urge to consume it made me think the bean was not related to the genie's power. Letting it sit in my palm, I scanned it, felt something organic inside, then scanned it again.

A calico cat from the sofa got up, stretched, and jumped into my lap. I could feel the skin of my forearms tingling, preparing to erupt into itchy red bumps.

In for a wish, in for a curse, I thought, and popped the bean into my mouth. It was chewy and sweet. A jumbo, coconut-flavored jelly bean. But inside…

A crunch. Shards of something hard and crispy caught in my teeth, scratched my tongue. I forced myself to keep chewing and gulp it down. The beer helped.

Before I'd taken a second swig of the beer, my sinuses cleared. My eyes stopped itching, and my skin settled down under the polyester tracksuit.

I took a deep, easy breath and smiled at him. "What was in there?"

"Owl vomit," he said.

"Ah."

"Mouse bones," he added.

I had another mouthful of beer, this time swishing it around longer before swallowing. I'd eaten worse. "Thank you," I said. "Is there a particular spell you cast to counteract the cat allergen, or—"

"Find yourself some owl pellets and give it a try." He sat in a wingback chair across from me and crossed his legs, moving more easily with each moment that passed. The house seemed to function as his fountain of youth. "I've found that mouse is best, as an ancient mammalian victim of the feline, but bird can be effective as well. You'll have to experiment."

"They have to be, uh, processed through the owl first?"

"Oh yes. Death gives its spirit strength. The victim seeks revenge, you see."

"But why not upon the owl?"

"I think you'll find yourself unbothered by owl allergen as well," he said. "Haven't you ever read LaRose's third volume on rodent remedies?"

I took another deep breath through my clear, cavernous nostrils. "No, but I will now."

He stood, walked over to a shelf, removed a compact yellow paperback, and brought it to me. "It was reprinted recently, and I picked up a second copy. You can borrow it. I've got the first edition." He retook his seat.

It was about the size of my hand, and after admiring it for a moment and nodding my thanks to him, I tucked it into the tracksuit jacket pocket. Maybe this was how he'd become so popular—giving books away. "Thank you very much." I wasn't excited about cooking with owl pellets, but the magic had worked so well I would start taking day hikes to search and collect the effective material as soon as possible.

"No drowsiness, either," he said. "Lets you keep your wits about you."

I risked stroking the cat in my lap, an act that usually gave me hives. "How did you see me through my cat shape?"

He tapped his black-rimmed glasses. "Always important to have a trick to see the world as it is." His gaze dropped to my throat where the copper ring hung on the chain around my neck. "That ring kept you hidden to the others, so don't worry."

I reached up and put my hand over it. "It hid my... human form?" I risked asking. He was obviously a respected source of knowledge, and I was always curious to a fault. I'd thought the ring only hid my demon ancestry.

"It hides whatever facet of your identity needs to be hidden," he said. "Quite a marvel, really. Where did you get it?"

I waited for a probing spell to strike, but he didn't use his power on me, which I appreciated. In his own home, I would be unlikely to be able to fight it off. "It's not my secret to share," I said.

He squinted intently at me, as if reading the small print on a vitamin bottle. Whatever he wanted from me had been valuable enough to pay a genie for. But why?

From the look of his home, he was a book collector or a scholar. The two witches behind me at the meeting had mentioned Lionel as the owner of a rare book on demon possession. Other witches had been deferential, polite, even affectionate. One had called him doctor.

"Forgive me, Witch Lionel, but why am I here?"

9

He lifted a book from the coffee table between us and held it out. "This belonged to your mother. Well, your human mother."

A chill ran through me. The cat, sensing my tension, jumped off my lap. I didn't reach for the book.

Lionel leaned closer, waving the book. "Take it," he said. "She lost interest in it, unfortunately, and left it here. I want you to have it." He set it on the table in front of me.

"How do you know who I am?" I asked. "Did— Was it —" I didn't want to mention Raynor's name, but he seemed the most likely source.

He shook his head. "I made a wish and I paid the price." He cleared his throat. "Unfortunately, that required my telling the jinn about your demon mother. She knew some of your history already, but she's greedy, of course, like all beings. She wanted it all."

"But... How can you... speak of... of her?" I braced myself for the genie's magic to clamp my mouth shut.

"We both know of her existence already, so her magic won't waste its effort on us."

I relaxed. It was a relief to meet another human being who knew about the genie, and I wasn't worried about her knowing my secrets. She had resources I couldn't fathom. If she was curious to know about me, she'd find out one way or another. Maybe she could share it with me.

But other witches... I didn't want them to know anything about me.

I scooted up to the edge of my seat and picked up the book, which was dark red and bore no text. It was old but in good condition. "Who else have you told?"

He leaned back and steepled his fingers. "No one. Please don't worry. I have no interest in sharing your secret with anyone else, or I would have done so already." He sighed. "You saw those witches tonight. Ravenous for any scrap of information about demon possession, no matter how foolish, Shadowed, or dangerous. Don't you realize I could've sold you to one of them? You were very vulnerable in your cat shape. A demonprinted specimen such as yourself, and a Bellrose to boot, neatly captured in a cat carrier—you could've earned me a nice bit of platinum."

Fear sent hot blood tingling through my veins. He was right. I'd been in more danger than I'd considered. Swallowing over a lump in my throat, I looked down, trying not to show my anxiety. Nobody had known about my demon-print until very recently; until then, I'd existed just like any other young witch, going to school, getting a job. I hadn't realized some witches might be curious about me, not as an agent of the Protectorate, destroying my career or locking me up, but as some kind of exploitable instrument of power. To those witches, my life was no more precious than the bones of a mouse processed in an owl's gut.

"Well," I said once I felt calm enough to speak. "Thank you for not doing that."

"You're welcome." He scratched his scalp and made a

face. "I hope you realize I'd never do such a thing. You've never heard of me?"

"Sorry, no."

"Witches from the East Bay find my library sooner or later, usually as teenagers. I've got a few books that make school a bit easier." He grinned, showing a flash of uneven teeth. His fountain of youth hadn't managed to fix his choppers. "Much easier."

"My mother was one of them?"

"Your human mother."

"The real one," I said.

He shrugged. "Hard to say what's real sometimes, don't you think?"

A revolting thought crossed my mind. My father had many faults, but he'd never been a predator.

So far as I knew.

"Was *she* a teenager?" I asked, my stomach clenching.

He tilted his head and looked me up and down with the same squinty look he'd given me at first. "About your age, I'd say. Perhaps exactly. The universe is filled with echoes, isn't it?"

"I have no interest in possession," I said.

"Very glad to hear it. Maybe you'll enjoy that book in a way others haven't been able to."

I looked down at the red book in my hand, then turned the cover to read the title page. *Warnings* was in large block letters. Then below in smaller type, *Regarding Possession by Demons and Other Immortal Spirit Beings*. No author was noted.

I thought about the conversation I'd overheard. "You show this to everyone who comes to your library," I said.

"I'm foolishly optimistic," he said. "But most only pretend to read it. It's just one more warning label to be dismissed. Like those big paper tags on a new pillow."

I turned the next page, then flipped through a few more. It was in a common witchy writing style, with a header above, details below, and an illustration on the opposite side. The first chapter was titled "Ethics." No wonder everyone stopped reading.

"I hear there's more than one book. Isn't this part of a set?" I studied an illustration of a child's innocent face as she gazed wonderingly at a spark in her hand. *The gift of Bright magic*, the caption read.

"Where did you hear that?" he asked sharply.

I looked up at him, debating telling him the truth, lying, or using it as leverage.

But before I could make up my mind what to tell him, he plucked the identities out of my memories. "Of course— Brayden and Trudy," he said, shaking his head. "You sat near them at the meeting. I never should've let them into my library, but they'd been coached. Older siblings get me into trouble sometimes. I've always been too sentimental about kin, which is one reason I'm talking to you."

"Tell me about my mother," I said.

"You didn't know her?" he asked, leaning toward me. "Not even her name?"

I felt odd, weightless, desperately curious. "Tell me," I said roughly. "Please."

"Look inside the back cover," he said.

Holding my breath, I turned the book over and looked inside. A block script in pencil—graphite, which gave it power—spelled the name POPPY ALMASI.

My vision shrank to a long, narrow tunnel. The letters grew into skyscrapers, the only thing I could see.

Almasi.

Alma.

Light-headed, I heard a buzzing in my ears. I regretted sucking down the beer so fast. Suddenly Lionel was there, putting a hand on my wrist, and I felt the world stabilize. Through my beaded bracelet, he was feeding me strength and calm.

"Almasi means 'diamond' in Arabic," he said.

I sucked in a deep breath and closed my eyes. Knowing I bore my mother's name all these years and hadn't known it knocked the breath out of me again.

"My apologies," he said. "I thought you must've already known her name."

I swallowed, took a shallow breath. "I didn't, actually."

My mother had been possessed by a demon, and their mutual existence had ended during my birth.

"You were born here in Berkeley," he continued.

I looked at him, tears burning in my eyes, overwhelmed to finally meet somebody who could tell me anything about her. "Thank you," I said. "I got that out of my father recently."

"But not your name?" Lionel asked.

With my fingertip, I caressed the inscribed name that was so like my own. "He wanted to forget, so he did. The demon probably helped him with the spell."

Lionel's fingers curled around my wrist, tight enough to hurt. His voice dropped. "You've met the demon?"

A minute ago he'd given me strength. Now he took it away. I gazed helplessly into his eyes as he pulled the words out of my mouth.

"She possessed my father again over the summer," I was forced to say. "She almost married him. She wanted to know me. She followed me and possessed my friend. Then she released her. I don't know where she is now."

Frowning, he watched my mouth as I spoke, scanning every syllable. "I heard about your father's wedding," he said. "Everyone heard about that wedding. It's why you're here now. I started asking questions about Malcolm's daughter, how old you were, what you looked like. You would've been born a year or two after I last saw Poppy."

I tried to pull away, but my hand felt as if it had been set in concrete.

Oh Brightness. Had my curiosity led me into a trap? Would the genie care if I suffered or died to fulfill my debt?

"You're hurting me," I said.

He looked down at his hand, and the clamp-like fingers loosened. "Forgive me," he said. "My emotions got the better of me. I've been afraid she'd gotten to you. I feel... responsible."

"Gotten to me," I asked, "or *in* me?"

He offered a brief, lopsided smile, released my wrist, and set my hand over the book with a pat. "You're obviously alone in there. I was very happy you came in cat form."

I began to breathe more steadily. "A possessed human can't shift?"

"It would take more experience and power than a witch of your age would have," he said. "The demon would make the transition, but you'd get lost behind, your spirit in a cold limbo. When you returned to your body behind my sofa, I was sure you were solo."

I shivered. Something else to worry about. If a demon ever possessed me without my knowing, I might get evicted from my own body when I shifted.

"Why would you feel responsible?" I asked.

He tapped the book with a gnarled finger, heavy with rings and inked with faded, illegible tattoos. "She'd bought that book at a yard sale. She brought it to me, thinking I'd tell her it was garbage, but..." He shook his head. "I told her *Warnings* was a famous book and all true. She hadn't known possession was real before then. Her witch parents were dead, and she'd been raised by nonmagical people with traditional beliefs."

I tried to imagine what it would've been like for her to find out the fantastic nightmares in the old book could really happen. "It must've seemed kind of exciting," I said.

"She became obsessed," he said. "I realized my mistake and tried to get through to her—I would read her the passages in *Warnings* to make my case—and she got angry and told me to keep it. The last time I saw her, she tried to convince me she wasn't going to pursue possession, but I knew she was lying."

Could I believe him? Maybe he'd helped her more than he was admitting. Maybe he felt guilty because she got what she wanted and then died. "Why didn't you find me earlier and tell me who she was? Nobody could tell me anything."

"I had no idea you existed. Until the word got out about Malcolm Bellrose's wedding and how his mysterious daughter was there to watch his demon bride's execution, I'd had no clue Poppy had had a child. It's not like she kept in touch."

"I'm hardly mysterious," I said. "Notorious, maybe. Criminal father, rejected from the Protectorate…"

"I learned that nobody, not even those who make it their business to find out, has ever known who your mother was," he said. "But what was more mysterious was that nobody was even curious."

I sighed and looked at the book again. "Poppy Almasi," I said quietly.

"She was an orphan," he said. "One of the prerequisites for a consensual possession."

I hadn't known that. "Do most witches know about the orphan rule?" I thought about all the witches at the meeting and hoped their parents were in good health. If the really nasty witches wanted to be possessed, they might try to help things along.

"No. Please keep that information to yourself. I don't

have the power anymore to cast lasting silence spells." He went back to his chair and sat down. "You saw what happens to me when I leave home—weak as a kitten. My magic is much the same. It's why I had to get the genie to bring you to me."

Helen would be expecting me, but I'd waited all my life to hear about my biological mother. "Tell me about Poppy."

He shrugged. "I'm sorry. In truth I never knew much about her, just what I've told you."

"But you paid a genie to bring me to you," I said. "Her wishes aren't cheap. You must've known enough to care about her."

"Her death remains a debt upon my soul," he said. "Young witches continue to be curious about demon possession. Because of your mother, I've done what I can to redirect their interests to more Bright pursuits. I try to save them the way I didn't save her. Every day I regret I was unable to reach her."

I wanted to believe him, but he was a witch. He might just be telling me what I wanted to hear. "Those two witches were talking about the other books in the set. Do you know where they are?"

Lionel smiled weakly and shook his head. "Witches have been sharing rumors about those other books for as long as I've lived here," he said. "One generation gives up, another picks up the quest."

"Have you ever seen them?"

He leaned back in his chair, regarding me over his nose. "I wouldn't tell you if I had."

At least he was honest about it. "Do you know if my mother found the other books? Is that how she... succeeded?"

"No," he said. "I believe, even after we'd argued, that she

would've shown them to me. She was so curious. She would've wanted my expertise in interpreting them."

Curiosity was the lifeblood of a witch—and a primary cause of death.

The books didn't interest me nearly as much as what he could tell me about Poppy as a human being. Maybe he didn't know much, but he knew more about her than anyone else I'd met.

"What did she... What did she look like?" I asked. "What kind of witch was she—metal? Kitchen? Or—"

Lionel got to his feet, pressing his fingers into his temple. Without warning, an invisible lever pushed me out of my chair and set me on my feet.

"I'm so sorry, Alma dear, but I've run out of time for today." He offered a strained smile. "I've exhausted myself this evening."

From the quick way he'd just stood up, he didn't look exhausted to me.

"Let me make you some tea," I said. "I have some spring-water in my car. Fresh from Silverpool. That's very refreshing." I wasn't ready to say goodbye. There was more to learn here, from him and from his books.

He shook his head, frowning. "I'm afraid I can't tonight, Alma."

"But you went to so much trouble to get me here. You'll want to get your wish's worth, right? Spend a little more time with me?"

He walked over to the front door and pulled it open. "You have the book. You've heard my warning. Now I can rest in peace." Then, in a louder voice that he directed to the outdoors, he said, "I consider the wish paid."

I tried to walk slowly, but his magic was overpowering. Within three seconds, I was standing on the sidewalk in front of his little yellow house. Two cats took turns snaking around his legs as he stood on his porch and waved at me. "Off you go," he said.

"But—" My legs in the tracksuit began walking swiftly down the hill toward where I'd parked my car. I was barefoot, but I was unable to make my stride slower and gentler to protect my tender sole and toes. I couldn't even look behind me. Lionel's magic kept my head locked and facing straight ahead.

I goose-stepped across the street, then pivoted ninety degrees and kept going. Even a block away, his spell forced my heel to land on a sharp piece of gravel. Exhausted? Hardly. He'd just wanted to get rid of me.

He'd wanted to make sure I had the book. I lifted it to my chest, held it there for a moment, then tucked it under my arm. The little book on rodent remedies was in my pocket, but *Warnings* was too large to fit inside with it.

Poppy Almasi.

When I reached my Jeep, I forgot I was wearing a vintage tracksuit, so I didn't change into the outfit I'd brought for the drive to San Francisco. I was too busy smiling. I was sad she was gone, but I had a name. I had so much more than I'd had before.

Lionel wasn't the only one who'd gotten his wish granted tonight. Would I have to pay a price for mine?

❧ 10 ❧

It was almost midnight when I drove over the Bay Bridge to San Francisco. The fairies were out in large numbers on the water, enjoying the storm blowing in, the holiday lights dotted along the bridge span, the impending solstice. Still caught up by what Lionel had told me, I was able to ignore them without casting any protective spells.

I got off the freeway and drove up and down the city streets, reflecting over what Helen was going to want to hear while also working on a spell to hide the parts I didn't want to share. I owed her an account of the meeting, but the information about Lionel and my mother, and how I felt about it, was mine alone.

Helen Mendoza lived in a large Victorian next door to the local Protectorate office on Diamond Street in Noe Valley. It was a picturesque, hilly area in the middle of the city; the witches shared the neighborhood with young tech workers, affluent families, and stubborn old-timers.

Helen was one of the latter. I parked several blocks away to evade Protectorate attention, then hid both books in the back of the Jeep under the box of kitty litter. I had indeed been forced to use it in my animal form. The smell would linger for weeks, but the power of my repulsion spell would be extraordinary. I didn't trust Helen not to steal the books if I brought them into her home.

With my overnight bag slung over my shoulder, I hiked up a street steep enough to have concrete steps set into the sidewalk. Enveloped in a camouflage spell—the agents next door were always watching Helen's house—I climbed her front stoop. The paint was peeling, the potted plants neglected, and the doorbell frequently broken, as it was tonight.

She didn't want any visitors. I stood and waited in silence, knowing she'd have a sensing spell on the landing to tell her I was there. Shivering in the cold wind that was cutting through the polyester of the tracksuit jacket, I glanced over at the Protectorate building, which looked like any other multimillion-dollar residence in San Francisco but in fact held dozens of the most powerful witches on the West Coast.

A black SUV pulled out in front of the Protectorate office and disappeared under a blanket of quick-moving fog. A second later, a row of cars, parked perpendicularly to the sidewalk, appeared in the empty spot.

Parking was tight. The only way to guarantee your spot was to make it look like it was already taken.

"What in Brightness are you looking at?"

I turned away from the Protectorate office to see Helen standing there in her doorway. She looked about sixty or so, with short white hair that tended to stick up. Tonight she wore a black velour robe and black sheepskin slippers, and held a shot glass of springwater.

"May I come in?" I asked. Even though she'd invited me, I'd be unable to enter without her express invitation.

She flung back the shot of wellspring water, nodded, and stepped aside. I carried my bag over the threshold, felt her scanning spell pick through it for valuables she might desire as well as objects of trouble, and followed her down the narrow hallway past the cluttered rooms of Victorian knick-knacks and furnishings. I was glad I'd left the books in the car. That scan would've spotted them immediately.

The center of her house, as well as her world, was the kitchen. It overlooked the deck and sloping backyard of her house, which was filled with professional-grade greenhouses. She made her living selling what she grew, along with secrets she collected from her vast network of friends, associates, and enemies.

I was an associate. There had been moments I'd thought we were friends, but she'd always done something to remind me of my place as a useful tool for her mercenary goals. She looked out for herself and wouldn't cut me any special deals just because she'd been nicer to me over the years since my first months as a trainee agent at the Protectorate next door.

"Sit," she said, pointing at a rickety white chair at the kitchen table, then she sat across from me. "Now spill."

Between us was a large, shallow bowl of water mixed with —I tapped it with a probing spell—a spoonful of honey, probably from her own bees. Honey was an old trick that would help her remember the secrets I shared with her. It was popular in school before big tests.

"There isn't much," I said.

Helen put her hands on either side of the bowl. "You might not know what you know. In fact, nobody does. It's up to the wise to see what's valuable. Only the wise can judge." She pointed at me. "So start talking."

"Nice to see you're in good health, by the way," I said. "I'm fine, in case you're wondering."

"Manners are for morons. It's late."

My mouth tasted like bugs, beer, and mouse bones, but I didn't trust her not to put something in even a glass of tap water, so I reached down to my overnight bag and took out a thermos of peppermint tea I'd brought with me. In between sips, I began to talk.

I told her everything, even Brayden and Trudy's conversation about the three books on possession and even how they mentioned Lionel owning the one that tried to warn witches away from it. I was very careful to keep my thoughts from drifting into what had happened later at Lionel's house, which might make her too curious, but I did have to tell her what I'd heard. My promise to her included anything at the meeting.

The owner of the house reciting the herbal textbook amused her, but she wasn't interested in any of the details, not even about the three books, which was old news to her. At first she was curious about Randy's declaration that the book *Instructions* had been found, but when she heard how many steps of separation there were between him and the person who might have seen it, she lost interest.

"There are always rumors about that book turning up," she said. "But it never does. If anyone has it, it'll be Lionel. Not some Berkeley kid with a big mouth."

I'd told her everything; now it was my turn. I'd have to feed her ego a little to get her to share information freely. "Lionel was like a local celebrity," I said. "Have you ever met him?"

"Of course I've met him," she said.

"But you don't really know him, right? He's so much older than you." I saw the satisfied curl of her lip and added, "Much, much older."

"It's true I'm many decades younger," she said. "But I know him well. He's a regular customer, in fact."

"Wow," I said. "Everyone seemed to really look up to him. Why is that? Does he deserve it?"

"Well, he's not that amazing," she said, "but he definitely knows books. If I had a question about books, he's the one I'd go to."

"Do you think he has the—?"

"Enough questions," Helen said. "Is that really all you witnessed at the meeting? A fire-eating showboat and a rumor about an old book?"

I let her truth probe drift over me but kept it carefully contained to the meeting and blocked every thought of Lionel except the way others had treated him.

She pushed to her feet, shaking her head, and brought the basin of honey over to the sink. "What a waste," she said, pouring it down the drain. "I should've waited for you to get your redwood staff back."

"But you didn't," I said quickly. "So my debt to you is paid."

She slumped against the counter and sighed. "I suppose."

"It is. Agree to it."

"It's paid," she said, rolling her eyes. "You can have the bedroom you used before. I might not see you in the morning. Saturdays are my day to sleep in. Don't think I'm making waffles."

"Got it," I said. "Thanks for letting me stay over."

She began to walk away, then paused in the doorway. "I suppose it's good news those crazy witches still haven't learned how to make a demon possess a person," she said.

"Agreed," I said.

She frowned. "Waste of my time, though. I'd hoped to make a little money off their latest theory."

"Too bad," I said. A few minutes later, I turned off the lights and found my bedroom upstairs.

In the morning, true to her promise, Helen did not get

up and make me breakfast. Just as well; anything she served was likely to be hexed to get secrets out of me.

The city was shrouded in a light rain when I hiked back to my car. The Jeep's interior reeked, even with the enchanted plant trying to filter the air, but the books were still there. I got behind the wheel and thought about Lionel's abrupt ending of our visit the night before.

He'd gone to tremendous trouble to get me to his house. Why had he been so rushed to get rid of me? Did he really only care about giving me the book and washing his hands of what had happened to my mother?

I had to talk to him again. Sonoma County was across the Golden Gate Bridge to the north, and Berkeley was over the Bay Bridge to the east—not at all on my route home—but I needed to see what else I could learn from him.

The Saturday morning traffic wasn't too bad going to Berkeley, and the early-morning light on the bay reminded me of an assignment I'd had as an agent, chasing after a witch in Oakland who'd screwed up a BART train with an invisibility spell. Drunk teenage witches were a menace. Luckily I'd found the ghost train speeding through San Leandro before anybody got killed.

I stopped at a bakery off San Pablo Avenue, then parked near Lionel's house. It was only nine on a Saturday morning, and I hoped the bagels and coffee I'd brought would make me welcome. But just as I picked up the bag and was climbing out of the Jeep, my phone rang.

I had to set everything back down to take the phone out of my pocket. When I saw it was Raynor calling, I rolled my eyes as I answered. "I'll tell you about the meeting when I get back to Silverpool. I'm still in—"

"Did you meet with the old witch Lionel last night?" he asked.

I hesitated, wanting to protect my privacy. Raynor didn't always respect my boundaries. "He was at the meeting."

"Don't lie to me. Did you *meet* with him?"

Anger surged through me. "I'm not lying. Why do you want to—"

"He's dead," Raynor said. "And it looks like murder."

Climbing back into my seat, I closed the door, tapped into my redwood necklace, and cast a stronger boundary spell around the Jeep. If a murderer was nearby, I needed to protect myself from both magical and physical attack.

The poor old man. Had one of the witches from the meeting followed him home?

Other than me, that is.

The implications of his death struck me. Other than my useless father, he'd been the only link to my mother. Now I might never get the answers to my questions about her.

"Where'd you sleep last night?" Raynor's voice was harsh in my ear.

Preoccupied about Poppy Almasi, I answered numbly. "San Francisco. At Helen Mendoza's house."

He let out his breath. "Good." As the former director on Diamond Street, he knew Helen well. They disliked each other intensely, but they knew each other. The troublesome witch next door to the Protectorate office was under constant surveillance—and vice versa. "The agents would've seen you arrive," he added. "You went there right after the meeting?"

I rubbed my eyes. There was no point lying to him, but I dreaded his reaction to the truth. "No, I went to Lionel's house first."

He swore. There was a silence, then the sound of him snorting some magic herbs up his nose. Finally he said, "Of course you did. A body turns up, look for Alma."

"Hey. He wanted me to have a book," I said. "After he gave it to me, I left."

"Demon's balls," Raynor said. "A book?"

I hadn't wanted to tell him the latest personal gossip, but a murder meant I had no choice. "He recognized me in my cat form at the meeting," I began, then told him about the allergy cure, both books, and his regrets about my biological mother.

I did not, however, tell him about the genie's role in bringing me and Lionel together. Her magic prevented me from mentioning her existence even if I'd wanted to.

As I spoke, he asked a few questions or muttered curses under his breath. When I stopped speaking, the line went quiet except for him sniffing another pinch of herbs up his nose.

"You have the book with you now?" he asked. "*Warnings*?"

"Yes," I said.

"For Brightness' sake, don't let Timms know you have it. It'll look too suspicious."

"Timms?"

"Director Edward Timms. My replacement. He called me this morning to find out if I had any leads for him." He sniffed again. "He's heading the investigation personally. At the house now with the response team. You're going to have to go talk to him."

I'd already put on my seat belt to drive home. "But—"

"They'll figure out you were there last night," he said. "Shifting from cat to human would've left a magical fingerprint, and you said you sat down and drank a beer, talked for a while."

For Brightness' sake. I was going to get mixed up in Protectorate business again. "Do I have to do it now? Can't I wait for them to come question me in Silverpool?"

"You'll want them to rule you out as a suspect as soon as possible," he said. "You didn't kill him, right?"

I sighed. If only I hadn't left him alone last night. Maybe I would've been able to protect him. "Not that I remember."

"Don't joke," he said.

"I don't want the new Director to find out about my demonprint."

"You're wearing the copper ring?" he asked.

I was grateful I could say yes.

"Good. Keep it on and use all your powers to hide it. Hopefully he'll be too curious about your cat shifting. I've already told him I sent you to the meeting to collect intelligence," he said. "Everyone knows Lionel was cat crazy. It makes sense he wanted to lure you home and talk to you about shifting."

I relaxed slightly under his reassurance. "Who found the body?"

"Don't know the name. A local teenager. One of the kids he lets use his library."

"I feel bad I didn't get to know Lionel better," I said. "He seemed like such a nice guy."

"I don't know about that. You never know with the really old ones what they get out of doing what they do," he said. "They certainly don't bother explaining themselves to anybody. It's as if after living that long they get bored with following the rules. I've met more than one old witch who thought their hundredth birthday was the perfect time to start exploring Shadow magic."

"You think something Shadow killed him?" I asked.

"He was at that meeting, wasn't he?"

❦

BEFORE I GOT out of the Jeep, I made sure the copper ring was on my finger and the sleeve of my sweater was pulled down over the tattoos on my forearm. Director Timms and his agents would turn their powers of inquiry on me, and I didn't want any unnecessary questions, especially about my heritage. I'd already come across one magic ring that could smell out my demon ancestry; I didn't know if there was another one on the finger of any of the witches at the crime scene.

I was relieved to see the man standing outside the house—Darius Ironford, my former partner. We'd had a rough time when we'd worked together, but recently we'd become uneasy friends. I respected him enormously, and his opinion of me had improved over the past year. Before that, he'd blamed me for letting Seth Dumont, who he'd thought was a demon, throw him into the San Francisco Bay. It was that incident that had led to me being declared unfit for the job as an agent of the Protectorate.

This morning Darius was pretending to be a flooring contractor on a lunch break, leaning against a Hardwoods and Carpet van in the driveway, holding a clipboard and a sandwich. The houses were so close together the usual crime scene methods of enchanting the property would be harder to pull off, so they'd doubled up with actual props as well. He saw me, groaned, and rolled his eyes.

"Raynor sent me," I told him.

"Of course he did. How did he— Never mind. I don't work for him anymore." He bit his sandwich. "Unlike you."

Thinking of how Raynor was finally, actually paying me, I shrugged. "I'm supposed to talk to the lead investigators and tell them I need to make a statement." I glanced at the house. "Should I give it to you?"

Darius folded up his sandwich and set it carefully inside on the seat of the van. "Why do you need to make a statement?" he asked warily.

To Darius, I was always showing up in the wrong place. I was supposed to safely be hours north in Silverpool, not popping up at crime scenes in Berkeley.

I cleared my throat. "I was here last night."

"Here in Berkeley, or *here* here?"

"Here, here," I said. "In the house. With the victim."

He rubbed his eyes. "He was alive then?"

"Of course he was alive. Can you please tell them I'm here so I only have to explain it once?"

After a pause, Darius sighed. "Timms will want to hear it directly. Director Timms. He arrived the day Raynor got sent away."

I leaned in, lowering my voice. "And? What's he like?" A Director of a Protectorate office had influence over the entire magic community in its region.

"Judge for yourself," he said.

"Come on."

He smiled and shrugged at the same time. "I like him. But you'll have to judge for yourself." He walked away and went into the bungalow.

A shaggy black cat mewed and peeked out at me with yellow eyes from behind a shrub. Two more cats, one white, one spotted gray, explored the yard. And then another black one, short-haired, trailed after Darius into the house.

I wondered what was going to happen to all the cats.

They'd lived with an old witch with all kinds of secrets; not just anybody would be allowed to adopt them.

A moment later, Darius came out again. As he walked over, he glanced up and down the street. "Follow the driveway and meet Timms in the back. Keep it casual. We don't want the neighbors to notice anything."

I nodded and stepped around the van, then up the cracked driveway lined with towering bamboo along the neighbor's property line. I could feel the boundary spell crackling with power between each tall, thin trunk.

The backyard was a lot like mine: a hundred-year-old detached garage, obviously no longer used for a car, and a messy garden and uneven patio under old trees. A balding man stood near a lemon tree, smelling the blossoms, and turned to greet me with a mild, polite smile.

"Alma Bellrose?" He held up a hand in greeting but made no move to shake my hand, which was kind of a man in his position to grant me my privacy. "I'm Director Timms," he said.

He was a medium-statured man in gray pants and a button-down blue shirt, a uniform that could've placed him in dozens of occupations—dentist, salesman, teacher. Given the spells available to witches, his age could've been anywhere between fifty and a hundred, but the wrinkles on his balding head made me think he'd kept his natural appearance, which probably put him around sixty.

"Brightness be upon you," I said, because Timms looked like an old-fashioned type who would appreciate traditional manners.

He held out both hands, palms up, and bowed—an old greeting showing he meant no harm. "Protector Raynor told me you had something to share with me."

I'd already decided it was safest to tell him everything. Well, almost everything. My impulse was to keep as many details as possible to myself, but that would only make me vulnerable to more questioning later. "Yes, Director. At Raynor's request, I came to Berkeley yesterday to attend a secret meeting of witches interested in the forbidden topic of demon possession. He wanted an eyewitness in case some of them came to Silverpool to cause trouble over the solstice. I attended in cat form, which is an ability of mine. After the meeting, the victim, Witch—I'm sorry, is he a doctor? I don't know his last name—"

"Nobody does. He's always just been Lionel. Some people add honorifics out of respect, but he doesn't seem to care—rather, he didn't." Timms swallowed hard. "Hard to believe he's gone."

I nodded. It was common to drop your surname if you didn't have an old family tree. "Lionel tempted me home with him, and I regained my human shape inside the house here—he gave me clothes—and talked for a while. I left—"

"What did you talk about?"

"Demon possession." I was going to admit to everything except my mother issues. "He'd been able to identify me in cat form and wanted to dissuade me from inviting demon possession."

"Did you need to be dissuaded?"

"No, Director. I'm no fan of the process."

"Your father's bride had to be put down at their wedding, I understand. A demon almost married a Bellrose. Hard to believe."

"It was awful," I said. His gentle scanning spell wafted over me and could feel my sincerity.

His expression softened. For the first time, I noticed his eyes, unlike the rest of him, were dazzling. Pure blue, clear and piercing. "I can't imagine. At least you have the comfort of knowing the union was unwilling and unconsummated," he said.

Not quite, I thought. My father had been willing—and there had definitely been some consummating—but he hadn't actually known she was a demon, and that was all that mattered to the Protectorate.

I nodded and looked uneasily at my feet. "I'm sorry about Lionel. I wish I'd met him before yesterday."

"Many generations of young witches have enjoyed his library over the years, including myself," he said. "That's who found him this morning, actually, a poor kid. We had to put him under a rest spell. He's sleeping it off at home. Local student."

"Must've been quite a shock," I said. "Was there evidence of violence on the body?"

Timms' eyebrows rose, then he shook his head. "Now, Bellrose, you're not an agent anymore, are you now? I can't tell you that sort of thing, and from what I understand from your file, you wouldn't want to hear it anyway. Not the violent type." He winked one of his bright blue eyes at me. "If only the rest of the world was made of up peaceniks like yourself. What a nice place that would be."

"I'm not exactly..." Peacenik sounded nerdy and old-fashioned—which also described Timms, so maybe he did mean it as a compliment.

"Now, how about you give a formal statement to Iron-ford and hit the road? You've got a long drive home, don't you?" He turned, absently scratching his forehead. "Protector Raynor can fill me on any details we forget to get from you today."

"Thank you, Director. I'd love to get going." Tension drained out of me. "The solstice is only the day after tomorrow."

"Hopefully Raynor has finally got a decent boundary put up. Too much trouble up there lately. Look out for yourself. Stay home if you can."

"Thanks. I plan on it."

He nodded at me, looking at the back door of the bungalow as if hesitant to go back inside. His pale face was drawn and sad.

"Did you know him well?" I asked.

He glanced at me. "When I was a student, which was more years ago than I'd like to admit. You won't be able to understand this until you're older, but it doesn't feel like more than a month or two. Time is the cruelest magic of all. The biggest Shadow hanging over all of us."

"I'm sorry for your loss."

"Thank you, but it's more of a loss for people your age. And younger. He was more generous with his time than other witches of his stature. Certainly more generous with his books. As long as you read them under his roof."

I nodded, blocking the memory of the books that were at that moment hidden under the seat of my Jeep just a block away. Timms hadn't become Director without having the ability to scan minds at least a little bit. He put on a good show of being a nice guy, but I was skeptical. He'd have to prove his niceness for me to believe a witch at his level was generous and sensitive.

A thought struck me. I *did* have a favor to ask. A concrete one.

"Excuse me, Director Timms...," I began.

He focused those brilliant blue eyes on me.

🦋 12 🦋

I waited for the shiver of a probe needling into me, but only sensed mild, distracted patience. "Yes, Alma?" Timms asked.

"During the recent incident in Silverpool, the Protectorate took something of mine. A redwood staff. The investigation is complete, but I never got it back."

He frowned. "A staff?"

"Yes, Director. I made it myself." It might offend him to complain about Protectorate policy of unlawful searches and seizures, so I only said, "Perhaps when the former director left and came to Silverpool, it was lost in the shuffle."

"You think the Protectorate still has it?"

"Yes. At the Diamond Street office. It's not valuable—as I said, I made it myself. It's not old or expensive—and I bet it just got forgotten in the broom closet or something."

"Broom closet," he said.

"Just a guess."

His eyebrows lifted. "And you've inquired before?"

"I'm afraid so."

He flashed a sour smile. "Right. Lost in the shuffle.

Perhaps one of the Flints has gotten a little attached to it. Completely unacceptable, of course, if it's your rightful property," he said. "I'll look into it. Is that all?"

"Yes, thank you. Sorry to bother you about it, it's just I made it—"

"Made it yourself. I understand. I made a wand once when I was a boy. Set the cat on fire." He looked around the garden. "Speaking of cats, he was always too fond of them. I'm allergic myself. Had to eat mouse bones to use the library here."

I smiled, about to tell him I had the same problem, then remembered he was an important man with a dead witch to mourn and investigate. "I'll give Darius my statement," I said.

Turning toward the house's back door, he lifted a hand in acknowledgment. "Have a safe drive home," he said.

I thanked him and walked back to the front yard where another van had arrived, this one labeled FELINE RESCUE—complete with a cartoon cat logo in a full-color wrap over the entire vehicle. Two women in beige jumpsuits were casting catnip spells and luring the animals into several carriers set in the garden.

Darius had stopped pretending to be a flooring contractor and was directing two agents to set up a hiding spell around the property. A guy riding by on a bike, suddenly confused, swerved and rolled up a driveway across the street, then checked his tire, shook his head, and got back on the road without ever looking our way.

"I'm supposed to give you a statement," I said.

Darius snapped at one of the witches to pull the spell in closer to the sidewalk—"We don't want to kill anybody, do we? More paperwork for all of us"—and then gave me an irritated nod.

We walked to the hardwood flooring van, where I told

him everything about my visit to the witch meeting and then Lionel's, skipping the part about my mother and the book.

"You didn't see anyone as you were leaving that would explain why he'd ended the visit so abruptly?" he asked.

"Nobody," I said. "Sorry."

"Did you get a good look at the witches at the meeting?" He wrote every word of my statement down in one of the notebooks he always carried.

"I think so, but I was in cat shape. I should be able to recognize them if they come to Silverpool," I said. "Sometimes I remember things that only a cat would notice."

"I suppose that's how Lionel recognized you," he said. "If you'd been a bird or a dog, he might not have been able to."

That surprised me. I'd thought Lionel had been able to see me because he had the power to identify humans in all shapes—not because I was specifically in cat form. "What do you mean?"

"Takes one to know one." He looked at the house with a sigh. "I'm going to miss that man."

"Lionel was a cat shifter?"

Nodding, he gestured at the cats around the yard. "Sure wasn't interested in dogs."

"I didn't realize…," I said, trailing off. Maybe he, too, had been allergic to cats, which was why he kept the magic antidote handy. "I'm sad I didn't get to talk to him longer."

Darius gave me a bleak look. "Yeah," he said, snapping his notebook shut. "I need to get back to work. We're all supposed to help collect the cats."

"What's going to happen to them?"

"Too many to go to Diamond Street, so they've got a warehouse in Richmond they're looking at."

"A warehouse?"

"Near the bridge. Industrial area. Nobody there will get too curious."

If I remembered right, there was a massive garbage dump and an oil refinery. "A warehouse? But they're living creatures."

"It's just for a day or two. They need a secure location to scan them."

Shivering in the cold breeze, I looked up at the cloudy sky. "It's December. They'll be miserable. They've been coddled their whole lives."

"The old witch is dead. Those Bright days are over for them."

"How can you be so cruel?"

Darius spun on me. "Something killed that man in his own home. Left his body on the floor like… like a *hair ball.* In his own home! The youth spell had worn off, of course, so he hadn't been able to retain even that small dignity. What I saw was more bones than flesh." He fell silent, scowling. "That old man never hurt a—" He turned away abruptly, falling silent.

I realized his gruff tone was because he cared too much, not too little. "You knew him."

He spun around. "Of course I knew him. My parents knew him. My grandparents knew him. He was an icon in the East Bay."

"I'm sorry for your loss."

He shook his head and rubbed his eyes. "Just go home."

"I really am sorry—"

"Please. I'll call if there's anything else I need in your statement."

I nodded and stepped back, almost crushing a cat that was curled up in a ball at my feet in a sunny patch on the sidewalk. While Darius strode away to the agents setting up the hiding spells, I bent down and stroked the wiry fur, whispering my condolences for its loss. The witches with animal carriers were hauling them into the van and taking out new ones as they cast more spells to trap the remaining cats.

I petted the sleeping cat's back, felt its fragile bones. It purred, got to its feet, and began snaking its body around my hand, wrist, and arm. A graceful tail stroked me under my nose.

I looked up at the Protectorate's animal control unit. The women were quick and efficient, but not as gentle as they should've been. Under the catnip spell, the cats were easily snatched and thrown into the cages. They might be in those carriers for days, even longer.

The cat under my hand collapsed on the sidewalk again, purring more loudly as it invited my touch.

Oh, demon's balls. I picked it up, tucked it into my jacket, and hurried across the street, casting a confusion spell of my own behind me.

Looked like I'd be adding mouse bones to my diet from now on.

๑๙๛

Although the drive through Marin County was sunny and clear, as soon as I turned off on the Riovaca Highway to reach rural western Sonoma County, heavy clouds appeared overhead. By the time I was driving over the Silverpool Bridge, a light rain had begun to fall.

I was glad to have made the drive in the daylight. With the impending solstice, celebrating fae had arrived in greater numbers and were haunting the wooded ravines to the side of the road, tempting drivers with their songs, twinkling lights, and misty dreams. Even with my most powerful wooded focus beads, I wasn't immune. Their temptations were far worse—much stronger—than on the San Francisco Bay. In fact, because I could see and hear the fae even when they hadn't intended for me to do so, I had to block out a cacophony of sensory distractions, which was hard enough to do anyway on a narrow mountain road with dozens of treacherous switchbacks along the river and redwoods.

The cat I'd rescued was curled up in my jacket on the back seat. I'd almost turned back twice to return it to Berkeley, but it looked so cozy and frail as it slept I hadn't had the heart.

Such an old cat, with the sense and skill to get a sentimental witch like me to adopt it, must've been with Lionel a long time. It had barely opened its eyes for the entire journey, and I'd kept reaching back to make sure it was still alive. Now, pulling into my driveway in Silverpool, the first thing I did was to feel the cat's breath. I'd had no choice but to rescue it. It never would've survived a night in a freezing warehouse.

I bundled the animal in my arms and walked into my backyard. My house was well guarded by my own spells, but Willy had stepped in a few times at unexpected moments to back me up—with shocking force—and I had learned not to offend him. We were allies, neighbors, and even friends, but I knew the bond was tenuous—and on his terms. If I was going to bring a new creature into the arrangement, he would appreciate my consulting him.

"Willy?" I called out. The animal in my arms was limp but purring.

The gnome appeared without flourish at my feet. Usually he pretended to walk out of a little door at the base of the redwood tree where he lived, but this afternoon he simply flashed into sight a few steps in front of me. He wore a red velvet jacket that looked a little different than usual—a brighter red and longer in the waist, though tighter.

"Only a moment am I having, Alma, for there is an important visitor and she is hot-tempered, quite difficult and impossible as everyone knows, and if I'm late, there won't be anything to be done but weep and drink rainwater." He looked up at the sky, and drizzle fell on his bearded face. "At least the weather is fine, at least there is that, I am thinking."

I wanted to ask questions about his visitor—he never had visitors, so that was exciting and I was dying to know more—but I was getting wet, and so was the cat. "I wanted to introduce you to a cat I'm bringing home today, Gnome Willy," I said, hoping the formal address would buy me a minute of his time. He was already turning away to go. "It seemed to adopt me, and I didn't have the heart to say no."

"It is a he, dearest Alma, which is so common among the forlorn, have you noticed? We are a sad lot, the he. The males. Our hearts are broken, our bodies are old, and"—he tugged at his velvet coat—"our buttons are too tight. How is this possible when I have kept it so carefully wrapped in leaves from the Old Home all these years? It has seen no sunlight, no rain. Until now, what a lovely day, the solstice is almost here. I must be going. She will not want to be waiting. She is often such an angry thing, as hot as the sun. Perhaps the long night of a big moon will soothe her fires."

Now I was *really* curious. "A… *female* gnome is visiting you?"

13

Willy pointed at the cat. "He is tired and thirsty and is not liking this water on his whiskers, Alma, please be having consideration. Cats are not gnomes. Not ever."

I looked down. The poor thing did look more miserable than he had a moment ago. Taking Willy's concern for his well-being as permission for him to live with us, I hugged the cat and turned to the house. "Thank you for the excellent advice as always, Willy. Good luck with your guest."

"I will be needing more luck than even a talented, kind-tempered witch such as yourself has available to offer, alas and terribly sad it is. But I thank you." He vanished.

I smiled, imagining Willy on a date. Apparently he had a lady friend, one he'd known for ages from the old country. He'd sung long ballads about his dead wife, whom he'd adored, but I would've remembered if he'd ever mentioned another female gnome from his past. There had been one in Mendocino who had helped me—was that his visitor? Had I somehow brought them together again?

Speaking of being brought back together—I missed my

dog. I texted Birdie that I was home, and a few minutes later I was inside with the kitty, setting up a padded area in the warmest spot in the living room. Under a pile of crumpled plastic bags under my sink, I found a can of cat food, something I'd bought for myself. Ugh. I didn't like to think about eating Tuna Delight every time I went looking for beans, so I'd put it with the cleaning supplies.

The cat opened an eye when I waved it in front of him, then ignored it and fell back asleep. I scraped it into a bowl and left it nearby with some water.

I wondered if I'd made a mistake taking him away from the other cats. Maybe he was friends with one or more of them. Familiar company.

But I reminded myself those animals would be sleeping on hard concrete in a drafty warehouse. The nights would be cold and lonely. Traumatic.

I scratched him—I'd need to come up with a name—behind the ears, smiling as he rolled onto his back and purred. He'd chosen me, perhaps with Lionel's spirit's help somehow, and I had to respect that. He might not last long, but at least I could keep him warm and safe. While he slept, I made myself a quesadilla and ate it at my kitchen table, thinking about Poppy Almasi, Lionel, the new Director, my father, the books, the secret meeting.

My mother, an orphan, had wanted a demon to possess her. Vera, for reasons of her own, had obliged. Now they were gone, and I was here with a cat who slept with his scraggly paws in the air like a dead bug.

I closed my eyes, feeling sad, angry, hurt, and confused. The only person I'd ever met who could tell me about Poppy had been murdered. I couldn't think of what the connection would be, but it was too much of a coincidence. Or had the genie been involved somehow?

When I got up to wash the dishes, there was a knock at

the door. I went over to find Birdie standing there with Random. My dog was restless and sniffing the threshold.

"You didn't have to bring him," I said. "I was going to come by."

"I was glad for the walk," Birdie said. "But I can't stay because I'm setting up the store, which is kind of an exaggeration because I only have nine shelves, but it's better than nothing, don't you think? I've already got people coming in, and I think they're witches, but I'm not good enough yet to be able to tell that, but what other tourists would be here when the weather is so bad?"

"Probably witches," I said. "Thanks so much—"

She was already jogging away, shouting over her shoulder. "You're welcome! Come by later, OK? I've got somebody working for me, and maybe you could check her out? Hope she's not a demon in disguise, right?"

"You hired somebody?" I asked, concerned she was too trusting, but she'd already turned the corner of my house and disappeared from sight.

I'd have to call her later. For now, I had to make sure there wasn't any conflict between Random and the cat—

An eerie howl drew me back into the house. I hurried over to the cat's makeshift bed and was relieved to see he was sleeping just as I'd left him. Random, however, was on his belly, facing the cat food, his shackles raised, ready to pounce. It was the same posture he assumed for gophers hiding in a hole at the park.

"Hey doggo, it's all right, that's a good boy." I picked up the cat food and put it on the kitchen counter, then poured Random some fresh kibble in his own bowl. He ran over, tongue lolling, and attacked the proper meal with gusto.

The food soothed him for only a few minutes. As soon as he'd relieved himself outside, Random was back in the living room, growling at the cat.

He'd adjust. He'd whined and pulled on the leash to get at cats before, but those were strangers' cats away from home. This one was ours, and he wasn't doing anything threatening, just sleeping and purring. I kicked back on the couch and patted the cushion for Random to join me just like he always did. He was a good dog. It wouldn't take long for him to follow my lead and accept our new friend.

৩৯৯

I SOON LEARNED it was going to take Random longer than I'd thought. Pretending to relax on the couch didn't work; he kept pacing around the living room, sniffing and whining. The cat opened an eye once or twice but went immediately back to sleep. It was a one-sided battle.

Around six o'clock, I got a text from Raynor, telling me to come to the winery and give him a full report.

I looked at my dog, who was in the process of jumping off the ottoman to the floor, then onto a chair, onto the floor, onto the ottoman, and back onto the couch next to me.

It wouldn't be safe to leave the old cat with a suspicious dog, so I wrote back, *I can't leave my house right now.*

My phone rang. Raynor was escalating it to a voice call. "Why can't you leave the house?" He sounded tense. "What happened?"

I hesitated. It was better not to tell him I'd absconded with one of the murdered witch's cats. "It's nothing you need to worry about. My dog isn't well. I need to stay with him."

He sighed. "All right. Write it up. I'm paying you now. Do a formal report."

That would actually be better than being interrogated in person. "Sure. No problem."

"I hope your dog gets better before tomorrow," he said.

"You need to look over the new witches in town and see if you recognize anyone from Berkeley."

I stroked Random's rigid body. He relaxed slightly. "He'll be fine."

"We'll start with the campground," Raynor said. "Then walk around downtown. Cypress, the taqueria, your friend's new store."

"We?"

"If there's trouble, I don't want you getting involved," he said. "You'll tell me, and I'll handle it."

"Works for me."

The line was quiet a moment, then he said, "New York hasn't told me anything." He sounded annoyed. "I think they're trying to make a point about my new position being less than my previous one, even though there isn't a witch in the country who wouldn't lick a toad's nostril for the chance to be Protector of Silverpool. A lifetime appointment, your own winery, short drive from the beach…"

"It's a great job. You must be really happy."

He was quiet. We both knew he was not. But he said, "They won't hear me complaining. Their murder isn't my problem."

"Exactly."

He snorted again. "That doesn't mean you don't have to write up a report for me," he said. "Whatever you told Timms. And whatever you didn't tell him. I want that too."

I respected his insights and would tell him as much as I could, but the genie's role and the emotional drama I was experiencing would remain my secret. "Of course."

"Nine tomorrow morning," he said. "Meet me at the coffee truck outside Cypress Hardware. I'd rather go earlier, but there'd be no point if our targets are all asleep."

"Are we going in your car? You don't want to swing by and pick me up?"

Instead of answering, he hung up. Smiling, I put the phone away. It had been embarrassing for the now-Protector of Silverpool to get hurled through the air by a little red-coated gnome—and maybe a little terrifying. The respect he and Darius now held for me in my house was satisfying.

I curled up in bed with both the books Lionel had given me and had to tie Random down next to me with a leash to help him settle. The rodent remedies book was surprisingly fascinating, but I had to set it aside; given the circumstances, the book about possession seemed more important.

Warnings, however, turned out to be as dull as a plastic rock. No wonder my mother hadn't wanted to keep it.

Beware the morning.

Beware the afternoon.

Beware the night.

But more than those three, beware dusk, dawn, and thee.

If you hear a pleasing song, plug your ears, for the music may be coming from Shadow.

If you hear a terrible song, plug your ears, for that music may be Shadow as well.

If it is a dark cloth, beware the Shadow.

If it is a white cloth, beware the Shadow.

I looked at Random, who was whining softly next to me on the bed. I'd moved the cat's bed to a spot I could see through the doorway and had put the food and water back on the floor, as well as a fresh litter box. For his sake, I'd kept the wall furnace running at a higher temperature than usual.

Stifling a yawn, I went back to reading. Other than several blank pages in the middle of the book, which could've been a printing error, there was little to excite my curiosity.

Beware the dew on the fox's paw, for it will attract the fairy who will attract the Shadow.

Beware the sunlight on the forest clover, for it will delight the fairy who will attract the Shadow.

Taste not the summer honeysuckle, for the fairies need it to repel Shadow.

Taste not the summer strawberry, for the fairies need it to repel Shadow.

Taste not the summer sage, for the fairies need it to repel Shadow.

"For Brightness' sake," I said to Random, slipping lower into my bed, yawning as I closed the book. "They take the fun out of everything."

❧ 14 ❧

At some point around midnight, the cat got up and joined me on the bed, settling just out of Random's reach. The sound of plaintive dog cries woke me, and I had to get up and soothe him with a biscuit.

Even then I had to arrange myself at the foot of the bed to get between them. I curled up around Random and assured him I loved him very much, he was a very good dog, on and off until the dawn finally came.

Random could learn to accept the cat in time, but I couldn't stay home today to work on building their relationship—I had to patrol around town with Raynor.

Maybe Willy would have some insight. Around seven-fifteen, after Random had his breakfast, I took him out into the backyard and stood before the massive redwood tree. The sun had just begun to rise, and the yard was gloomy with fog and shadows.

"Willy?" I set down a small package of peanut butter sandwich cookies, which I knew he loved. "Could I ask you something?" I nudged Random's nose away from the cookies because he loved them too.

Willy flashed into sight a few feet in front of me, wearing a red velvet coat with a brown, bulbous seed of a California buckeye dangling from the buttonhole. It was an odd choice —they looked like fuzzy elk eyeballs and were as big as a baby's fist. His hair was slicked back, a distracting style that made me try to remember if I'd ever seen him without his hat on. His skull was as knobby as a walnut.

"Is your short life in its final moments?" he asked quickly, eyes blazing. The brown irises were flecked with gold and grass green.

"No, I'm fine, Willy," I said. "It's about the cat I brought home. Random is having trouble—I'm sorry, is this a bad time?"

"It indeed is being a very, very, extremely bad time this moment, Alma Bellrose." He spat on his palm and ran it over his head, gazing past me toward the house next door. "But tell me, female, though you are female of the human people, do I look pleasing to you this morning?"

I turned to look at Seth's house. The yard and garden between our houses had become overgrown, leaving many hiding places for all kinds of wildlife and fae, as I'd planned. Adding to its fairy appeal was that Seth had originally been fae himself.

Had another gnome moved in? Perhaps a female one?

"You look very handsome, Willy," I assured him.

He nodded absently, then flashed a nervous smile. "I am very thankful to hear that and also for the hard round cakes you offer. Hope is with me that they will be pleasing to others and not just my own self." He adjusted his coat. "Not all of my kind has been living here in the times long enough to become enjoying the new tastes. Peanut is one. This might be making her disgusted."

"Your friend is from the old country?" I asked.

His eyes widened. "There are no friends here but you,

95

Alma. I am thanking you for not calling others that. It would be good I think if you were going inside and not using that word anymore where it might cause the trouble."

"Sorry," I said quickly. "But do you think you could give me any advice about Random and the cat—"

"I am having none of the time to fix a situation that is hopeless, very much a problem, sadly for the new one."

"I won't keep you, I promise—but aren't you worried the cat is, I don't know, dangerous—?"

He gave me a pitying look. "He is dangerous if your short life is hurting to be reminded of its shortness. He is a very old creature. Very old. Not long for this realm."

"Right," I said. "So, not a threat. Why then is Random so upset about him?"

"It is known among some wise folk that a dog and a cat will not be so loving with each other," he said. "Is this wisdom you are lacking when you come here and use my time, which I am needing to prepare for other, more enjoyable, I hope, conversations?"

I bowed my head. "Thanks. Of course. I'm so used to magic I start thinking everything has some secret meaning behind it." My dog didn't like the old cat I'd brought home —I shouldn't have thought he would.

"Are you being sure the coat is pleasing on this body?" Willy asked, holding his arms out in a T.

"It's very pleasing. The velvet is... sharp."

"But you distress me, for velvet is being soft, not sharp, and—"

"Sharp as in handsome. Snazzy. Chic." I wasn't always able to keep a straight face with Willy, but his vulnerable face kept me from laughing.

A car honked from the road. I looked over my shoulder, but the house blocked my view. When I turned back, Willy was gone.

"Thanks again for talking to me," I said to the empty air. Then I took Random inside and peeked out the front windows to see who was honking.

Parked across from Seth's house was a black SUV, which usually meant a Protectorate agent. In no hurry to talk to any of those, I stayed where I was, watching from behind the curtains.

But it was Darius who got out. He walked around to the back, lifted the hatch, and took out...

My staff!

I yanked open my front door and ran outside. "Darius! Welcome to Silverpool!" I let Random come outside with me and closed the door.

Darius hefted the staff up and waved at me with it, keeping his distance. Because I was so glad he'd brought me the staff, I didn't tease him about being afraid of coming near my house. Random ran out to greet him first, who he'd met before and judged excellent, like all humans, including many who didn't deserve it.

I walked over. "Wow, talk about service," I said. The best I'd hoped for was the permission to come to San Francisco and pick it up myself.

Darius, in a dark fleece jacket and jeans, petted Random hello and then took out his notebook. Adopting a formal tone, he read from his notebook while holding the staff rigidly out to me. "Witch Alma Bellrose, please accept the apology of the Protectorate for the delay in restoring your magical property to you. Sincerely, Director Edward Timms, Diamond Street Office, San Francisco."

I grinned, made an exaggerated bow, and plucked the staff out of his hand.

A warm surge of magic ran out from my house, through the ground, and up into my body, leaving me tingling all over. Random, who didn't like the staff, ran back into the yard to pee on something.

"Thank you," I said, sighing with pleasure. From now on, I'd keep the staff with me as much as possible. Maybe all those times I'd left it at home had weakened my bond with it. I'd be sure to treat it with more respect going forward. Nobody liked being left behind.

Frowning, Darius shoved his notebook back into his pocket and leaned against the SUV. I wondered if he was angry at me again.

"I'm sorry you had to come all this way just to bring it to me," I said. "For what it's worth, I really appreciate it."

He rubbed his eyes. His posture and his bleary expression suggested he hadn't slept the night before. "It's not that. But you're welcome."

"Up all night with the dead body?" I asked. "Scanning the crime scene? Or were you on cat-sitting duty in that warehouse?" Since I hadn't slept well myself, I empathized.

"I would've been happy to do any of those things. But no. I've been sent to this Shadowed place again." He cast a spell of angry sparks at the road, and they sputtered and sizzled for a few seconds.

"Sent...?" I hugged the staff against my chest. If he was angry enough to start little fires in broad daylight, with nonmagical humans nearby, maybe he'd accidentally snap an enchanted hunk of redwood. "Sent for good?"

"If I quit the Protectorate entirely, they might let me go somewhere else," he said. "But as long as I want a job, I'm here. Working for Raynor. The new Protector needs underlings, apparently."

"They didn't give you a choice?"

"None. And if that wasn't bad enough, my sister is quitting to work for our parents' accounting firm." His furious look made me flinch.

"Rochelle quit?" I asked. His little sister had been a Flint agent like I'd been. But unlike me, she'd seemed determined to stay—ambitious and serious about her assignments. "Why?"

"No good reason."

I'd known Darius for long enough to guess what that meant. "Is there a man involved?"

He snorted. "She claims not. Says she's been having doubts for a while, which is demonspit. She would've told me."

"That week in Mendocino was stressful for all of us," I said.

"She said it has nothing to do with trauma. Nothing about death, demons, even magic. It's financial. She wants to buy a house, which isn't possible in the Bay Area on an agent's salary for at least a decade."

Darius' sister clearly idolized him, and I worried about him hurting her feelings with his judgment. He didn't always express himself with subtlety. "Does she know you think she should stick it out as an agent?" I asked. "Maybe if she had your support—"

"I don't care if she works for the Protectorate or not," he said. "If she's unhappy, she should leave. But working as an accountant? Living a nonmagical life? No way."

"There's not much else available," I said, gesturing at my humble cottage.

"She could go to grad school," he said. "Teach. Study. Something other than spreadsheets. So what if tax prep pays the bills? She'll die of boredom."

"You told me the same thing, if you remember," I said.

"You worked for my parents?"

"I moved to Silverpool, where you said I'd die of boredom." I thought of all the hexes and murders I'd dealt with the past year. "Quite the contrary—I've nearly died of excitement."

"Only because you seek it out," he said, "which proves my point. You need a challenge. And so does my sister."

"Nothing is permanent. She can change her mind if she gets bored."

"I suppose." He gestured at the staff in my hand. "I'm glad you got that back. I'd submitted a statement confirming it was yours, but they didn't want to give it up until Timms got involved."

I stroked the warm wood. A residue of the scans done by Emerald witches at Diamond Street remained on its surface, eating away at the enchantment I'd cast on it when I'd made it. Redwood was a soft, easily splintered wood, and I'd needed to use magic to keep it strong. "I'll have to use it more to wipe off the Protectorate cooties they left all over it."

"I wrapped it in a velvet blanket in the car," he said. "I didn't want you giving me a hard time for doing something to it."

Poor Darius. He'd followed all the rules, but they'd put him in Silverpool, far from where he wanted to be. "Thanks so much for delivering it. I know I can trust you." I fought off the impulse to give him a hug. "It means a lot to me."

The corner of his mouth flicked upward in a quick, half-hearted smile. "You're welcome. If you need me, I'll be drinking myself under the tasting bar at the winery."

"Sounds like a plan."

He smiled more broadly, then got in the SUV and drove away. I stayed on the road, watching him drive out of sight. Something made me stay there instead of going back inside. Seth's house was dark and quiet, but I felt something…

I looked up into the low, thick branch of an oak tree in Seth's front yard. A female gnome in a brown dress sat there in a side-saddle position, as if riding a pony. Like her clothes, her hair and skin were brown. Her round-toed boots were a mossy green. Where Willy stood out with his bright colors and jaunty cap and pipe, she blended into the natural background.

She looked concerned. Her gaze kept darting over to the end of the road where Darius had gone.

"That witch won't hurt you," I said. When she didn't move, I added, "And neither will I."

In a flash, she left the tree and appeared beside me in the road. Her expression was hard to read, but I would guess she was curious. She tilted her head back and forth, up and down, studying me. The braids wrapped around her head bobbed slightly with the movement.

I remembered the first day I'd met Willy—well, the first day he'd shown himself to me. My small gesture had cemented a friendship that had possibly saved my life once or twice. She'd shown herself to me now, and I wanted to display my gratitude for the honor as I'd done then.

"Will you wait a moment? I have something for you." I said, putting a hand over my heart. I paused to make sure she wasn't going to disappear, then bent down and plucked a big three-leaved redwood sorrel stem from amid the sword ferns. It was an enchantment I'd practiced many times for Willy's sake, and I was able to cast it instantly. Then I bent on one knee and held out the four-leaved clover to the visitor.

She raised an eyebrow, looked at me, then took it. Unlike Willy, she didn't fall over herself thanking me. I had the impression that if she'd been human, she would've rolled her eyes.

But she gave me a polite bow of her head and tucked it in her buttonhole, just as Willy liked to do. As she faded away —she didn't flash out of sight, but drifted away like the tree-tops in fog—she said, "Call me Olive."

❧ 15 ❧

I t was almost eight thirty, and Raynor was expecting me, but I still couldn't leave the animals alone in the house. Random just couldn't settle down. So I called Birdie.

"I wonder if I could ask you a really, really big favor," I said.

"Sure," she said, breathing heavily. It sounded like she was already hard at work. There were banging, tearing, and thumping sounds in the background.

"I rescued an old cat," I said. "Long story. It was an impulse. But Random is upset, and I have to go—"

"Bring me the cat!" I heard a grunt, then a loud thud. "Perfect timing. That's just what we're missing. Every bookstore needs a cat. Especially a witch bookstore, right? I made actual money yesterday, can you believe that? I sold one of the necklaces you said I could sell, and that was great except now I don't have anything to put on the display. Can you make me another one?"

"Of course. I'd love to. Especially if you take the cat for a little while. It isn't permanent—unless you really click, then of course." I leaned down and stroked the cat's bony head. "I should tell you, though, this cat used to live with a powerful old witch. And, ah… he was murdered."

"What? Again?"

I flinched. My life was not normal. "It was in Berkeley," I said, as if that explained everything. "The Protectorate is investigating, and they weren't nice to the cats, so I took him."

"Of course you did. Of course."

"So, I don't *think* the cat is dangerous, but there's never a guarantee with—"

"I don't care. Bring her—him? Except I don't have a litter b—"

"He's a he. I'll bring the box. If it doesn't work out, no problem. Random just needs time to adjust."

She continued to agree, claiming it was fate, so I packed up the car with the box, fresh litter, food, and a blanket. Then I lifted the cat in my arms, wished Random well, and left him there to enjoy the empty house.

I drove into town and parked on the side street next to Birdie's store. She must've seen me drive by, because she hurried out, waving, with another woman I didn't recognize right behind her. The cat was on a blanket behind my seat, and I got out and lifted him out while Birdie chattered away. The furry thing curled up in my arms, purring. I felt bad to leave him with Birdie but didn't know what else I could do.

"This is Joanna," Birdie said. "Joanna, this is Alma. And there is our new cat, or Alma's cat, or the dead guy's cat. He's his own cat. What's his name? He doesn't have one? Look at how bony he is. But his fur is really soft. Feel him, Joanna, isn't that soft? I bet he's cold, so let's bring him inside. I think we should call him Frank. Is that OK? OK, Frank it is. I learned a warming spell that shouldn't set anything on fire, but maybe you could check it out, Alma? It'll be great for the kitty. I cast it in the middle of the store so people are drawn in to shop. I think ambience is so important, don't you? Even if it's not magic…"

She continued speaking as she took the cat—Frank—out of my arms and into the building. Joanna, a thirtyish fair-skinned woman with her blond hair styled into two space buns, helped me carry in the gear. She wore jeans and a sweatshirt adorned with a large cat face. There was glitter.

"You like cats?" I asked.

She lifted her hand and laughed into her palm, as if she were a kid in math class afraid of getting into trouble. "Yes," she said, lowering her hand and shoving it in her pocket.

My impression of Birdie's new hire was that she was a witch of above-average skill and below-average sophistication.

I walked around the store, impressed by how much Birdie had done in just a few days. The space had been an abandoned travel agency for years, but she'd gotten help cleaning up, emptying out the dusty old furniture, and setting up some bookshelves and comfortable chairs. The customer-service counter was near the front door, flanked by a slipcovered sofa. An enchanted bouquet of dried lavender hung from a copper wire above the doorway, cleaning the air with each visitor.

It was still a skeleton of what it could be, but the store was already welcoming in an eccentric, witchy way. The second floor was a separate two-bedroom apartment where Birdie had moved last month. Since then, she'd been working to cast several boundary spells marking the entire building as her home, but she was still new to magic, and I felt the holes where visiting witches had left their magical fingerprints just yesterday.

She had much more to do, and learn, to make it secure. It was tricky to have a boundary that allowed so many witches inside—necessary in retail—before knowing if they were safe or not.

"I'll come back in a few hours to make sure everything's going all right," I said. "I can take Frank back home with me if it's not w—"

"Look at him." Birdie pointed at the couch where Joanna held Frank against her cheek. Actually, she wasn't doing much holding—Frank had climbed up onto the cushions so he could balance on her shoulder. One of her buns had come loose, nestling Frank under a shank of hair. I could hear the purring from several paces away.

I smiled at Joanna. "Good thing you like cats."

Her eyes were half-closed, enjoying Frank's attention, and she didn't say anything. My guilt eased a bit.

With a start, I realized the time, thanked them both again, and ran out to the street. Rather than drive one block, I jogged to the Cypress Hardware parking lot. Raynor was waiting for me next to the coffee truck, his big shoulders hunched up to his ears in the cold.

"It's nine-oh-nine," he said.

I sucked in my breath. "Sorry. I had— Something came up."

"At Birdie's?"

Raynor was still an agent, a demon hunter, an Emerald witch, a former Director, and the Protector of Silverpool. He didn't miss much.

"Yes," I said, stepping over to the truck to order myself a hot chocolate. I'd given up coffee, but a dark morning in December needed something.

"She has a new witch in there with her," he said when I rejoined him. "Did you check her out?"

I flushed, realizing I hadn't given her a proper scan because I'd been distracted by the cat, the store, and my hurry to meet him. "She likes cats," I said, licking the swiftly melting whipped cream on my breakfast.

He raised an unimpressed eyebrow. "Imagine that. I thought she wore cat illustrations on her clothing because she wanted to repel them."

"If you'd met her already, why did you ask if I had?"

"Your perspective might've been useful," he said. "I'm capable of admitting my limitations. You and she have a lot in common. Maybe you noticed something."

My ego recoiled. He hadn't said his beautiful girlfriend and I had a lot in common, but sure, me and the socially awkward cat girl were like twins. "I'll look at her more closely next time. I was in a hurry to meet you."

We got into his car. He frowned at my drink, so I put the lid back on, silently mourning my tongue's loss of access to the whipped cream. I reached for a new topic. "I was already running late because Darius came by," I said. "Did you put in the request for him to be assigned to you?"

"I wouldn't do that to him," he said. "And they wouldn't listen if I had. I'm not their favorite Emerald right now."

"What do you think of Timms?"

"He's all right, I guess." He frowned again at my hot chocolate, and I felt a protective spell waft over, wiping away the drops that threatened to fall from the edges. "He doesn't make waves. Follows the rules. He says he'll give me my independence up here, but we'll see if he means it. He's coming up tomorrow for the solstice. New York seems to think I'm too new to the job to handle the big event myself."

"He seems nice. He gave me my staff back," I said.

"Careful he's not trying to get something from you."

"That's what I was afraid of," I said. "But Emeralds like you two do that anyway." I sipped my hot chocolate, smiling silently to myself. I'd likened him to a witch in a way he wouldn't find complimentary, just as he'd done with me.

As we drove by Birdie's bookstore, I saw Joanna in the window, setting up a display. Through the glass, which had been touched by Birdie's spells, I noticed something I hadn't seen in person.

Ears. Pointy, furry ones, on top of her head, right where the space buns had been. The reflection of the glass also distorted her features into a white blur marked by two dark, shining eyes.

"Stop the car," I said.

❧ 16 ❧

Raynor didn't question me, which I appreciated, just pulled over into the next gap at the curb.

"Birdie's new assistant can shift into a cat," I said.

"You scanned her in the window just now," he said. Not a question.

"Didn't have to. I just saw it."

"Good work," he said. "I missed that."

"Thanks. Maybe it takes one to know one."

"See? I knew you two had a bond of some kind."

I rolled my eyes. Maybe he was right. "Listen, I'd like to go out to the encampment by myself."

"We had a plan. Like last time—"

"Last time I didn't have a magical antihistamine," I said.

He scratched his bald head. "You're going to shift?"

Seeing Joanna had given me the idea. If I was going to be a witness, I should be the best I could be, even if I didn't enjoy shifting. "I'll have the same perspective as I did at the meeting."

"But it takes hours for your mind to catch up. And doesn't it drain you? The solstice is tomorrow. If any—"

"Look around," I said. "It's deserted. There wasn't anyone at the coffee truck but us. The bookstore was empty. At nine in the morning, most witches are still asleep, especially the demon-loving kind. They were probably up late, casting spells at the moon and stars. In a few hours, when they get out of their tents and start walking around, I'll be ready."

He frowned but said, "Fine. But I want a report as soon as possible. If any of them are bringing demons into my town, I need to know."

I opened the door and stepped out. "Of course, Protector." I smiled, glad he was taking some pride in the job he didn't want.

"Call me as soon as you're human again," he said.

"Will do."

A moment later, he drove off. I got into my Jeep and headed west, nursing the last of my hot chocolate. From the lack of symptoms I'd had around Frank, I knew the magic of Lionel's mouse bones were still working.

A jolt of anger struck me. Somebody had killed the old witch in his own home, ending his kindness, his wisdom, the unique flame of his magic. I accelerated, suddenly motivated to get to the witches' encampment faster. If any of them had anything to do with his death, I'd find them.

That is, after I wandered around the field and woods for a few hours, killing birds and eating things I didn't want to remember. I found a woodsy turnout to park the Jeep near the encampment, undressed, and shifted before I could give in to any doubts.

When I regained my human consciousness, the sun had passed midday. Rain clouds were rolling in, about to shroud Silverpool in gloom. I was sitting on the bank above the flowing river, playing with a dead field mouse. That was an unusual prey for me, and I wondered if the remains of the bones in my spiritual bloodstream had made me hunger for it again. Perhaps it would become a new staple in my diet in both shapes—a thought that gave me no pleasure.

I lifted my nose and tasted humans and magic in the air. The campground wasn't far. It took me a few minutes to remember to let my cat form move on its own without my input—otherwise I'd start doing dumb things like stepping over branches instead of leaping or crawling—and by the time I was walking between human legs, glancing up at witches' faces, I was graceful again.

There were at least two dozen tents, four RVs, several trailers, and nineteen cars spread out in a grassy, open field above the river—twice as many since a few days ago. I'd expected the crowds as we got closer to the solstice. In spite of their counterculture ambitions, the witches I saw—and rubbed against—were ordinary humans with jobs and mundane responsibilities that didn't allow them to drop everything and take a week off looking for fae and demons in Sonoma County.

When it began to rain, the witches pretended not to care. A few umbrellas came out, but others let the rain soak their hair and shoulders, occasionally looking up into the sky and smiling as if the ordeals of existence only made them more powerful while they sipped their camp stove coffee.

Maybe I was being judgmental because being wet made me more miserable as a cat than I'd ever felt in my human form. It took every magical atom of my human brain power to keep walking around, looking up at faces, instead of running into a dry tent and making some stupid person cuddle and feed me.

There was a long-legged man with dreadlocks and a pink umbrella, who looked youthful until he bent down to pet me, and a closer look showed he was pushing eighty. He was wearing a white T-shirt with the same distorted yin-yang symbol I'd seen at the Berkeley meeting. A female witch with a head-to-toe raincoat around her short, round body smelled promising, reminding me of the owner of the Berkeley house, but when I rubbed up against the raincoat, she kicked me.

"I'll bite you, kitty," came a horrible, growling voice from above. I looked up into a sneering face—beautiful but scary—that I'd never seen before. Glad to remain strangers, I ran away, finally giving in to the seduction of a dry tent.

At first I thought the cozy space was empty, but then I felt a hand come down on my back. Arching into her palm, I looked into the face of the woman who'd been sitting behind me at the Berkeley meeting, the one who'd known Lionel and talked about his books. And the other clothes in the tent smelled the same as the man at the meeting. My cat brain couldn't remember her name, but Lionel had mentioned both of them. Jaden and Tanya? No... Aidan and Candy?

I rubbed up against her, drawing upon her witch power to enhance my memory. *Brayden and Trudy.* Yes.

Trudy was the one with nice fingernails who'd scratched my back as nicely as she was doing now. I purred without shame and climbed into a fluffy sleeping bag with her.

"You poor thing," Trudy said, stroking my head as she yawned. "Who brought you here? They're a monster."

I purred some more.

"Well, sorry, but you can't stay here. You're getting mud on my boyfriend's bag."

I flopped onto my back and gave her a seductive yawn.

"Nice try," she said. "Still no." She lifted me, pushed me out of the tent, and zipped up the flap behind me.

Well, how nice could she really be if she wanted a demon possession? I went on to look for other familiar faces.

As I walked around, I detected the scent of two other

beings I thought were familiar, but I was unable to find the individuals who matched the scents, and staying in cat form while focusing so intently was exhausting me. Lionel had helped me recover from the meeting in Berkeley, but I didn't feel the same endurance now. Plus it was still raining, which was increasingly intolerable.

I decided I'd done all I could do under the circumstances and went back to the car. I looked up at the rear window, far above my head, that I'd primed with a half-finished opening spell for my cat self to get back in. But I couldn't muster the strength I needed to leap that high and do magic at the same time.

The rain continued to pelt my miserable body, so I crawled under the Jeep. I found a promising spot directly below the magic beads, herbs, and amulets I'd stored beneath the driver's seat.

A few minutes later, after I'd drawn from its power, I was able to find the strength to slink back out into the rain, open the window, and leap inside.

I shook, hating my life and all humans.

And then I shifted back into my human form and narrowed down the objects of my resentment to Shadow witches, witches who came to Silverpool, witches who went to meetings about demon possession, witches with tents, and rain. Also Raynor.

Being back in my human form was a relief, but I was still exhausted. I huddled in a ball under the quilt kept in the car until I stopped shaking. It became clear that the strength of Lionel's anti-allergy owl vomit was wearing off; a sneezing fit struck me, and itchy, coin-sized welts appeared on my skin.

I should've found more owl pellets before shifting. Yawning and sneezing at the same time, I fumbled into my clothes and climbed into the front seat. Then I rested my head back and fought the delicious temptation of falling into a coma.

The shift had drained me utterly. Instead of hot chocolate, I should've indulged in a double espresso.

I opened my eyes and blinked rapidly to stay awake. If I went home, I'd just fall asleep until my body and well of power recovered naturally, which from the way I felt, could take all day and all night. I'd be too late to get the information to Raynor at a useful time. There weren't any herbs or spells I'd found that could give me what I myself was lacking —it would be like trying to pick yourself up by your own bootstraps. Scientifically impossible.

But the power of the tide, especially the day before the solstice...

If I found the sweet spot between ocean waves and dry land...

That power would help. It would be worth a drive to the coast. It wasn't far from the encampment, which was probably why the witches loved the spot, placed halfway between the wellspring and the sea.

I rolled down the windows for the bracing fresh air and again drove west. As I drove, I sucked on my redwood beaded necklace and widened my eyes as much as possible. I probably looked like a surprised toddler, but the close contact between my bloodstream and the magical redwood kept me awake. With its help, I reached Highway 1 on the coast and turned left. Already feeling refreshed by the sea air, I drove south along the rugged cliffs until the shoulder was wide enough for me to park and get out.

Cold rain spattered me in the face, waking me further. I walked to the boulders alongside the road, tripping in my weakened state, until I found a hidden path down to a private beach that I knew about.

I wiped the rain out of my eyes and reached out for

balance as I climbed down. Below me, the storm had created a high surf that was washing piles of kelp and debris ashore. If I found driftwood in the best zone between tide and land, it would help me recover even faster; seeing how much material was on the sand, I felt optimistic I'd find what I needed.

Just before I reached the beach, I stumbled the last few feet and landed on my hands and knees. Damp hair into my eyes, blocking my sight, but I was happy to feel the cold, damp sand under my palms and fingers. It was in the zone. The liminal zone, betwixt and between, wet and dry, up and down, land and sea. The zone driven as much by the moon as it was by the earth.

I bent down and rested my forehead in the sand, inhaling wonderfully salty, fishy air. Energy flowed up my hands and into my arms and legs, my torso, my chest, my head. For several minutes, I drank in the power.

When I was refreshed, I pushed up onto my knees to look up at the rain the way the encampment witches had done and say hello—directly and fearlessly—to the sky.

But it was Seth who stood above me. Smiling, he took a sip from a stainless steel bottle in his hand.

"Fancy meeting you here," he said.

❧ 17 ❧

I wiped the rain out of my face and got to my feet. My head was clear, my legs steady. "Were you following me?"

He held out his bottle to me. "You look like you could use a drink. Rough day?"

"The usual." I studied the bottle. "Is that something hot?"

"Sorry," he said. "Springwater."

I wrapped my arms around myself and shook my head. My jacket had a hood, but the cold wind was blowing rain into my face. "That won't do it for me."

"Such a shame," he said. "It does everything for me." A lake fairy by birth, Seth was deeply affected by the magic in the wellspring. In fact, he'd told me his mother had warned him to never drink it because it would make him dependent and vulnerable. He'd finally given in to the temptation recently.

"Tell me you weren't following me," I said.

"I wasn't following you." He smiled. "I would've, though. You could've shared my picnic."

I pulled the hood over my eyes, hunching into the wind. "Lovely day for it."

He grinned widely. "Isn't it?" Water in all forms made him happy.

Having received the energy I needed, I turned and began climbing back up to the road. "Well, I've got to be going. Enjoy your picnic."

"Don't go," he said. "Here, does that help?"

"Does what—" I began, then stopped when I realized the rain was no longer landing on me. He'd put a bubble of dry, warm air around my body. I'd been too drained of magic to do it for myself.

I turned, frowning. "I'd rather you didn't use your weird fae enchantments on me without my permission."

"What I did had nothing to do with you. You're just the same. It's the water around you that's changed." He sipped the springwater and shrugged. "And maybe a little tiny bit of the air. You looked cold. It was making me uncomfortable."

It did feel good to be in a warm, dry bubble. "Thanks. I *was* cold."

"I heard about the old witch," he said. "The murdered one. Did it have anything to do with you going to Berkeley the day before yesterday?"

It annoyed me he kept track of my movements. "Why do you know that?"

He looked away, stroking his jaw. His dark hair gave him an attractive shadow. "Sorry. Sometimes I can't help what I know."

"Couldn't help? Or couldn't stop yourself?"

He turned back to me. "Just like I couldn't help but notice you face-planted in the sand there a minute ago, I couldn't help noticing the smell of University Avenue on your tires when you drove back into town." His gaze held mine. "There's a bond between us. You feel it too."

A shiver ran down my back. He was right. The demon in me and the fae in him were drawn to each other, but was that a good thing? Demons ate fairies for sport.

So then why did I always feel like prey?

There was an old fallen tree near us. I sat down on it, too shaken to care if Seth's fairy bubble would keep my pants dry.

"Who told you about Lionel?" I asked, negotiating a safer subject. "I'm not accusing you of anything. I'm just curious." I did trust Seth, but he still loved to hide things from me. His fae powers were mysterious, filtered as they were by a human body and the death of the human who'd owned it briefly at birth.

"A table of drunk witches from out of town were talking about it at Taco Perdido." He sat next to me. "Your beefy boss dude should tell them to keep it down. The nonmagical folks were probably getting creeped out. Aren't you supposed to keep your magical wiles a secret?"

"Beefy boss?" I had to smile. "Do you mean Raynor?"

His face remained serious. "It's his job to keep the peace for all humans, not just the witchy ones. You should remind him of that. There are a lot of normal people in Silverpool who shouldn't have to hear about demon possession while they're eating their nachos supreme."

His vehemence surprised me. In spite of his constant joking, Seth had a serious core.

"Did you recognize any of the witches?" I asked. "Maybe you could ask the river fairy if he'd seen any witches leave the night Lionel was killed. Or maybe you could use your fae talents to see if any of them have the taste of University Avenue on their tires."

"The tires weren't inside the taqueria," he said. "But yes, I'd say you weren't the only one who'd been to the East Bay, but I'm not attuned to them the way I am to you." He held my gaze again.

I regarded him openly, giving in to my curiosity. Rain seemed to land directly on him, but he remained dry. The dark hair, the long nose, the dimple in his chin—human but inhuman, thirty but ageless.

"I don't like Raynor's girlfriend," I said suddenly.

Finally breaking his gaze, he looked down at his hands. The bottle had been replaced by the remains of a tiny, fragile crab shell. "Maybe you're jealous," he said.

My heart was beating too fast. What were we playing at? "Maybe," I said.

Still looking down, he smiled. The shell, thin as paper, blew off his palm into the beach grass on the slope behind us.

"When you figure that out, let me know," he said, then blinked out of sight.

Rain began spattering me in the face again.

◊❦◊

I DIDN'T FEEL like writing a report or being grilled over the phone, so I went directly to the winery to meet with Raynor in person. He could scan me and get the two women's faces from my memories, check them out himself, leave me out of it. The sea had refreshed me, but Seth had drained me again, and I needed my house to truly recover.

It was already dark when I parked next to the winery residence and got out. The rain had weakened to a drizzle, and the wind had died down, but the night was cold. My stomach growled, reminding me I hadn't eaten all day— except for whatever my cat stomach had enjoyed. On the other side of the driveway, above the rows of dormant grapevines, was the small building for visitors. I wondered if Darius had drunk himself under the tasting bar as he'd promised. For his sake, I hoped so. The man needed a vacation.

I walked over to the house. As soon as my foot touched the welcome mat, the front door opened on its own. An invitation. I stepped over the threshold, feeling the tingle of a scan far stronger than Birdie's had been, and headed deeper inside.

Memories struck me. Before Raynor, the Protector of Silverpool had been a witch named Tristan Price. He'd been a friend of mine, a boyfriend. He'd also been murdered, and solving the crime had shown me I'd never be able to escape supernatural threats. Although I'd ended my dangerous career with the Protectorate, I'd chosen to settle near a wellspring. I'd thought it was because of the beautiful redwoods, but now I had to admit to myself it was because I hadn't been willing to completely leave magical society. And magical society meant danger. It just did.

I followed the sounds of movement to a small room Tristan had used for storage. "Raynor? It's me, Alma. I'm here to give you—"

I turned the corner and saw Raynor's girlfriend, Kelly, standing behind a desk covered with books. She wore pink jeans and a dark T-shirt, and her hair was wrapped under a white silk scarf. A shimmering cloud of magic clung to her fingers—a dusting spell.

She was an author of magical reference work, so I wasn't surprised to find her with old books. "Hi," I said. "Sorry to bother you, I was—"

"He's not here," she said.

I felt my face get hot. It wasn't as if I made a habit of dropping in on her boyfriend. "Sorry," I said again. "When the door opened, I figured Raynor—"

"I'm expecting the pizza guy." She dropped the heavy book she'd been holding onto the desk. It was a striking yellow color with a three-inch binding; I recognized Tristan's favorite textbook from high school.

Pizza guy? She was lucky I wasn't a stranger with ill intent. Raynor needed to explain to her the dangers of living with a Protector near a wellspring.

On the floor at her feet was a pile of books as high as her knees, sloping to one side. If they were all Tristan's books, they were magical texts, some old enough to be valuable.

"Do you know where he is?" I asked. I could call him, but I wanted an excuse to learn what she was doing. Why was she going through the books by herself? She was clearly sorting them into categories of some kind—a pile here, a stack there.

After he'd died, I'd found a collection of Tristan's Shadow-market trinkets and amulets, and the Protectorate had quickly confiscated them. Looking at these books, I wondered why they were still at the winery. Birdie had inherited the estate after Tristan's death; if the Protectorate hadn't wanted them, they should've gone to her.

"He's probably still at the store," she said. "He's been watching witches coming and going there all day." She cracked open another book and studied its pages, barely glancing at me.

"Cypress Hardware?"

"That's the one." She brought the book to her nose, sniffed, and wrinkled her nose. "I can't believe Tristan kept this garbage."

"So...," I began. "They belonged to the previous Protector?"

"I assume so," she said. "I found them in a closet."

I cast out a quick scan. The book was old, smelling of lilac and... bumblebees. "May I?" I asked, holding out my hand.

She shrugged and let me take the thin hardcover out of

her fingers. It was a lovely book, once red and now pink, and although its gold foil engraving had worn off, the enchantment of spring flowers was as strong as the sunny morning when the spell had been cast. "It's beautiful," I said. Inside were illustrations of English gardens in the eighteenth century, each page infused with the scent of the plant or flower it represented.

"Take it," Kelly said. "Raynor said I could choose. We only want the good stuff."

I held it against my chest and stared blankly at her. "Good stuff?"

"You know, for a library," she said. "The winery should have references on metal, gemstone, and mineral technologies, don't you think? Or at least for the witches stuck here to have something to read."

Although I was very happy to keep the book, I couldn't resist needling her about her magical prejudices. "Don't you think growing grapes requires a knowledge of botanical magic?"

"The winery people grow the grapes. That's their job." She picked up another book, her face brightening. "Here's a good one—silver containers for potions made at dusk. That's what I'm talking about."

I walked over and picked up another book she'd discarded. *Fae and Flora of the Cape*, the yellowed paperback read. It looked like an encyclopedia about the fae known to prefer certain perennials. The book was focused on South Africa, which had the same kind of summer-dry climate as California. "Can I have this one too?"

"You can have anything on the floor," she said. "You'll be doing me a favor. I don't know who would want that old stuff."

Thinking about Birdie and myself, I said, "I do. Don't throw anything away."

She shrugged and picked up another book. "Suit yourself."

I picked up one of the empty boxes. "Can I use this?" She nodded, and I began scooping the books inside. About two dozen books of all sizes, young and old, in various states of condition, went into the box.

I eyed the ones in a pile behind her she'd yet to sort. "I'll come by tomorrow and see if you have any more you want to get rid of."

"They're all just hearth magic," she said. "Herbs and gardens. My granny would've said they were old-fashioned."

"Perfect," I said, and picked them up. "I'll come by tomorrow for any others."

She nodded without looking up. She'd found an encyclopedia of rocks and minerals, and was scanning it for inherent power with a charm she wore hanging from her belt on a long gold chain.

Her attitude about hearth magic was familiar to me, and I decided to take advantage of it. One person's treasure and all that.

I carried my box away, deciding to bring them to Birdie. She needed them more than I did. At the threshold, I paused to close up the box, protecting it from the rain, then hurried over to the car. Maybe I could keep just the bumblebee-scented one. How had the witch infused such a subtle scent into paper and cardboard? It was the sort of puzzle I lived for.

Right now, however, I couldn't afford to indulge in intellectual exercises; I needed to find Raynor. He didn't answer his cell, so I drove to Cypress Hardware, hoping he was still there. As I drove, I saw the river below the bridge was gushing and tumbling along, rising to flood levels. My headlights fell upon a solitary witch in a yellow raincoat who stood on the bridge walkway with her mouth open. I slowed, cracking my window, and heard her singing to the fae.

To her left, sitting on the railing—she could've reached out and touched him, had she seen him—was the green-skinned river fairy. As I drove by, I got a glimpse of his bewildered face as he stared at her. They didn't understand us any better than we understood them.

I hadn't seen the river fairy since he'd sent up the alarm about the demon-summoning witches the other day. Usually he stayed out of sight, hiding under the bridge. He wasn't articulate like Willy, but he was more verbal than most of the wood sprites nearby, who were only interested in their own company and were quick to fly into a panic when magical threats were around. Tonight his face was confused but calm, which assured me the witch wasn't casting any spell that was terribly dangerous.

At the Cypress parking lot, I was happy to see Raynor's car was still there. I parked next to him and went inside.

But before I had passed the customer-service desk near the front door, the new store manager, Nico, appeared from nowhere in front of me.

Startled, I stopped walking. He wore a fuzzy red holiday sweater over khakis, which should've made him look harmless but somehow made him seem sinister. Perhaps it was the six-inch metal wand he pointed at me, a metal I couldn't even identify. It looked like a fancy pen but was definitely not for writing.

And his smile made my blood tingle in my veins.

"What do you want here?" he asked.

❦ 18 ❦

I resisted the urge to grab my necklace, which might escalate our encounter into a conflict I hadn't intended and wasn't prepared for.

"Just shopping," I said, patting my thighs and glancing at the pen thing. It was giving off little waves of power. Although he was human, I trusted the genie more than this guy. "Is Jen around? As long as I'm here, I should say hello. We're kind of friends. Definitely friends."

He tilted his head slightly. "You don't say."

Having regained my composure, I straightened my shoulders and looked him directly in the eye. Talking to the genie would give me the opportunity to find out more about Lionel, if I had anything of value to give her. "Yes. She wouldn't want you pointing that thing at me."

He rolled the wand between his fingers, looking me over. "What did you come here to buy?"

A smoky haze filled my vision, and I found myself starting to say, "Noth—" before I fought off his truth spell. "Just browsing," I gasped, clenching my fists. The effort took the breath out of me, and a headache began to form behind my eyebrows.

"Perhaps you should go home." His cold voice pierced the spot between my eyebrows precisely where my headache was forming. "Now."

No longer controlling my limbs, I pivoted on my heels and faced the sliding doors to the parking lot. "Hey—"

"Happy holidays," he said fake-sweetly behind me.

My legs, stiff and numb, marched me toward the doors, which slid open just in time, then out into the cold, wet night. An animated reindeer constructed of wire and green lights nodded its antlers at me as I passed it on the sidewalk.

As soon as the doors shut behind me, my power came rushing back into my body, and I was able to stop walking. I spun around, fingers flexed, and pointed at the figure rapidly coming up behind me—

But it was Raynor. "Where are you going?" he asked. "Kelly said you were coming here to talk to me."

Breathing hard, I looked into the store to see if Nico was watching. I wanted to knock him down or at least steal that pen. Nobody messed with my bodily autonomy like that. I hadn't even done anything. Who did he think he—?

"Alma," Raynor said. "Talk to me."

I put my hand on my forehead and massaged the sore spot above my eyes. How embarrassing to let one witch take over my body so quickly. It had to be the genie's power, amplifying his, and forgetting the enchantment that prevented me from talking about her, I began to say, "There's a—"

My voice left me. My throat, my lips, the air in my lungs were paralyzed. I had to consciously reassure the forces acting upon me that I remembered my vow of silence to the genie before I could draw air back into my lungs.

He put his hand over my arm and pulled me away from

the store to his car. The driver's side door popped open, and he reached inside and drew out a small vial, which he gave to me. "Drink."

"Springwater doesn't—"

"I know," he said. "It's not from the wellspring. Drink it. All of it."

Hands shaking, I pulled the cork and poured the contents of the tiny bottle onto my tongue. A fragrant sweetness rose up into my sinuses, tickling my brain, and the tightness inside me relaxed. One of these days, I'd have to explore the potion arts myself.

I thought about what I could say, testing the words in my mouth before trying to speak them, discovering I could say, "The new store manager didn't want me to come in. Nico."

"Nico?" Raynor asked. A funny look came into his eyes —unfocused, distant—and he said, "Nico, yes. He's been kicking out witches all day."

I stared at him, chilled by how easily the genie had touched his mind. Raynor was an Emerald, powerful and experienced—with a demonprint like mine. Had she manipulated me as easily?

Intimidated, I hugged my arms around myself and glanced warily at the store. I imagined Jen watching us with her ancient eyes.

"I wish he'd make allowances for locals," Raynor continued, "but you can't blame him for being cautious. He's the manager. The solstice is tomorrow."

"I can blame him," I said, licking my lips. The potion was working throughout my system, erasing every bit of Nico's hex as well as my worry about Jen. It was a potion I'd had before—a former friend had been good at making them —and it brought me back to full power. Wonderful stuff. "I'm going to have to learn how to make that."

"Give me good intel, and maybe I'll share the recipe with

you." He looked at the sky. "Get in. We'll talk in my car. It's starting to rain again."

For the second time that day, I climbed into his passenger seat and closed the door. I handed him the empty vial, including the cork. "There were two witches there I recognized from Berkeley," I said. "Boyfriend and girlfriend. I actually only saw the woman today, but the tent smelled like him. Lionel said their names are Trudy and Brayden."

"Excellent work. Are you going to let me peek in your brain for their faces?"

I closed my eyes and grabbed the door handle, bracing myself. "Do it. Hopefully it won't get lost in translation from my cat brain."

His scan came over me like a lint roller, gentle but sticky, picking up the images of two faces I held in my mind. The sensation made my stomach lurch. I hunched over, clutching my abdomen, hoping I didn't vomit. Spilling my guts would be a lot worse than spilling hot chocolate.

"Got it," he said as my nausea faded. "What was the color of their tent?"

Memories came to me of a puffy sleeping bag and excellent fingernails. "I don't know."

"That would've been helpful."

"Sorry," I said. "It was a small tent. Like for backpacking. Two-person maybe. Not one of those giant things you can put furniture inside."

He sniffed a pinch of herbs into his nose. "This information would've been more useful before the sun went down."

"I did the best I could."

"It's all right. You found two," he said, wiping his nose. "That's even better than I'd hoped. How do you feel?"

"Fine now, thanks. Have you heard anything about the investigation? Any reason Lionel would be m—"

"Not my problem," he said. "I couldn't care less, and it

feels great. My job is here. Protecting Silverpool. Keeping these stupid witches from messing up my first solstice." The door at my side popped open, telling me it was time to get out and leave him alone.

"You don't mean that," I said. "Darius said Lionel was a pillar of the community. People are really sad he's gone, and we don't know—"

"We will," he said. "Timms will figure it out. Or maybe he won't. Either way, we keep our eye on the prize. No possessions or violence in Silverpool while I'm in charge. That's all I have to worry about."

❧

RANDOM WAS hungry when I got home. I felt terrible for leaving him alone locked up in the house all day, so I gave him a good meal, fed myself, and then took him out for a walk. I was tired, and it was dark, cold, and wet, but he needed the exercise. While I walked, I checked in with Birdie, who assured me Frank was doing fine. With a little more time, I was sure I could teach Random to accept a cat's company. He was comfortable with *me*, and I must've reeked of cat after shifting.

The stars were out. Realizing the storm had passed, I pushed back my hood and inhaled clean air deep into my lungs. The branches of the tree along the road, normally dotted with wood sprites and other fae, were dark and empty. The solstice was hours away, and they were probably gathering near the wellspring, preparing the height of their celebrations for tomorrow night.

It was strange how dark and quiet it was. I forgot sometimes how used to the fae I was, silently—or not so silently— existing in the background. Like crows and sparrows, or butterflies and mosquitoes. Their absence was usually more noticeable than their presence.

Because Random was a black dog who didn't always come when I called, I didn't let him off leash at night. He was invisible except for the glint of his collar or his eyes in the starlight; the risk was too high of a drunk tourist driving around on unfamiliar roads, looking for the famous pool of magic springwater.

We reached the end of my street and turned up the hill, away from the river and downtown. The darkness grew thicker. I paused to take out my phone to use as a flashlight, a nonmagical light source that wouldn't drain me. Rainwater was pouring down the street, filling the ditches and potholes to either side on its journey to the river. Magic was pulling water from the leaves overhead to increase the flow, to guarantee the river flooded, to trigger the blossoming of the wellspring.

The air was sweet with magic, shimmering with the taste of dreams and laughter. The fae had begun their parties. When the pull of their charms broke my concentration and I stumbled, Random turned and jumped on my legs, whimpering to get my attention—a magical service dog.

Because of the beauty of the night, we walked longer than usual, and by the time we were back on my little street, passing the Souters' house at the end, I was half asleep.

The darkness had grown deeper since we'd set out. The Souters' porch light didn't flicker into action when we walked by the way it usually did. Seth's house, usually glowing with some indoor light, was invisible in the darkness, as was my own house beyond.

A gentle touch tickled the back of my neck. I reached up, telling myself it was just a strand of hair that had come loose from my ponytail, and rubbed the bare skin where I'd felt it.

Still no fae in the trees. Was it normal for there to be

none at all? Had it been that way last year? In my unlucky experience, a lack of fairies meant a demon was nearby, either in its spiritual form or while possessing a human.

My throat went dry. The fatigue I'd been feeling left me. I grabbed the redwood beads at my throat and cast out a probing spell for threats, bodied or bodiless.

Nothing.

My heart was thudding, but I still wasn't convinced there was anything to fear. It had been just a touch. My magical senses didn't detect a supernatural threat, and I didn't hear any human sounds at all, no footsteps or wheels or TV through a living room window. Other than the Souters, I was the only human on the street. It was late. They were probably sleeping.

I kept walking. It had been a long day. I was tired. In a few minutes, I'd be safe inside my house, a happier dog at my side, lowering my head to a cool, fluffy pillow—

A stream of light appeared over my house. It came from above, pointing at my house like a tractor beam from a flying saucer in an old sci-fi show.

I stopped walking.

Demon's balls. I just wanted to sleep. What now? Aliens?

Random, tail wagging low the way it usually did after a good walk, tugged at the leash to go home. Whatever was going on in my backyard, it couldn't be too bad, at least not for dogs. I cast a spell of protection around us and continued walking.

The beam of light pointing at my house was a cool, flickering white. Given the benign oddness of it, I hoped it was something fae. It was the right night for it. A million microscopic fairies looking for the wellspring, perhaps. But then why was it at my house?

I paused at my driveway, holding Random back, then stepped over the boundary onto my property. The light stretched overhead. As I walked, I studied the point where it broke through a gap in the trees and pointed at the sky. And then—

And then I saw the stars. Our galaxy, a cloud of galaxies, billions of suns and planets and space dust, blazing in the sky. The light pollution of human civilization, our atmosphere, our moon—shrouded for now, allowing the blinding energy of the wider world to shine down in a tunnel of light between the trees, to illuminate...

I broke into a jog. Random, always game, ran with me. We rounded the corner of my house, and then we stopped, chests heaving for breath, to stare at the small figures beneath the redwood tree.

Willy wore his red velvet coat and light-colored pants, and his knobby head was bare. Olive wore a brown dress, the same plain one as before, but now a chain of white camellia blossoms was draped around her neck.

They faced each other, holding hands, their arms outstretched. The blinding starlight fell around them in a circle, casting the rest of the planet into blackness.

I swallowed, then let my mouth fall open. This was private. I shouldn't be watching this.

But I reminded myself Willy had the power to hide himself from me; if he'd wanted his date to be private, he wouldn't have drawn me to witness it.

Willy bowed. Olive curtseyed. And then they began to dance, still at arm's length, their feet barely moving. I caught a flash of Willy's smile, saw the hopefulness of it, and couldn't allow myself to watch anymore. If I was able to see their private moment, it might only be because Willy was too overwhelmed with emotion to stop me.

As quietly as I could, I took Random with me into the house and closed the door.

19

The next morning, solstice day, I drove to Birdie's bookstore to check on Frank and give her the books.

Respecting Willy and Olive's privacy the night before hadn't been easy. I'd managed to stop myself from spying out the window with the help of an herbal concoction to knock me out and a charm on the bedroom doorknob to prevent me from opening it.

The mystical scene continued to haunt me even by the light of day. Looking at the stars through the hole in the sky had filled me with a bodiless hunger to swim in the inhuman darkness with the universe—not just once but for all time. What did it mean to be Alma? Nothing. Compared to a galaxy of galaxies, I was utterly insignificant.

At the bottom of the hill, I braked at the stop sign and frowned at two outsider witches gathered on the bridge. I still felt disconnected from myself. Whatever I'd witnessed last night had been too much for my human eyes to absorb.

I realized I was idling at the stop sign, staring at the gray sky through the trees. It was almost noon, and I'd overslept—

a combination of my exhaustion from shifting and contagious overwhelm from the hot gnome date. I had to shake it off and get ahold of myself. Today wasn't a day to drop my guard.

I looked again more closely at the witches on the bridge.

They weren't tourists; they were Protectorate agents, both novice Flints in unadorned black leather jackets. A black SUV was parked on the shoulder on the opposite side.

Raynor had said Director Timms would be coming up today. He must've chosen apprentice agents to make the trip with him. They seemed to be enjoying themselves, too, taking pictures of each other and the town with their phones.

The important day had drawn all kinds of visitors to Silverpool, and as I drove down Main Street, I got stuck in a traffic jam of cars, SUVs, campers, pickup trucks, motorcycles, bicycles, scooters, and jaywalking pedestrians. The nonmagical residents in town must be wondering why everyone came here for their Christmas shopping after avoiding us the rest of the year. The empty lot past Cypress was a makeshift farmer's market with stalls of candied popcorn, steamed tamales, savory pies, cases of oranges, and an assortment of popular nonmagical products—from an herb grown locally—that were supposed to be restricted more carefully by the authorities.

The closest I could park to Birdie's bookstore was on a hill two blocks away. Hefting the box in my arms, I began walking down the hill to the store. When I turned the corner, I noticed an old blue minivan facing away from me. Its wheels weren't angled toward the curb, which was unsafe on such a steep, rain-slicked street. If its brakes didn't hold—and from the peeling trim and many dents, it looked poorly maintained—it would roll directly into the crowded intersection below.

Before I could cast a well-meaning wheel-tilt spell, a

fluffy white cat trotted out from behind a tall hedge and sat near the back of the van. Something about the cat's posture as it sat there, its tail at an oddly rigid angle, made me step off the sidewalk and hide behind the hedge.

I recognized a kindred spirit. Was it Joanna?

Shifting the heavy box to my hip, I peered out from behind the bush. I felt a little guilty to spy on her, but I was curious to see it from the outside. While I watched, the white cat slid into the shape of a naked human woman, who then promptly opened the hatch of the van and took out some clothes.

I averted my eyes while she got dressed. When she turned to put on her shoes, I saw the cat-and-glitter design on her sweatshirt.

Joanna sure liked those cat sweatshirts. It was even a different color than yesterday's, which meant she had more than one.

Was it a coincidence a cat-shifting witch had appeared so soon after Lionel's murder? Then again, of all the animals to transform into, cats were common. Maybe I was being paranoid.

But being paranoid was smart. I'd have to talk to Birdie.

Before Joanna closed the hatch, I saw a pile of books mixed in with the empty grocery bags, shipping boxes, a suitcase, other clothes. While she was distracted putting on her shoes, I cast a distant probing spell and felt an aura of magic around the books. They weren't everyday beach reads.

Was she stealing from Birdie? Contributing to the inventory?

I waited behind the bushes until she walked away, then stepped out and scanned her minivan. It had driven up from San Francisco, but it had also been up and down the coast. The dealer tags on the license plate were from Sacramento.

From what I could sense, she didn't stay in one place for long. A nomad. But I couldn't detect any Shadow.

I walked the rest of the way to the store, keeping a safe distance from Joanna, who turned out to be a slow walker. Shape-shifting probably exhausted her as it did me. When I finally stepped inside the shop a few minutes after her, my arms were aching from the weight of the box, and I was happy to set it down near the wall.

Birdie was taking cash from a middle-aged witch with long blond hair and lace-up stiletto boots. From the look of the customer's platinum-and-gemstone tiara—imperfectly camouflaged with a hiding spell—she appeared too wealthy to have slept in the wet campground. Although a few houses in town converted into bed-and-breakfasts for the season, I guessed she'd stayed in an expensive hotel on the coast and driven into Silverpool early that morning.

The store was filled with similarly interesting, unfamiliar witches. One was reading on the couch with Frank, who was cuddled in a boy's lap next to his mother; another was picking through the books on the new shelves; others were meeting in chattering clusters around the half-empty space.

If Birdie could have this many customers year-round, her business would've thrived, but this was a holiday crowd. Luckily, because of her inheritance, she wouldn't need to make a profit.

The tiara-wearing customer left, and Joanna took over the register. Birdie, face glowing, ran over and gave me a hug.

"Can you believe this?" she whispered in my ear. "Look at all these people!"

I squeezed her shoulder, giving her a tap of supportive magic to improve her defenses. So many witches in the store were drawing on her power just by existing, and she wasn't experienced enough yet to block them all.

"How's Frank doing?" I asked.

"Great! He slept at the foot of my bed," she said. "He ate a little. I've got an appointment at the vet next week."

That was a relief. "I've got something for you," I said. "They were at the winery. They should've gone to you directly, but that's witches for you. Sticky fingers."

She looked down and saw my box. "Books! Just what I need! I want to sell what I have, of course, but if I sell them all, then I won't look like a real bookstore, even though people seem to like buying the other stuff just as much. Did you know how much people like calendars? I had no idea. And those little chocolate balls—"

"Don't sell them until you look them over. You might want to keep something for yourself." I felt bad about interrupting her, but she had a tendency to talk forever, and the store needed her attention.

Joanna was watching us from behind the register. The current customer checking out was a local nonmagical woman I'd seen at the supermarket, one who I suspected knew about us and enjoyed the thrill. She was buying a crystal key chain and a coffee-table book about ancient herb gardens.

"You're doing great," I whispered to Birdie. "Listen, I need to talk to you alone. Just for a second."

Birdie opened her mouth and was about to ask something like "*Alone?*" in a loud voice, but recent months had taught her to be more cautious, so she snapped her mouth shut, nodded, and walked over to the exit.

I followed, and we stepped through one door into another, which led to her private apartment upstairs. The boundary spells she'd set up when moving in were much stronger here. We faced each other on the bottom steps.

"Did you know Joanna has books in her car?" I asked.

Birdie frowned. "Is that a problem?"

"So you knew?"

"She's helping me set up the store. She said she had a collection she wanted to try to sell on consignment."

I smiled. "That's what I hoped. Great. I just wanted to make sure..."

"Make sure I wasn't being a sucker," she said.

I scratched my jaw, feeling embarrassed. Sometimes I was maybe, perhaps, a little overprotective. As the first to introduce her to the witch world, I felt responsible for her safety. "How well do you really know her?" I asked. "Did you know, for instance, she—"

"I never could've gotten the store set up for today without her," Birdie said. "She stayed up late, arranging shelves and putting out the books in the categories she said were taught in witch schools. I didn't know *anything* about that stuff."

I felt my face flush. There was so much I could teach her —but I'd been so busy. "That's great you had her then. It's just—she appeared so quickly, out of nowhere, right at the moment you needed someone most."

"Is luck always bad? Is that how you see the world?" Birdie's tone wasn't angry, but wasn't joking, either. Her optimistic personality was always going to conflict with my default negativity sooner or later.

"With witches," I said carefully, "luck usually *is* bad, yes."

"People, magical or not, usually find what they're looking for," she said. "If you look for the worst in people, that's what you'll get."

I pressed my lips together, floundering on what to say next. We'd never discussed shifting, and now wasn't the time; she was busy, annoyed with me, and Joanna was just a few feet away. If the woman could shift into a cat, she might have other powers I couldn't measure, such as eavesdropping.

With a sigh, I touched Birdie's arm to defuse the situation. "I'm sorry. I really didn't mean to upset you. I trust your judgment."

She blinked. "You do?"

I smiled. "Well, I'll try."

"I trust Joanna," she said.

My friendship with Birdie was more important than proving I was right. "All right, then so do I." I could check up on Joanna without Birdie knowing.

Birdie flung her arms around me and squeezed. "I'm so sorry, it's just that I'm really stressed. What if people figure out I don't know what I'm doing? What qualifications do I have? I was bad at school. I hated math, but English was even worse. I just can't write those papers they need you to write. I get so freaked out whenever I see a blank screen, you know? I'm hopeless. So what business do I have owning a bookstore? I should've done something else. A bakery. Dog grooming. This is just embarrassing—"

"Birdie, stop. You're great. Books are your dream. You're doing great." I gave her a magical jolt, stronger than the last one. "What were you just telling me about being positive? You can do this. You've got a big day ahead, but you've got this. You've got this."

Her eyes flickered as my supportive can-do spell poured into her veins. A weak smile formed on her lips. "I can do this."

"Yes. And you will. Go back there and rock on, witch lady." Holding her shoulders, I turned her around and pushed her toward the store. "Enjoy yourself. Remember— you want to do this. You are doing this."

Nodding her head, she pumped her fist in the air, shot me a smile, and pushed through the doors to return to her new business.

I didn't follow. Anything I did now might look like inter- ference, triggering her again. Letting out my breath, I left the store with one of the nonmagical customers. From the sidewalk, I looked up at the gray sky, imagining the universe beyond.

I hoped the remaining hours of the shortest day of the year would be peaceful.

20

Raynor hadn't asked me to do it, but I walked around town and scanned the visitors with my most suspicious eyes. It was lunchtime, and the taqueria had a line out the door. Too bad for me; I'd thought about grabbing a burrito. The Thai place down the street was also packed with all its tables filled and a crowd out front.

Among them was a nondescript older man in a trench coat. Director Timms. He was squinting at the menu posted at the door and didn't seem to see me. I maneuvered through the bodies on the sidewalk to approach him. Thanks to him, my staff was back home.

"Welcome to Silverpool," I said. "I wanted to thank you."

He lowered his reading glasses and smiled at me. An Emerald witch, he had the skill—and probably amulets—to stifle any magic he was performing. All I could detect was a normal human being with an appetite for pad Thai.

"I was hoping I'd see you, Alma," he said. "You got your property back?"

"Yes. Thanks so much."

"Of course. The Protectorate can't act like common

thieves." Then, to his credit, his smile fell as he remembered who he was talking to. "I beg your pardon."

I smiled tightly. There was no escaping my father's infamy. "No problem." Maybe because my ego had been stung, I went on the offensive. "Did you catch Lionel's murderer yet?"

"No," he said. He didn't seem offended, just sad. "But we will."

Ashamed of my callousness, I nodded and plotted my escape. "Well, I'll let you get your lunch. Looks like you're next in line."

"Enjoy the holiday," he said, waving.

I hurried away and headed for the car. From there, I texted Raynor a message that I hadn't seen any menacing events downtown, in case he wanted my opinion, and went home.

Previous years on solstice night, I'd driven as close as I'd dared to the wellspring and crafted my redwood bead necklaces under the moon. The power of the singing fae, especially after the sun went down, could linger in jewelry for years if harnessed carefully. I'd hoped to make matching bracelets and hair combs this year, but my instincts told me it would be better to stay home. Maybe it was the light rain that had begun to fall, or the fear of Raynor's irritation if he found me trespassing near the wellspring. Or maybe I was just worn out. Whatever it was, I put on sweats and savored the feel of staying secluded.

The first thing I did was to make a big pot of chicken soup. Random enjoyed his bowl as much as I did. At dusk, I went out into the fog and walked to one of the redwood trees along the road—I didn't want to offend Willy—and peeled a small piece of shaggy bark off the trunk. The blanket of coastal fog blocked my view of the sky, but the tree knew the day had been the shortest of the year, and the bark it gave me was tingling with energy. Every moment from now it would grow stronger with the increasing length of the days, and I would harness it for my own use.

I brought it to my nose, inhaling its woodsy scent. It wasn't as delicious as cedar, but I loved it. My toolbox was in the garage with an old quilt, and Random and I went to collect them together. I set up my alfresco workstation in the center of the backyard where I'd seen the gnomes dancing. A mystical energy remained in the spot, interesting me as well as Random, who sniffed it eagerly. I hoped it would improve my craftsmanship.

After rubbing the bark in the patchy mud—I'd never had much of a lawn—I looped copper wire around it, forming a teardrop-shaped pendant about the size of my big toe. Because of the darkness, the pattern of the curving wires was uneven, but it would hold the magic to the wood until I could do precise work later.

"Hello, dearest Alma, you are going inside now, I am hoping."

I dropped my pliers, startled by Willy's sudden appearance. He stood at my left elbow, wearing a shockingly white jacket.

"Sure, of course." I picked up the pendant I'd dropped. "Can I have just a few more minutes?" If I stopped now, I'd lose some of the enchantment.

"It was being better a few minutes ago, it is the truth," he said. "You are very much in a wrong place and time, and I am wishing you stand up with your animal and with all the things you are doing as soon as now or even earlier."

I felt an odd pressure in my fingers, and then they were picking up my pliers, spool of wire, and leather rag without my conscious intent.

Willy had power I didn't understand, and I didn't want to confront him and discover the hard way how far it went. "As fast as I can move, Willy," I said, struggling to my feet. "Please let me move my own body. It'll be faster. I'm sure you want me to go as quickly as possible."

He flashed me a nervous smile, and his power over my limbs ceased. "You are being correct. Thanks be to you, who is moving in the best direction and I am appreciating also you remove the fabric with you." He glanced off to one side, his smile faltering. "There are those who are not so fond of humans, but she has said you will be acceptable, which is generous. Her words have hurt many witches' ears for many years in many places, even when we were young."

I bundled the old blanket under my arm, picked up my toolbox and jewelry, and scurried off the special ground. His girlfriend sounded difficult, and I kind of hoped it didn't last. But—since they were young? That meant he'd known her before he married his wife.

"Happy solstice, Willy," I called out over my shoulder. Manipulated by Willy, Random was already pawing at the door to go inside.

The moment we were both in the kitchen with the door closed, the beam of light from above began to pour down through the trees again. I dropped the blanket on the floor and set up my workstation on the kitchen table. Facing the window with its view of the glowing backyard, I sat and picked up my redwood bark again.

I worked for a few minutes, trying to focus on the wood fibers, how they pulled at the magic of the earth and my soul, but I couldn't stop staring out the window.

What if this was the last time I'd ever get to see gnomes courting under a solstice sky?

A minute went by. The wire spool rolled off the table, and I didn't pick it up; the shimmering beam landing on my dead grass was the most beautiful thing I'd ever seen.

Another minute went by. It might have been an hour.

Random curled up on the floor beside me and fell asleep with his chin on my toes. I was as immovable as a couch cushion.

At school, I'd heard about fairy lights having unique powers of illumination—of magic, objects, ideas. Something hidden by the greatest human magic could be effortlessly exposed under its light.

More time, long enough for Random to move to my other foot, went by as I stared and had dreamy thoughts about the mysteries of the universe. Life and death, love and evil...

I thought of Birdie's bookstore, the books I'd carried, Kelly going through the books, the books in Lionel's library, the books on herbs he'd given me, the book of warnings...

I snapped out of my daze. *Warnings* had blank pages in the middle I'd thought might've been a printing error, but what if they'd been enchanted?

I jumped up and ran into the bedroom to get the book. Random plodded after me—uninterested in literature, he jumped on the bed and went to sleep. With *Warnings* in my hand, I went to my back door and paused, knowing I only had a moment before Willy drove me back inside. I'd have to be ready.

I flipped through the book to find the blank pages, and with the spool of wire I reclaimed from the floor, wrapped the book open at the key section. The force of that light and Willy's annoyance might knock it out of my hands. I just needed a moment to read what was written there. If anything was.

The redwood bark was already singing to me from its half-finished state on the table. I picked it up, pressed it to my forehead, and cast a spell to give me visual memory far superior to my normal state.

Heart pounding, I turned the doorknob, flung the door

open, and ran out with the book in front of me, pinned open in my hands.

Willy and Olive were dancing again, both in white garments that matched the blinding stars above. Still engrossed with each other, their heads didn't turn, at least not at first. There was one second, then two...

I jogged forward, holding the book out in the beam of light. As soon as the pages were illuminated, black text jumped into view. Paragraphs of it. Spidery letters, elaborately scripted by hand. I stared at the book, afraid I wouldn't have time to see it all before—

Whoosh. I was flying through the air. The book, attached to my jeans belt loop by a double strand of wire, flapped violently at my hip. The door yawned open, I careened through the doorway, and then I fell on my kitchen floor. Stars flashed in my eyes—from pain, not mystical, celestial light.

I heard the door slam and a picture frame shatter to the floor. Random barked from the safety of the bed but didn't join me—apparently, if I'd been stupid enough to go up against Willy, I was on my own.

I rolled onto my back, gasping for breath, but I was smiling. It had only been a second, but I could still see each of the pages recorded like photographs in my mind.

There had been the usual warnings typical in the rest of the book. Don't do this, don't do that. Demons are bad. Blah, blah, blah.

But then, bracketed in parentheses, was a mention of the two other books, *Temptations* and *Instructions*. A few words jumped out at me as if highlighted by magical neon:

"Many will fail to heed these Warnings. For this reason, where one be, there cannot, will not, be the other. In this manner the final foolishness is therefore prevented."

Aha. The two other books were enchanted to remain

apart from each other. If a witch held *Temptations*, he or she wouldn't be able to have *Instructions*. They might not ever know why they were unable to acquire the other book, no matter how hard they tried. The witches at the meeting had alluded to how difficult it was to get them.

Had Lionel tried to find the other books, but the magic kept him from getting them? He'd had *Warnings*—did he have either of the other two? Maybe he'd guessed about the enchantment and had hoped by giving me one of the books, he'd be able to finally get the others—

I shook my head and rolled over to get to my feet. Whatever had driven Lionel was pure speculation on my part. Maybe Darius knew more.

Rubbing my sore hip—landing on the tile had hurt—I walked over to the window and pulled the curtains shut. Hopefully Willy would forgive me tomorrow.

If the books were cursed, a witch who acquired both of them, expressly forbidden, might be in danger. He might, for instance, die suddenly in a violent way.

Had a visitor brought Lionel one of the books, say, the one they talked about at the meeting, and it killed him because he also had the others?

If so, where was it now?

❧ 21 ❧

I had a nightmare about books chasing me down the street and pushing me in the Vago River while the green-faced river fairy, dancing under the bridge, watched and laughed. When I woke, I was sleeping with one foot on the floor, a sign I was under way too much stress.

And my head hurt. The spell to remember the book had left a throbbing ache between my eyes. Even after I took a hot shower and got dressed, I still felt drowsy, so I unlocked my filing cabinet for an herbal remedy. Caffeine wouldn't touch magical hangover, but candied rosemary and habanero tea might.

I was brewing a cup in the kitchen when my front doorbell rang. I cast out a spell to see if I needed to grab my staff, but it was only my neighbor Madge Souter.

That was a bad sign. Madge was sociable but usually stayed home and preferred to visit in her kitchen—which I could relate to. If she'd left her house at this early hour, something was wrong.

I hurried over and opened the door. "Hi, is everything all—"

"Oh, Alma, don't come out," she said. "There's a killer on the loose. Did you hear?"

"A killer?" I began to worry less about Chuck and more about Madge. She was still sharp and usually beat Birdie at their weekly game nights, but anybody could snap eventually, especially with gnomes and demons and witches prowling about on solstice night.

"Birdie's new girl was found behind the dumpster," Madge went on. "It's just horrible. Horrible. I don't know what's happening to Silverpool. It's horrible."

My stomach lurched. "Joanna?" What could she possibly have done to lead to her death?

I needed to see Birdie right away.

Madge ran a hand over her short, pinkish-red hair. "I think that's her name. I hadn't met her yet. Birdie told me about her."

Chuck appeared behind her in the road, approaching as quickly as he could and looking upset. "I told you to wait for me."

Madge patted my arm and hurried out to her husband, who had reached my driveway. My magic wards didn't affect them—they screened for magic or evil intent, neither of which the Souters had.

"I knew you were right behind me," she told Chuck. "I had to make sure Alma had her door locked."

"And so you went running out by yourself? There's a nutjob out here killing women and Lord knows what else." He waved at me. "Poor Birdie's got bad luck, huh?"

I flinched at the words that were so much like what I'd said to her yesterday. "Looks like it," I said, my mind racing. If the Souters had heard about it, the nonmagical police—probably from Riovaca—were involved. Only after they'd been there could the Protectorate move in. "Did you hear anything else? Any idea of the cause of death? Suspected witnesses? Last time the victim was seen?"

When both gave me an odd look, I realized I might've sounded too businesslike for a twentysomething girl who made wooden bead jewelry for her meager living.

"The garbage man found her. That's all I heard," Madge said. "My sister's son-in-law heard it on the police scanner. He's always glued to that thing."

Trying to recover my ordinary cred, I said, "Poor Birdie. I better call her." What I was really going to do, however, was get my staff, my strongest necklace, a vial of springwater, call Raynor and Darius, and go over there in person.

"She doesn't have any family, you know," Madge said. "Find out if there's anything we can do for her."

"I'll do that," I said.

"After they catch the guy," Chuck said, putting an arm around Madge and turning her away. "Bye then, Alma. Lock up."

"I will."

When they were safely back in their house, I called Birdie, but she didn't answer. What if she'd been hurt too? Had anyone checked on her?

I grabbed my staff and coat, put a leash on Random, and drove downtown. I went past the store, pulled a U-turn at the stop sign, and parked on the other side of the street to watch from a safe distance before approaching.

As I'd expected, the Riovaca police had taped off the parking lot and alley behind the store, and nonmagical men in blue were ignoring the curious, gawking people gathered on the sidewalk. The cops wouldn't know the spectators were witches, but the cloud of magic rising up from the corner made my hair stand up from a half block away. The witches were casting probing spells, trying to figure out what had

GRETCHEN GALWAY

happened—the innocent ones, anyway. The killer, presumably, already knew.

It might not be a human killer; if Joanna had been like the witches at the Berkeley meeting, she could've died from a failed summoning. The world was unpredictable on the solstice, as I'd seen with the beam of starlight in my backyard. Only a Protectorate investigation could determine her true cause of death. But unless she was behind the dumpster when she'd cast a deadly spell, the placement of her body behind it suggested another human had been involved.

The Protectorate would push everyone away as soon as the nonmagical cops left. I got out of the Jeep with Random and walked across the street, joining the crowd for a moment before walking around to Birdie's private door.

A young cop with a crew cut and a poker face stood on the sidewalk. He didn't seem to know it, but he had a tattoo on his forearm that made his muscles appear larger than they actually were. I wondered if the tattoo artist, obviously a witch, had been in love with him; there was a tang of unrequited longing in the enchantment. Random looked up at the guy, hoping for a neck scratch, but he was disappointed.

"I'm here to see Elizabeth Crow, the owner of the bookstore," I told him. "She lives up—"

"Sorry, ma'am. Nobody can go in right now."

"I just want to talk to her," I said. "I'm her friend. She might need me."

He shrugged and looked away. After he'd ignored a friendly dog, I hadn't expected him to be very nice to me either.

It wasn't worth the energy to try to convince him. In a few minutes, all the cops would probably get the urge to drive back to Riovaca, and the cause of death for the body they'd taken away would be something noncriminal and uncomplicated.

150

I stepped away from the cop and looked up at the windows of the second-floor apartment, but all the witches sending up a cloud of spells of their own made it impossible for me to detect anything. I couldn't even determine if Birdie was up there, let alone how she was doing emotionally.

Thwarted for now, I went back to my Jeep and called Raynor again. No answer. Then I called Darius, who did pick up that time.

"I see you," he said. "Please go home."

"You see me?" I looked up and down the street. "Where are you?"

He paused, and I thought I heard the sound of eating or drinking. "Taking a day off."

I cast out a probing spell. Far enough from the bookstore, I was able to detect him in the deli that was the closest thing Silverpool had to a café. "Good for you. Enjoy yourself." Then I hung up, grabbed Random's leash again, and walked up the street to join him, hoping they didn't have a problem with dogs.

The café was dim, and soft classical music played. Darius was near the door, hunched over the bar overlooking the street, a paper coffee cup in his hands.

"Go away," he said.

"We can enjoy our days off together." I smiled at him, glanced at the counter to see if anyone was going to hassle me about Random, saw that it was empty. "Where is everybody?"

"They're closed," he said, sipping his coffee.

"You broke in?"

"I didn't break a thing." He leaned on his elbows and stared out the window.

"You look forlorn," I said.

"I am forlorn."

"It's not that bad in Silverpool," I said. "You'll learn to love it."

He snorted into his coffee.

"Where's Raynor?" I asked.

"Busy keeping that mob of witches from setting this cursed town on fire." He gestured at an empty storefront near the Jeep, which I'd been too preoccupied with the bookstore to look at carefully when I'd parked. Now I could sense a screen of distraction in front of it. Raynor must've seen me park and walk around, and still he ignored my call. "He's also trying to keep the cops from destroying any magical traces they don't understand."

"Why aren't you helping him?" I asked.

"Timms ordered us to stay out of the way," Darius said. "He says murder investigations aren't the role of a Protector. A few Diamond Street agents came up with him yesterday, and *they* will be the ones to scan the scene." His tone was bitter.

"But Raynor—" I began.

"Is violating orders. He feels responsible for Joanna's death. He feels guilty he didn't protect her."

"It was the solstice," I said. "He had his hands full."

"Doesn't matter. Somebody died on his watch." Darius's lips flattened, suggesting he felt responsible as well. "Right now he's working to keep the nonmag cops away from your friend Birdie," he said.

I thought of the blank-faced young guy standing guard outside her door. "Raynor hexed the Riovaca cops?"

"Nothing the cops do here will matter. They'll lose interest in Joanna's tragic death as soon as Timms enchants them," he said. "But Birdie doesn't know that. She grew up nonmag. She might worry. No reason to put her through that."

He didn't seem like a softie, but Darius was a really nice

guy under the rule-following, gruff exterior. "That's sweet of you. Thanks."

"Thank Raynor when you see him." He shook his head. "I'm not doing a Shadowed thing."

"You're talking to me, which I appreciate. I was worried about Birdie."

"Go home, Alma. It's a mess. You don't want to get involved in this one." He frowned at me. "Or you shouldn't want to. They'll probably send an agent to come by to warn you once they process the crime scene."

"Warn me about what?"

"The victim could shift into a cat," he said. "Raynor told me you could tell just looking at her."

"Yes, so?"

"She's the second cat-crazy witch to die a violent death this week," he said. "Think about it."

I bent over and scratched Random's soft head. "They're going to interrogate all the suspicious dogs?"

His voice lowered. "Come on, Alma."

I stared at him, genuinely confused. Associating cats with Shadow magic was an old prejudice. Surely he was too modern to buy into such a damaging stereotype. "What?"

He got to his feet and put his hand on my shoulder— which was alarming, given how rarely he'd ever touched me.

"You might be next," he said.

❧ 22 ❧

"That doesn't make any sense," I said. "Why would anyone want to kill witches who can take a cat shape?"

"The alternative doesn't look good for you either," he said.

That one had already occurred to me. Director Timms would wonder why I was so close to two separate murder scenes—again. I'd hoped to have him as an ally in the Diamond Street office. If he suspected me of murder, that was unlikely.

"I'd never met either victim until right before they died," I said.

"You might not want to emphasize that point," he said. "Somehow it sounds worse."

"There's got to be a different connection. Demon possession. The solstice. Raynor. The Protectorate. The meeting in Berkeley." I ran a hand through my hair, pulling nervously. Would Timms and his agents trace Joanna's movements yesterday and find evidence of me spying on her? How closely I followed her for several blocks?

"Let's hope they find something like that," he said. "She showed up around the same time he died. What do you know about— Never mind. It's not my case. They've made that clear. When I got kicked off Lionel's murder case, I thought—OK, maybe it's because I'm too close. I knew the man. I loved him. Raynor put in a word for me, so they sent me up here."

"He didn't ask for you to be here. He knows you hate it," I said.

He waved that aside. "But then a murder happens right here." He pointed toward the bookstore. "Right under my nose. I'm ready to go, eager to help. But Timms wants me to stay at the winery. Why?"

I felt bad for him. Unlike me, he had big dreams of achieving Emerald or even Sapphire status and working at the highest levels of the Protectorate. That was unlikely to happen if he got stuck in Silverpool. "If they think the cases are linked, your connection to Lionel might be the only reason. It's not your fault."

He dropped his empty cup in the garbage and pulled open the door. "You don't know that. I don't know that. Maybe I screwed up, and this is their way of telling me."

"You haven't screwed up," I said, chasing after him. The deli fell into darkness, the door locking behind us from Darius' spell. "You never screw up. You're the perfect agent. Everybody thinks so. How many people came up to tell you how sorry they were you'd been stuck with me after I got fired?"

His lip twitched in a brief smile, so I went on.

"And when Timms started as Director," I said, "he *must*'ve heard great things about you to bring you to the Berkeley crime scene at first," I said. "It was only after they learned you'd known Lionel that you got kicked off the case."

He sighed, drawing a hand over his hair. "Maybe you're

right. But I'm right here, watching from the sidelines," he said. "Timms could find *some* way to make me useful. Why keep me on the bench while those idiots are trampling evidence?"

We looked down the street where the police and spectators were still gathered around the bookstore.

"Raynor is making sure that doesn't happen," I said.

"I should be helping him."

"You'll help him protect Silverpool." I zipped my jacket to my chin, looking to the west. The witches I'd recognized from Berkeley, Trudy and Brayden, weren't gathered in front of the bookstore with the others. What were they up to? "There are witches here trying to summon demons. One witch's death won't stop that."

The actual day of the solstice was over, but the wellspring's power was still at a peak. Joanna's death was a dangerous distraction. While Raynor was watching Birdie's store, who was watching the town's boundaries?

"Do you...?" He trailed off and scratched his chin, looking unusually uncomfortable.

"Do I what?"

"Do you, uh, feel anything? From the fairies?" He waved his hand around in the air.

"There are a few sitting on your head, but they're harmless," I said.

His jaw tightened, but self-control kept him from swatting the air around his head. "I'm having a difficult day, and I'd appreciate it if you didn't make it worse."

"Sorry," I said, biting back a laugh. Then I felt bad, remembering poor Joanna had been killed just a few steps away. "Really, I'm sorry. They're not on your head. They're mostly over there." I pointed at the Vago River running parallel to Main Street behind the stores and restaurants. The trees were vibrating with clouds of fae, the little finch-sized ones who wore brown and green tunics. They'd never spoken to me, but some witches put out bowls of honey-sweetened water and sliced fruit to protect their gardens—and in some tragic cases, their small pets. The fae didn't share human morality.

"When Raynor told me a body had turned up, he said we'd have to find out if any of those witches you'd recognized were still in town."

"See?" I said. "You've got work to do. Would you rather dig through garbage in the dumpster? You'll be searching the whole town. You'll have the chance to find evidence that matters."

"I doubt those crazy Berkeley witches murdered anyone," he said. "Raynor's just humoring me. He wants to make sure I don't quit. Misery loves company."

I took in a deep breath, enjoying the damp, woodsy air, confounded by the fact they'd rather live somewhere else. "It's only been a week."

He bent over and scratched Random's back. "Yeah."

"I think you'll survive," I said.

Giving Random a final scratch, he straightened. "Speaking of survival, I'm serious about what I said. You should go home. It's not safe."

"It's never safe."

"Don't you have beads to carve or something?" he asked.

I thought about the project I'd had to interrupt because of the dancing gnomes. It wasn't too late to capture some of the solstice energy. Every day it grew weaker, and soon I'd have to wait until summer or next winter to use it again.

"I have to try to help Birdie," I said. "She'll need me."

"Having you around is only going to look worse for her," he said. "If you really care, you should keep your distance."

I flinched. He had a point. The Protectorate would interrogate Birdie, which was sure to be unpleasant, but it would be longer and more intrusive if they thought I'd coached her on what to say. Director Timms had been working for the Protectorate a long time and was less likely to have something to prove. Maybe he wouldn't make it too difficult on her.

I should keep my distance until after she'd been questioned by Diamond Street. "You're probably right."

"You're in the same boat as me," Darius said. "How about that?"

"Will you keep an eye out for her? Go up to her place, see if you can do anything for her? Steal her something from the deli?"

He held my gaze. "You'll go home?"

"I'll go," I said, casting a half-truth spell; I would leave, but not for home.

TAKING side streets so Darius wouldn't see me, I turned around and headed west toward the wellspring.

When I'd first moved to town, I'd expected the Protectorate to set up agents around the wellspring itself, especially on important days like the solstice. But instead, official policy was to avoid the ravine where the magical water pooled in the winter. Hidden by enchantments, the wellspring would be more vulnerable, not less, if high-visibility Protectorate witches got too close to it. The policy was to draw a boundary around the entire town, which confused humans but was effective guardianship. Even now that more witches had learned there was a secret wellspring in Silverpool, they still didn't know precisely where it was. They would feel the magic in the river and hike around town, collecting vials from flooded streets and creeks, but they wouldn't know where the mouth of the spring was. The last place Raynor and Darius could afford to go was the ravine on the west side of town. Every witch in the campground would race to follow.

But *I* knew how to find it, even when the bluffs of the ravine and curve of the creeks and river changed. The Protectorate had set up confusion spells as well as physical obstacles —enchantments of overgrown blackberry brambles, for instance—but I'd learned to plow through them.

The first trick was watching the fairies. They always knew where the wellspring was. If I listened to their songs, watched their dancing in the trees, and followed the smell of the blossoms and woodsmoke, I'd remember the way.

Random had also become a useful guide. He wasn't distracted by the fairies, although the quivering, shaking brambles could scare him.

I turned off the highway on the narrow road near the wellspring, parked on the shoulder behind a hedge, and took a few minutes to prepare a few items before I got out. Random would be better off without a leash so he could run to safety if necessary. I'd be better off with my staff.

The witches posing the biggest threat to Silverpool wouldn't be the gawkers watching Birdie's bookstore but those who could find the wellspring. If I found any there, I'd tell Darius so he could look good—and feel good— confronting them. If nobody was here, no harm done; I'd collect a few vials of solstice-drawn spring water and go home.

Random and I got out and walked toward an ancient live oak that was currently providing shelter for a magical fairy bonfire. Using my staff, I shielded Random from the fairies' attention—he was bigger than their usual prey, but I wasn't taking chances—and cut to the left to put more space between us. The fae under the tree canopy were my least favorite; wood sprites like them had driven me off the road over the summer, almost totaling my Jeep. This morning they seemed to be focused mostly on the sky, which was a clear, crisp blue, and we were able to slip by without enduring too many sticks and leaves thrown at us.

"Stay close," I said to my dog, overly optimistic he'd listen. My father, his original owner, had trained and enchanted him for his criminal enterprises, but I'd broken that bond. Out of Malcolm Bellrose's reach, Random was just a dog who did what he liked, which at the moment was peeing on the same stick he'd peed on last month.

The slopes of the ravine were slicked back from a recent deluge of flowing water. The high tides this time of year prevented the river from draining quickly enough to prevent local flooding. The creek was a little lower now, but still a dark, murky gray tearing through what had been a dry creek bed just weeks ago. The river was on the other side of the highway, but the pool formed here.

Muddy footprints told me I wasn't the only one to know where the wellspring was, although they were partially hidden by an invisibility spell.

I paused, feeling for danger. The witch nearby was strong… but alone.

The trees above me were flickering with the wings of tiny leaf people, the fae who always reminded me of dragonflies, and I could still hear the singing of the wood sprites under the oak tree.

Their presence relaxed me; if demons had been summoned, or if the witch ahead of me at the wellspring was possessed, the fae would have fled. Or been eaten already.

Using my staff, I cast a powerful cloaking spell around me and Random, then continued walking.

Twice I was distracted by the Protectorate enchantment: once to go back into town for some pad Thai with shrimp, which I loved, and then to drive out to the coast and see if I could find Seth, who I lo—

Well, that was annoying. I did care about him, but love? I pushed that thought aside, tapped into more mental clarity from my staff, and climbed around a patch of blackberry brambles.

Then I saw her.

I'd expected one of the Berkeley witches, but it was Kelly. She stood to the side of a bend in the creek where the water formed a wide, still pool. Unlike the fast-moving water that ran through the ravine, the pool was as clear as Lake Tahoe, blue and deep. Its surface glowed in a spiral pattern.

Kelly, absorbed with the pool, didn't notice me. She wasn't doing anything I could see or sense; even with my staff, I detected no magic coming from her. She was just standing there, one hand pressed against a tree for balance, staring down into the water. The blue glow of the pool reflected off her beautiful face, slack with wonder.

Suddenly I felt bad for intruding. I remembered the first time I'd visited the wellspring, and I'd felt the way she looked right now. It would've embarrassed me to think anyone was watching me.

Random had lingered behind me, sniffing and lifting his leg, and I cast a spell to stop him from getting any closer. Then I turned and carefully went back the way I'd come.

There was no benefit to confronting Kelly here. What right did I have to bother her? Her boyfriend was the Protector. I held no position of authority. It only felt as if I did.

I jogged past the fae, who pelted me and Random with balls of mud as we jumped into the Jeep. Random got more slime on the seats and then on me as he lunged over to lick my face. The fairies freaked him out. I was tired from using the staff to hide us on our walk to the wellspring, so I didn't waste what energy I had left on magic protection. Letting the mud splatter my paint job, I turned around and drove away.

23

On my way back home, orange cones and detour signs, warning of a flood, directed me around Main Street. I didn't think anything of it until I was pulling into my driveway and the protective spells around my house erased the Protectorate enchantment.

Agents must've arrived in Silverpool and taken over the crime scene.

I hosed off Random's paws before letting him inside, then ran in for a towel. By the time I was kicking off my own muddy boots in the kitchen, I was ready to collapse with a cup of hot—

"Good afternoon," Raynor called out from the living room.

I yelped and dropped the towel. And then, belatedly, cast a defensive spell around myself.

"How did you get in here?" I yanked the towel away from Random, who thought it was a game. Nobody should've been able to get through my boundary spells, not even Raynor.

"Your gnome friend let me in," he said. "He said he

didn't want me darkening your doorstep. I think, though, he really just wanted his privacy. He was making something out of flowers in your front yard."

I put my hand on my chest, begging my lungs to return to normal functioning. Willy's romantic life was going to kill me. "You shouldn't have come in without my permission."

"You shouldn't have come into any building, even your own home, without scanning for danger first."

He was right, which only made me angrier. I marched into the living room and pointed at him where he sat in my favorite slipcovered chair. "You should be out there making sure Birdie is OK."

"I did what I could. Timms is questioning her now." He made no move to get up. "Darius said you were looking for me. I thought I'd drop by, see how you're doing, make sure you didn't feel the urge to, ah, help. The solstice is over. With Timms, all his agents, and Darius, we've got this under control. Enjoy the holidays."

"Birdie needs a lawyer," I said. "The Protectorate needs to join civilized society and stop imprisoning and interrogating people without due cause."

He leaned back and crossed an ankle over his knee. "I'll do what I can, but I'm not exactly at the top of my power game at the moment." He shrugged. "She'll probably be fine. There wasn't any trace of her magic anywhere near the body. They'll be looking for demons, Shadow, solstice tourists. If anyone should be worried, it's you. Joanna was a cat shifter."

"That doesn't mean anything. It's the most popular type of shape-shifting."

"Maybe for women," he said. "I've known more men who trained to shift into birds. Who can resist the urge to learn how to fly?"

I thought of the birds at the Berkeley meeting. Had any

of them come to Silverpool in human form? "Cats kill birds," I said absently.

"My grandfather took the shape of a golden eagle. No house cat could've taken *him* down."

"You've never mentioned your family before," I said. Suddenly I remembered what Lionel had said about demon possession and shifting. "Sounds like he wasn't your demon ancestor then, was he?"

He stared at me and said nothing.

"I've heard you can't shape-shift if you're possessed," I continued. "Had you heard that?"

"I try not to have conversations with other witches about the finer details of demon possession. It looks suspicious." He scowled. "Who have *you* been discussing it with?"

"Lionel," I said.

He looked away, shrugging. "Oh. Well. I suppose that doesn't matter now."

Maybe it was because Raynor was in my home, his shoes off, his khakis wrinkled, but I suddenly had the urge to confide in him. "He knew my mother," I said. "My real mother."

He took out a velvet pouch from his pants pocket and removed a pinch of herbs. "And?" he asked, sniffing them up into his nose.

"What do those things do for you, anyway?" I asked.

It took him a moment to recover from whatever he'd snorted. He'd shielded it from detection, so I was unable to identify the individual plants. "Focuses my mind," he said.

"Any side effects?"

"There's a price to everything."

"Like what?" I asked. "Nosebleeds? Insomnia?"

He raised an eyebrow. "If you didn't want to talk about your mother, why did you bring her up?"

I did want to talk about her, but it was difficult. I

reminded myself that with his connections, he might be able to find out more about her. Maybe he'd already heard of her.

Nudging Random aside, I sat on the couch. "Her name was Poppy Almasi. She was a student. He was afraid she was interested in demon possession, tried to talk her out of it, she ignored him."

"What a coincidence for you to end up at that meeting at the same time he did."

Was he suggesting I'd sought out Lionel? "You're the one who sent me," I said.

"And he invited you to his house. Right before he was killed." He sniffed and wiped his nose. "You didn't tell Timms about this, I assume?"

"Not about my mother, no. He knew about my father's"—I hated to talk about it, even with Raynor—"uh, wedding." Such a disaster, I hated to even call it that.

"Every witch in the world knows about that wedding," he said. "Sorry to say."

"He put two and two together. I'm the right age to have been her daughter."

"That's a big leap for him to make," Raynor said. "There had to be something else that made him think you were... What did you say her name was?"

"Poppy Almasi."

"Oh well. There's the name. I guess that was it." He smiled. "Your secret's safe with me."

A tingling in my cheeks told me a tendril of magic had entered my home and was swirling between us. It folded the words of our conversation, making it difficult to remember what we'd been talking about.

Still smiling, Raynor got to his feet. "Now why did I come here? Something... Oh, right. The cops. They've gone back to Riovaca with the body. It's already been dismissed as a drug overdose."

I cast out my senses, traced the swirl of power to the window, and felt the genie's unique fingerprint. Although I pushed against it, locking her out for now, Raynor's mind had already been touched. His curiosity about why Lionel would want to meet me was gone.

"The Protectorate loves to blame drugs," I said, watching him.

He ran a hand over his bald head, unaware it had been breached. "She was too young for a heart attack."

"You nearly gave me one when I walked in here," I said.

"Apparently it was a lesson you needed to learn. You need to be more careful," he said. I fought the urge to tell him he'd been invaded himself in a worse way. "Whoever is killing witches this time around, they've got a taste for the cat lovers. Stay home. Put up your guard. Ask the gnome to help. But don't go looking around for trouble."

"I don't think me being a cat shape-shifter means I'm in danger. You'll need me to keep an eye out for trouble. At the very least, the Berkeley witches—"

"No," he said. "The big night is over. I can keep an eye on them myself with Darius. Until Timms finds what killed Joanna, stay here."

I looked at the floor. There was no point arguing when he'd made up his mind. He could give me all the advice he wanted. One beautiful thing about my freelance status: I didn't have to obey.

"You're vulnerable, Alma. As a suspect and as a victim." He tucked the velvet pouch of herbs in his pocket, walked to the front door, and put on his shoes. "If Timms is any good, he'll find the killer. And if he doesn't... and I do"—he grinned and opened the door—"then odds are I can get my old job back. Being Protector for life is an optional perk, not a requirement."

I followed him out into the garden and watched him

walk away down the street. The winery wasn't far, but he usually drove. I wondered if Kelly had dropped him off. Did he know she'd been hanging out at the wellspring today? I walked over to the far corner of my garden and began picking a bouquet of sad, soggy lavender. I could dry it out, mix it with some spit, melt it into a candle at midnight.

What else had Kelly found at the winery while he was out—more books? Had she found other objects Tristan had left behind that she'd decided to keep for herself? Something about her reminded me of my father. Her arrogance, her charm, her good looks, her air of greed.

Seth suddenly appeared in front of me. "You're jealous of Raynor's girlfriend. I can feel your thoughts."

Looking down, I saw I'd accidentally wandered onto his property. Not wanting to give him the satisfaction, I stayed where I was. "I'm not jealous. I'm suspicious."

"You're suspicious because you're jealous."

"I'm suspicious because Raynor isn't. Two people are dead, and I keep finding her sneaking around."

"While you're sneaking around yourself, I bet," he said.

"I know *I* didn't kill anyone." Pretending it wasn't intentional, I took a step back onto my property, where his unpredictable knack for mind-reading would hopefully be thwarted. "Do you know anything about the witch they found behind the dumpster this morning?"

His air of mockery faded. "I know she was a cat witch like you."

"I'm not a cat witch. I'm a witch who can turn into a cat. Big difference."

"Raynor told you to stay home," he said. "Right?"

"What do you care what Raynor says?" The two were enemies. Hunter and prey seldom became buddies.

"We both share a preference for your continued well-being." He pointed at his house, and the indoor lights popped on. A warm, yellow glow surrounded the bungalow, gently lighting the low-hanging branches of the trees. The odor of baking bread wafted out an open window. "I'll be moving back in to help keep that a reality."

I took another step away from him, deeper into the enchantments of my home, burying the feelings that were churning inside me.

It felt good to have him nearby. Something about him had always felt... right. We fit. He said it was the fairy in him and the demon in me coming together in some ancient, cosmic pairing. I thought it was more base than that: I was lonely, and he, handsome and charming, made me feel special.

When he wasn't annoying the Shadow out of me.

"Perfect timing to return to Silverpool," I said. "The Director of the Protectorate, who wants to kill you, is here with a team of agents. Not to mention Raynor."

"I did mention Raynor," he said.

"This isn't a joke!"

He tilted his head, smiling. "I used to hate you trying to take care of me." His voice dropped. "But now I like it."

I shivered. What if Raynor was pressured by Timms and other Protectorate bosses to finally get rid of the changeling in Silverpool?

He stepped over my property line, which I knew was uncomfortable for him, and looked down at me. "You're trembling."

"It's cold. We might have a frost tonight."

He glanced up at the weak December sun, and then I felt warmth on my cheeks, all over my skin, my flesh, my bones.

"Is that better?" he asked softly.

"You shouldn't be able to do that on my property," I said.

"I've been practicing."

My breathing was tight, shallow, anticipatory. "You're in

more danger than I am," I said. "Please go. You're not stuck here anymore. The Protectorate—"

"They won't be a problem. They have other priorities right now." He didn't move, but I felt a fingertip brush the hair out of my eyes. "And so do I."

❦ 24 ❦

Just before sunset, Birdie arrived at my house with Frank and an overnight bag. I got her and the cat inside and made a pot of peppermint tea spiked with enchanted blueberry leaves to help her recover from the shock.

"The boss man was pretty nice," she said, sinking onto the couch. "But it took forever. They asked me questions, did that scan thing, asked me again. I guess they were satisfied. I'm not supposed to leave town until they say so."

Random wasn't happy to see the cat again, but having his beloved Birdie there distracted him. Frank was as sleepy as ever, barely peeking out from the padded laundry basket Birdie had brought him in. I set it on the coffee table between us and made sure Random didn't get too close.

"Did you say you made an appointment at the vet?" I said. "I want to make sure he's OK."

Birdie hugged a pillow to her chest. "He said he was just old and tired."

"Who said? You already brought him in?"

She sipped the tea. "No, Frank said it. Not to me, of

course, I don't speak cat. But Joanna—" Face twisting, she set the tea down. "Oh God, she's dead. Why do I keep forgetting? It's like amnesia. I think of her and start crying, but then I get all soft and dreamy and feel better. Until then something reminds me again." She buried her face in her hands and began to cry.

I was tempted to soothe her with magic, but she'd already been overspelled by the Protectorate when they'd interrogated her. "They hexed you," I said. "To keep you calm so they could get all the information possible out of you."

She looked up in surprise. "I didn't feel anything. The Tim guy was nerdy. He reminded me of my math teacher in high school."

"Timms. He's an Emerald. They're powerful."

"More powerful than you?" she asked.

I smiled. A year ago, I would've laughed. *Way more*, I would've said. But now... Since the summer, I'd learned power couldn't be pigeonholed into the linear categories of Flint, Emerald, or Sapphire. Still, I didn't have the training to compete with an Emerald on intrusive magic like interrogation. "In some ways, they're much, much more powerful."

"But in other ways you are?"

I remembered some of the conflicts with other witches I'd had recently. For a peaceful witch who was unable to kill things, I had a ruthless track record of coming out on top. More than one witch had fallen dead in my wake. "In some ways, I think I am," I said. "Yes."

"Cool. I think so too. I feel much safer being here than at the store. One of the agents said Joanna had suspicious books in her car, lots of them. He said she was trying to get a demon to possess her and something went wrong, but that seems crazy. You saw her. She didn't have the courage for that. She liked books and cats and, I mean, those sweatshirts —did you know she made them herself? She tried to sell me one. I told her it would be fine to put them out on a rack and sell them at the store, but I don't think anyone will actually buy one. She'll be"—she flinched—"no, she won't be anything. She's dead."

Murmuring comforting noises, I waited for her to recover before asking, "She claimed Frank spoke to her?"

Birdie wiped her eyes. "You don't believe her?"

"Well, I don't know. What did it look like when they were supposed to be communicating?"

"I didn't see anything. She just came over to me when I was vacuuming—those tourist witches drag in so much mud, it's really annoying—and said, 'Frank told me he's old and tired.'"

"That's it?"

"And that he missed his family."

A pang of grief struck me. Lionel's home of cats would never be the same. I reached out and stroked his back. "Poor guy."

"So you believe Joanna could understand him?" Birdie asked.

"I guess. But it doesn't seem to have anything to do with her death."

Birdie picked up her tea and sipped. "They think it's something to do with her books. Maybe she stole one? I don't know, but they were obsessed with sorting them out into ones she'd brought, ones you'd brought, and ones I'd ordered myself."

I perked up. The witches in Berkeley, Frank, even Raynor's girlfriend—all had something going on with books. "What were they looking for? What did you hear?"

"They were really suspicious when I said you'd brought me some books from the winery, but then they looked through them and kind of laughed." She made a face. "Actually, I was offended on your behalf, and on mine, since they came from my biological father, right? They said you'd unloaded your recycling on me and I might want to reconsider our friendship, which was super annoying, and now that you tell me I was hexed, it makes a lot of sense, because I would've smacked that guy."

"What was his name?"

"Nobody I'd met before. A Flint, I think. They sent him out for coffee."

I made a face. It didn't matter who he was; his prejudicial attitude toward the botanical arts was typical. "What did they find in Joanna's books?"

"Well, that's the thing. When they found it—I think it was just one, but I guess it could've been more than one—they put up this big cloud of smoke, and I couldn't see or hear anything anymore. It was on a shelf in the back with other spell books. They wouldn't let me go back there again—in fact, that was right before they told me to pack a bag and go somewhere else for the night. They made me put my hands on a piece of metal, this big flat thing—"

"Zinc?" I asked.

"I have no idea. How do you tell what kind of metal is what?"

I took a deep breath. "Practice." A zinc plate could work as a combination of control, restricting her behavior, and as a screen, reading her magical fingerprint to compare against objects and places in their investigation. If she'd wiped her hands with sage and spit, the spell wouldn't be able to control her as well, but Birdie wouldn't know that. They had a metal plate at the entrance of the Diamond Street office as a security measure. I'd hacked it once, happily for me.

"Do you have any idea what the book was?" I asked.

Birdie leaned back on the couch, stroking Random, her expression softening. "I'm so sleepy. I was up late last night with the solstice. We had customers at midnight."

"Birdie," I said sharply. The Protectorate charm was working to erase her memory. I leaned over and put my hand on her knee, pushing magic under her skin and up to her heart and brain. "Remember."

"Well, there was this one book," she said, yawning. "They brought it over to me while another witch was holding a cold chain against my cheek. She was wearing metal with a lot of stones on it. A bracelet."

I got up, pushed Random aside, and sat next to her, our legs touching. The wooden beads she wore had come from my workshop, and I'd infused them with protective magic as well as a strand of her own hair. I set my fingertip on it and fought to unlock the confusion inside her mind.

The man at the Berkeley meeting had said the third book, *Instructions,* had been found, but Helen had been skeptical because false rumors had been flying around about it for years.

Very gently I added to the power I was pushing into Birdie's memories. "Did the book have a name?"

Her eyes widened. "Yes! I thought they were joking because it sounded like a romance novel, which I would like, but he really didn't look like the type to read romance, although I admit I'm new to owning a bookstore, so maybe I haven't learned how to interpret people and I shouldn't judge until—"

"Birdie," I said. "The book. What was it called?"

"*Temptations.*" She laughed. "Doesn't that sound sexy?"

I lessened the force of my spell, a little disappointed. "Are you sure?" I asked, but of course she was sure. Even without my magic senses, I could feel the truth of her recollection.

Somebody had put the second book in the trilogy in Birdie's bookstore.

"They wanted to know where I'd gotten it," she said. "When I could prove I'd never seen or touched it, he was satisfied. I'd say he was really happy about it, actually. That's when they told me to go." Birdie gave an enormous yawn and closed her eyes, and a moment later, drained from the competing energies inside her, fell asleep and began to breathe softly.

Why would Joanna put the second book of the set in Birdie's bookstore? Why not keep it for herself? Or sell it and keep the money, which would be much greater than any percentage of a consignment sale?

I looked at Birdie's sleeping face. Her mascara had smudged around her eyes from crying. It didn't make me feel good that I'd been right about distrusting Joanna. I wished the world was as good as Birdie thought it was.

Frank stirred in his basket and opened one sleepy eye. Random lifted his head, looked at me, then put it down on the floor with a sigh.

Suddenly Birdie sat up, eyes wide. "They said some bad things about Joanna and told me not to be so trusting in the future."

I froze, not wanting to disturb her while the memory was flowing through. "Bad things about her wanting demon possession?" I asked quietly.

She blinked. "Worse."

"Worse?" It was hard to imagine that awkward woman doing much of anything. "Like what?"

"They said she killed the old guy in Berkeley."

I stared at her in shock. "Lionel? But why?"

"For that book, *Temptations*. They said it was his. They think she killed him to get it."

✿ 25 ✿

Before dawn the next morning, I was on the road to Armstrong Woods, the state park holding a grove of old-growth coastal redwoods near Guerneville. Exhausted and magic-drained, Birdie had gone to bed early the night before. I'd been unable to get much more out of her about what had happened at the bookstore. The agents had found *Temptations*, the second in the demon-possession trilogy, and blamed Joanna for stealing it from Lionel and putting it there. I had *Warnings*, the first.

But where was *Instructions*, the third book? Did the Protectorate already have it? Had Lionel? Was the curse involved with the two deaths?

I hadn't told Raynor about the curse I'd read there. I should've told him, and maybe I still would.

But with two murders associated with it, I knew the Protectorate would take it from me. And it was...

It was the only object of my mother's I owned. I felt a deep, wordless desire to keep it private. It was bad enough to have a demon possession in your ancestry, but to have your own mother, a woman whose name you'd just learned, have sought it out intentionally... Well, it hurt. Maybe it was shame. Whatever the reason, I wasn't ready to discuss it with anyone.

Nobody living, that is.

The old-growth redwoods would give me the power to reach a spirit who was willing to be reached. I had to leave Silverpool, which was warded by old and new spells working to block any communication with demons. And even if I could have blasted those wards apart, the odds were the wrong demons would surge into town. I only wanted one in particular.

Vera. She would love for me to call her Mother, but that was never going to happen. Even if she *had* succeeded in marrying my father at their infamous wedding, that would've made her my *step*mother at most.

I left my Jeep beside the road walked into the park, using my staff to weave an invisible charm around myself. Sometimes nonmagical rangers went for moonlit walks, and I didn't want to be seen.

I hiked down a path and through the ferny undergrowth until I came to an unnamed tree. The really big ones had names and plaques, and tourists gaped and laughed and took pictures, amazed at how impossibly large they were. This one, however, was a daughter of one of those famous trees, overlooked in its shadow.

Perfect for me.

I'd need to set up my Summoning Circle before dawn when the barriers between our worlds would be at their weakest. The backpack I'd brought held nine candles—beeswax, not LED—and five flat river stones. If anyone saw the fire, alarms would go up and my Summoning would be ruined, so I used my staff to hide me and my objects from nonmagical eyes. As long as I didn't screw up and set the forest on fire, the rangers wouldn't notice me.

When my Circle was established, the candles burning, I stepped inside it and tapped my staff in the earth three times.

"Hi, Vera, you there?" I didn't buy into pompous, archaic, or flowery language. It was the thought that counted.

"Darling! How wonderful!" said a voice. It was the same as the woman who had been engaged to my father—Vera Vanders.

I edged over to one side of the Circle, avoiding the candle flame. "Will you join me for a little talk?"

The space in front of me shimmered like dust motes in a sunbeam, and then a faint figure appeared—first a long-haired young man, then a bird, then a horse, then a woman, middle-aged and ordinary-looking. I recognized her as the Vera I'd known.

"Oh, baby," she said, rubbing her hands together. "I only have a moment. I'm... still weak. Still... resting."

The last time I'd seen her, I'd had to drive her out of an innocent human being who needed her body back. Each death or exorcism drained Vera's resources for doing it again for a while. When I'd been born, the death of my biological mother had led to two decades of her trapped in a bodiless state, waiting until she could return and—

Ugh. I didn't like to think about it. She'd said she wanted to provide the mothering I'd lacked throughout my life. When, as a little girl, I'd imagined my mommy, a bodiless demon wasn't what I'd had in mind.

"I need to ask you about my real mother," I said. "Was she—"

"I'm as much your real mother as anyone, honey. I worry so much about you. Are you sure you should be out in the middle of the night? You look tired. Are you sleeping well?"

"Poppy Almasi," I said. "Was that her name?"

Pouting, she looked down and began playing with the

zipper of the intangible, semitransparent fleece jacket she wore. "It was my name too."

It infuriated me that she believed she was entitled to possess human beings, but I struggled not to show it. "Did she use a book to summon you?"

Vera stopped fiddling with her jacket and looked at me with shimmering gray eyes. "You spoke to Lionel."

My heart beat faster. I was on the right track. "Yes. He wanted to meet me." I rushed on, afraid she might disappear before I had my answers. "You knew him?"

"Poppy knew him," she said. "He tried to talk her out of fulfilling her destiny."

"I bet that made you mad," I said.

"It made Poppy angry, and I felt what Poppy felt," she said. "It's not his place to tell other people what to do just because he's older."

"Actually, he's dead," I said.

"Lionel is dead?" She sounded surprised.

"Somebody killed him."

She stared off into the forest, her mouth forming a black hole in the pale glow of her illuminated form. "He was very intelligent."

I pressed on, knowing time was limited. Her figure was already paler than it had been at first. "Did he give my mother the book that summoned you?"

She turned to me. "There are three books," she said.

"Yes, yes, I know." The Protectorate was chasing a murderer, but I was trying to unravel a personal mystery. Had Lionel given my mother the tool that had enabled her death? Maybe he'd been more responsible that he'd let on. "Did he give them to Poppy?"

"She didn't need the books," she said. "Once she learned of the possibilities, she had the gifts to make it happen."

Without Lionel's library, she might not have learned of

those possibilities, I thought. "I'm not sure it's a gift to be able to summon demons so easily."

"Lucky for her, it was me who answered her summons and not—well, spirits aren't always kind."

My stomach tightened. "She's dead. That wasn't very lucky for her."

"We were very happy together. And both of us were so delighted to have you. It made it all worthwhile."

I had to look away to regain my composure. No matter how willing Poppy had been to be possessed by a demon at the time, she hadn't known she was going to die. The thought of her life draining away just as I came into the world made me want to kick each of the candles into the undergrowth and start a raging wildfire.

When my breathing had steadied, I looked at Vera again. She was disappearing into the darkness, so I drew upon the candles' magic and fed the power summoning the demon who claimed to love me. Her outline solidified—now including a thicker jacket and a scarf.

"Do you know where the third book is?" I asked. "*Instructions*? Did Lionel ever have it? Did—"

"Why are you so curious? You're not seeking possession, are you? That would complicate our relationship."

"No, definitely not," I snapped.

"That's good. But if you were, you wouldn't need the book either." She gestured at the Circle around us, then tapped her chest. "Here I am. You're a natural. Like she was. I was fading away a moment ago, but you brought me back quite easily."

She meant it as a compliment, but it felt like a curse. "I only want to find out who killed Lionel and Joanna."

"Who is Joanna?"

I studied her face, wondering if its illusion could give away lies or truth. "The other witch who was killed. The second book was near her body. It's possible she killed Lionel for it."

"I don't know why anyone would kill for that one," Vera said. "Its promises are repeated elsewhere."

"But they would kill for *Instructions*?"

"Oh yes. And many have. But—are you sure you don't need a sweater, honey? Your skin is covered with goose bumps."

I just couldn't figure out why Joanna was dead. Was it all a distraction from something else?

"I'm very tired, hon," Vera said. "Taking two bodies lately was a bit of a stretch. Forgive me, but I can't hold on any longer without a host body to energize me. I'm... so sad... I have to... to say goodbye—" Her voice caught, and dewy tears glimmered on her cheeks.

"Thank you for talking to me." I didn't know what to feel —part of me wanted to keep talking to her because I was curious and lonely, but she'd done such a horrible thing and was likely to do it again.

She reached out to me with bodiless hands. "I want to be with you so much."

"Don't possess anyone else," I said. "It's not right."

I watched her scarf disappear, then her jacket. The bobbed hair morphed into a crew cut and then took on the texture of the bark of the redwood behind her. Moonlight shone through her chest, and her shins became sword ferns.

I stood, watching the flickering candlelight, and it took me a full minute before I realized she was gone.

A cold grief struck me.

Alone again.

❧ 26 ❧

The sun was just rising when I got back to Silverpool. Low on the horizon behind the trees, its light hadn't yet reached my quiet street, dark in the winter gloom. My headlights lit upon a still figure standing in the middle of the road in front of my house, his arm raised in greeting. Seth.

I braked and rolled down my window, and he walked over. Some of my sour mood lightened at the sight of his mocking smile.

"Where've you been now, witchy demon girl?" he asked, leaning down. "Or should I say, demony witch girl? Girly witch demon?"

"Alma will do," I said. I was in no mood to argue, not even playfully. With the window open, I got a good lungful of the fresh Silverpool air. It tasted delicious, like redwood, sea spray, cedar, and home. "Want to come over for a cup of tea? I might be able to find a few frozen waffles I could toast up for us."

He laughed. "It's never too late to learn how to cook, you know. As a kitchen witch, you might want to learn how to make something other than potions and spells in those caul-drons of yours."

"I don't even own a cauldron," I said—though I did want to get one. A cast-iron pot would hold more than my frying pan. "How about it? Cup of tea?" I inhaled another deep breath, trying to drive away the dark feelings clinging to my soul after seeing Vera. I felt more of a connection to her than I wanted to.

"With the gnome courting, I can't get any closer than this. Why don't you come over to my place? Bring Random. He's going crazy without you."

I looked over at my house and saw Random's frantic face in the living room window, peeking out from under the curtains. Hopefully he hadn't barked and woken Birdie.

I turned to Seth. "OK, I'll be over in a minute."

He smiled, thumped the Jeep's hood, and vanished.

I addressed the empty air: "Maybe you should walk away like a normal person." Then I saw a face in the woods, watching me from her seat on a log. With both hands, she held a pipe as large as her arm. It sent up a spiral of white smoke that moved sideways toward my house. Another stream of smoke, coming from my backyard, met it halfway.

"Good morning," I said, bowing my head.

She raised an eyebrow and sucked on the pipe. I waited a moment, feeling awkward. If it had been up to me, I would've set Willy up with a more friendly creature. I turned away and drove the Jeep up my driveway to park. When I got out, I saw Willy sitting cross-legged on the back patio. Next to him was an old red cooler from my childhood that I'd stuck in the garage. As I walked to my kitchen door, I saw it was filled with dried leaves, pine needles, sticks, and acorns.

"Good morning, Willy," I said, bowing my head to him.

"I am very sorry to be asking, as you are living in your

box near mine, which is your home, but this is my home also and privacy is a lovely gift—"

"No problem. I'm only here for a minute." I waved as I hurried inside. His dating life was stressing me out.

Random ran to meet me, giving me the joy only a dog could give. Birdie's bedroom door was closed, and the house was still dark without any lights on. I hoped she was still sleeping. To make sure Random didn't disturb her, I hooked the leash on him and took him with me. This time I took the front door and didn't bother to greet Olive as we walked by.

Seth immediately welcomed us inside. Like mine, his house was a two-bedroom bungalow, but his always looked and smelled as if it had just been staged by the best professional real estate fluffers in the world. I filled my lungs with welcoming air and felt the tension drain out of me.

"Are you baking cinnamon rolls?" I asked.

His blue eyes went out of focus a moment, and he smiled. "I am now."

His fairy abilities were supposedly limited since he'd been trapped forever in a human body, but I'd yet to see how. "What can't you do?" I asked.

He leaned against the doorway to the kitchen, tilting his head as he regarded me with a grin. "I'm trying to find out."

I looked down at my feet and considered returning to my house. My morning had been full enough already, and what I really needed was to relax, not contemplate the depths or boundaries of my feelings for a supernatural Minnesotan with bedroom eyes.

"I'm sorry," he said. "Too soon. Sit in the living room, and I'll leave you alone. Random, come with me, buddy. Cheese? You still like cheese?"

I watched my dog, who hadn't yet had breakfast, gallop into the kitchen with Seth. My stomach rumbled from the smell of baking pastries, and I kicked off my shoes.

I didn't know what I was doing, but if I thought about it too hard, I wouldn't get cinnamon rolls. The white slipcover chair with the hand-crocheted, multicolored velour blanket seemed the most appealing, so I walked over and collapsed into it. Then I pulled the blanket around my shoulders and let the fae magic of Seth's house wear down my defenses.

My mother had wanted Vera to possess her. Somehow, when I'd first discovered I had demon ancestry and then learned that it was so recent, I'd consoled myself with the assumption it hadn't been voluntary. My biological mother had been a victim of Shadow, and that Shadow had killed her.

But now it looked as if Poppy had been as eager to give her life to a demon as those witches at the Berkeley meeting. She'd been just like them. Maybe she'd even come to Silverpool and camped out in the field, waiting for the solstice, hiding from the Protector a quarter-century ago.

It wasn't her open-minded attitude that bothered me. It was that she'd been more eager to know demonic powers than she'd been to know *me*.

Seth appeared with a silver tray decorated with embroidered linens that would've impressed a duchess. He set it on the coffee table and left without flirting or making any jokes, which I mostly appreciated. I regarded the tray before me: a steaming cinnamon roll, a soft-boiled egg, a china teacup with a matching pot, a tiny pitcher of cream, a crystal vase holding a stem of orange blossoms.

From speakers I couldn't see, a string quartet played Mozart.

Maybe they weren't speakers. Maybe I was hearing talented, classically trained fairies from Vienna. They were there now, their music captured in another time, another dimension, reaching me through the unknowable powers of a man born fae.

As the music soothed away my mommy issues, the pillow behind my head invited me to rest. I drifted off.

When I woke, Random was asleep on the couch nearest to me. As I stirred, his eyes opened and his tail wagged. He'd been on guard duty and was glad to see me move again. I smiled, yawning. Seth wasn't in sight, but I knew he was there. I reached forward to lift the tray into my lap, only surprised for a second that the roll and tea were still steaming hot.

"I summoned my mother," I said to the empty room, lifting a chunk of cinnamon roll. "We talked."

Seth appeared in the doorway. "I'm glad. I was wondering where you'd been."

"Were you really? Can't you tell by sniffing my tires or something?"

He ran a hand through his hair. It was messier than usual, and his jaw was dark with whiskers that were on the verge of being a beard. "I know you don't like that."

"How much did you guess?"

"I could tell you'd been with some very old trees, burning beeswax candles, and one of the types of creatures I normally avoid."

"I normally avoid demons too, but she had some information I needed and I didn't know how else to get it."

He came over and sat on the couch near me. A teacup appeared in his hand, and he sipped it. I could sense spring-water mixed with lemon. "What did she tell you?"

"She's weak," I said. "She admitted my mother's name was Poppy Almasi and claimed—"

"Hold on. When did you learn your human mother's name?"

"My mother's name. My only mother."

He raised an eyebrow and sipped his tea again. "All right. And…"

"Lionel told me about her. He was afraid I might choose the same path and try to summon a demon." I ate a bite of egg, more cinnamon roll, then some tea. "Thank you for this. It's delicious."

"You're not eating properly."

"You sound like Vera," I said, shoving another chunk of pastry into my mouth. Frosting melted onto my tongue.

"Speaking of whom, what else did she say? Does she know who killed Lionel or the other cat witch?"

I chewed and swallowed. Each bite made me feel less alone, and I wondered if it was the sugar or the fairy magic, if there was a difference. "She didn't seem to know anything about what's been going on."

"Do you believe her?"

"I think so. She was weak and could only talk a few minutes. Wherever she came from, it was far."

"She loves you enough to make a difficult journey that cost her a few more years of rest," he said.

"She said my mother was a natural at summoning her, that she was so, so happy to be possessed." Sick at the idea, I picked up the tray and put it on the coffee table.

"Does it bother you that it might be true, or that it might not be?"

I pulled the blanket around my shoulders. "There's no point talking about that," I said. "One useful thing she told me—the book they found at Birdie's bookstore—wait, do you know about that?"

"I'd hope she has books. First rule of a bookstore, I imagine. But I'm old-fashioned."

"One of them they think was stolen from Lionel. There are three, all on demon possession. The first book is called *Warnings*, the second is *Temptations*, and the third, *Instructions*—"

"Is the one everyone wants," Seth said.

I stared at him. "Am I the only person on the planet who hasn't heard of those books? I mean… My father is a professional thief. Rare and valuable magic objects are just the sort of thing he would track down and steal. So why haven't I heard of them?"

He shrugged. "Did he ever steal books before? I thought he was more of a metal and stone guy."

That was true. I couldn't remember a time he'd taken an interest in paper. "You're probably right. Well, I have the first one now, because Lionel gave it to me to prevent me from following my mother's path. And the Protectorate found the second, which they think was stolen from Lionel, in Birdie's bookstore."

"And nobody knows where the other one is," he said.

"Right. The Protectorate suspects Joanna of killing Lionel for the second book."

"But who killed her?"

"There's a curse—I read it in *Warnings* during the solstice —that *Temptations* and *Instructions* can't be together at the same time."

"So maybe she did have both but was killed for the most desirable one." Seth poured tea from my pot into his cup. "Or the demon got her."

"What demon?"

"They're everywhere around the border," he said. "I had trouble getting back into town because I didn't want to get too close."

"Her body was found in town, though, not outside it."

"It was just an idea," he said.

For a few seconds we both watched Random, who was licking his paws. Finally I said, "It must've been a witch."

"Or a normal person who didn't like her taste in fashion," he said.

I kicked him in the leg. "She's been killed."

"Sorry," he said. "Now that I'm stuck in a mortal body, I have to make jokes about death."

I imagined Joanna's body dumped in the alley. It didn't seem like a demonic hit. And why would a nonmagical person hurt her on the night of the solstice?

"It was a witch," I said. "It must've been."

"She killed Lionel, somebody killed her?"

"Maybe." I thought about Lionel in his house, how he'd suddenly sent me away. Would he have been so eager to meet Joanna? It didn't seem to fit.

"By the way, I talked to the river fairy like you asked," he said. "He remembers somebody leaving town and coming back that night. And then the same car returned before you did."

"Why didn't you tell me earlier? That's great—"

"But he also remembers somebody leaving town and coming back every night," he said. "Multiple somebodies. Usually for work."

"OK, so maybe it's not important, but it's worth following up on." I moved to the edge of the chair, ready to get going, figure things out before another witch with a cat-shifting habit turned up dead. "Whose car was it?"

"No idea," he said. "Sorry."

I got to my feet. "Guess I'll have to find out."

27

Birdie was still asleep when I got home. Afraid she might be ill, I walked over to the bed, using a silence spell I'd learned as an apprentice to my burglar father. She was flopped on her back with her arms over her head. Her breathing was steady, and her cheeks a healthy pink. I held a hand over her chest to confirm she was clear of hexes.

Yes, she seemed all right. The Protectorate interrogation had simply left her with a terrible magical hangover. Random jumped up on the bed and flopped next to her, then looked at me with big brown eyes that swore to look after her.

Deciding that being under my roof was probably the safest place in the world for her right now, I gave Random a thankful scratch, grabbed my staff, and left the house on foot to walk to the business district. Silverpool had a low enough population that I thought I might be able to identify a car or truck that I'd never seen before, especially using magic. Most of the visitors had cleared out yesterday, so there were fewer vehicles to investigate. I could walk around the two blocks of shops and restaurants, casting probes over bumpers and tires that looked unfamiliar, and possibly detect the car that had followed me to Berkeley.

If a car had followed me to Berkeley. It could've been a coincidence. But if I did find a suspicious vehicle, it would give me something to work on. There had to be something I could do.

I started on the north side of Main Street, walking past the taqueria and deli, then forced to cross the street at Birdie's bookstore which was surrounded by Protectorate wards.

The cars gave little away. Some were from San Francisco or Sacramento, some from Oregon, LA, Denver, even Chicago, but they didn't give off any magic aura that reminded me of the Berkeley meeting. I wondered if Raynor had found the two witches I'd recognized, what he'd learned about them. If I asked him, though, he'd scold me for getting involved.

I did recognize a Mazda outside the Thai restaurant, and then I looked inside and saw, sitting at a table by herself, the witch Trudy I had nicknamed Good Fingernails. I already knew she came from Berkeley, so sensing that on her car didn't tell me anything new. The solstice was over, but she'd stuck around. Why?

I continued walking and scanning the cars along the road. When I got to the Cypress Hardware parking lot, I finally discovered something interesting. A forest-green Alpha Romeo was parked behind a protective spell near the garden center. The unfamiliar Italian car stood out like a panther in Alaska; if it had ever been in Silverpool before, I would've remembered it. The owner had to be a witch, because it was protected with magic.

I stood at the bumper, looked around, then tapped the rear left wheel with my staff. A prickly energy pushed me back on my heels. Staggering, I lifted my staff and cast out a curtain of magic that both protected me and gave me a view of what was hiding in the spell.

It was Nico's car. I felt his hostility, his strength. And...

I walked around to the driver's side door and brushed my fingers along the handle.

Well, well—Berkeley. And something old... an object... pages? No, faces. Pages of faces?

The ward finally overcame my spying and knocked me away. I fell to one knee, panting and bracing my weight against my staff, waiting for my head to stop spinning.

All right, so Nico was bad news. I'd thought that from the moment I met him. But was he a killer?

When I'd recovered my strength, I stood up and went into the garden center. Nico was probably at the main door and would need a few minutes to hurry over here to confront me. In those few seconds, I thought I could try to contact Jen directly—

A sharp pain struck me in the center of my chest, kicking me back a step. Nico came out from behind a row of ceramic pots on industrial shelving, pointing his small metal wand at me.

"You're not welcome here." He wore reindeer antlers adorned with tiny silver bells and green pom-poms—whimsical fun that didn't match his cold expression.

I braced my legs. "Why did you go to Berkeley last—"

He poked his wand at me again, but this time I was ready with my staff. The garden center was open to the outdoors, which gave me more contact to my house up the hill. I pressed my staff into the concrete and pulled a sheet of thin protective energy between us. I didn't think Jen would appreciate my hurting her underling, so I had to be gentle. Defense, not offense.

This time it was Nico who fell back a step. The bells on

his headband tinkled in the quiet garden center. He lowered his arm.

Smiling at him, I took out the redwood pendant I'd made on solstice night. It was unfinished, but the power was complete, possibly even stronger for the lack of time I'd spent working on it and disturbing its raw essence.

"I wish I knew if Nico was responsible for killing Lionel," I said loudly, holding the pendant out in my palm. If I asked for too much information, the pendant wouldn't cover the cost. I didn't want to risk losing my staff again.

The pendant vanished.

"Alma," Jen said behind me. "Come. Let's talk in my office."

I was now surrounded by the two of them and my path to the exit blocked. The look on Nico's face wasn't aggressive anymore; it was soft with adoration. The look he gave Jen was pure love. I almost saw bluebirds and tiny red hearts fluttering around his head.

I put a second hand on my staff and turned to Jen. "Can I see you alone? We can talk right here."

"She invited you to her office," Nico snapped.

"That's all right, Nico," Jen said. "You can go."

He immediately bowed his head and walked away. Proof of his subservience, he didn't even grumble or throw any dark looks at me.

"Thanks," I told Jen.

"He didn't kill anyone," she said.

I let out my breath. It would've been so nice to blame Nico for everything.

But I still had questions. "Will that pendant cover the cost of explaining why he went to Berkeley the same night you sent me there? The Protectorate might discover the same residue on his car that I did. He'll need to explain himself."

The pendant appeared in her hand. She stroked it,

frowning—then smiled. "Yes. As it happens, you do have enough credit."

A queasy feeling opened up in my stomach. In my haste, I might've just given her something more powerful than I'd meant to.

Too late now. "Did you send him to follow me?"

"Not exactly," Jen said. "You see... Lionel made a wish for you to visit him. Due to his advanced age, he was unable to travel here and meet you. When you arrived on his doorstep, my service to him was provided. Nico was there to collect his payment and close the deal."

I cast my thoughts back to the images I'd seen when touching Nico's car. Faces. Pages of faces.

I thought about what the jinn valued. Her biggest deals with me had hinged on her maintaining her privacy. Evading discovery. She'd lived for generations in Silverpool, pretending to be the youngest in the matriarchal line of women who'd owned and managed the biggest store in town. Older residents in town remembered her mother and grand-mother. I'd seen a photograph from decades ago with her face identical to today's.

Pages of faces...

"Did he have a photo album?" I asked. "Pictures of you from the old days?"

She nodded and tucked a dark strand of hair—not a strand of gray—behind her ear. "It's all the old days to me," she said. "There. You have your wish. I could've told anyone who asked that it was my great-grandmother, and my grand-mother, and although nonmagical humans would of course believe me, witches are always sniffing around suspiciously for that sort of thing. I accepted his offer. Nico collected the album from Lionel's mailbox, never setting foot on his prop-erty. He has no idea if the old witch was living or dead when he visited."

"When exactly did he—" I began.

Jen closed her fingers around the pendant, then opened them again and showed me her empty palm. "Your balance has run to zero again, I'm afraid. Did you want to replenish your account?" Her eyes darted to the staff in my hand.

I tightened my fingers around it. "No. Thank you. Goodbye." I turned on my heel and strode out of the store, my heart thudding in my chest. She looked nice, but I didn't know what kind of limits her power had, and it terrified me.

I gave the Alpha Romeo a wide berth and hurried across the parking lot, eager to get off Cypress Hardware property.

Nico was just a loyal servant, following orders, sent to Berkeley by others, just as I was.

But unlike me, he was driven by love. Given the look on his face, he'd do anything to make Jen happy. What had he thought when he'd realized Lionel had owned a photo album implicating her? Maybe he'd become worried about Lionel keeping the secret, even after handing over the album. He might do anything to guarantee her safety, her happiness, her continued existence where he could serve her.

Jen had said Nico hadn't killed Lionel, but maybe she didn't know everything. If she did, she would've known about the existence of the album in the first place and had the power to destroy it. Her powers were vast—but as she'd told me once, she could only do what she'd been paid to do. Her existence itself relied on fulfilled transactions.

What if Nico had taken it upon himself to silence the man who'd blackmailed his beloved master?

❦ 28 ❧

I was about to cross at the stop sign on Main Street near the Silverpool Bridge when Kelly zoomed by on her white motorcycle, heading west.

What was she up to now? For a romantic couple, she and Raynor didn't seem to spend much time together. I knew Raynor was busy with making sure all the demons stayed out of town and the boundary spells held as the visiting witches departed, and of course there was a murder investigation with Timms and his agents staying at the winery. But I didn't get the impression Kelly was feeling neglected. If anything, she was taking advantage of her solitude.

I wished I'd taken the Jeep so I could follow. I jogged into the intersection, tapped my staff against the asphalt where I thought her bike's wheels had crossed, and cast a tracking spell. Then I turned onto my street and ran uphill to home, cursing my weak athletic conditioning.

While I struggled to keep my pace, afraid Kelly was getting too far ahead to follow, Birdie's Toyota appeared at the top of the hill heading toward me. I flagged her down and went over to the window.

"Are you sure you feel good enough to leave?" I asked, panting on her.

"I have to. I have to be home. What if they decide they don't want to leave my store, that it belongs to the Protectorate now?" She put her hand on her own redwood bead necklace. "You've told me a million times how important it is to occupy your space and not let other witches get their magic all over it. I've worked so hard, you know? I can't let them ruin it, even if Joanna is dead, and I feel terrible she's dead, but how will it help her if I'm just hiding in bed? And—"

"It's OK, Birdie," I said, squeezing her arm. "Of course you want to go home. I don't mind."

She blinked away tears, looking relieved. "Anyway, Frank and Random don't get along."

I looked past her to the laundry basket wedged on the floor in front of the passenger seat. Frank regarded me from under heavily lidded eyes.

"I wonder if he hates me," I said. "I thought he wanted me to take him home with me, but maybe he was just saying hello."

"Of course he doesn't hate you," Birdie said. "He just misses his human. Cats grieve too, you know."

"Right," I said. "That's probably it." Distracted by the thought of Kelly's increasing distance, I told Birdie to take it easy, avoid as many witches as she could, and we both went on our way.

I jogged past Seth's house with a shielding spell around me that I hoped prevented him from meddling in my affairs, at least for now. He had weird fae powers of apparition and inanimate object manipulation, but my self-defense magic had always been a match for him.

Inside my house, I collected Random and got in the Jeep with him to go look for Kelly. He could always be my excuse for why I was wandering around somewhere. Dogs needed their exercise. Wiping off my sweaty upper lip as I turned onto Main Street, I admitted the same went for me.

I held the staff in one hand as I drove, feeling for the tracking spell, but it was weak. Kelly had driven around town before, and I could be picking up an old trail. I drove first to the wellspring, parked, and walked around, feeling for evidence of her motorcycle, footprints, anything that felt like the Kelly I'd met. Nothing fresh struck me.

Random, who I'd left locked in the car, panted at the window, protesting his imprisonment. I decided to drive on to the makeshift campground to the west and look for her there. While Random begged me, I put my hand on my necklace and cast a camouflage spell around my Jeep. The proximity of the wellspring seemed to drain my strength faster than usual, and I tripped as I climbed back in behind the wheel. Hopefully it would give me a few minutes before she saw through it.

I drove out to the field the witches had turned into a campground. This time I found a parking spot on the same side of the road as the campers, next to a retro trailer shaped like a metallic egg. From the safety of my enchanted Jeep, I scanned the gravel shoulder, the field, the surrounded forest. There were several motorcycles parked in a turnout, but no fewer than three of them were white. There must've been a witch fashion for white motorcycles that I hadn't been aware of. I'd walk over and scan them after I saw as much as I could from the hidden safety of the Jeep.

Most of the witches seemed to have packed up and left already, but I recognized the tent I'd climbed into as a cat. Where I'd enjoyed Trudy's good fingernails. Now that I saw the nylon dome with my human eyes, I realized the tent was bright yellow. My cat eyes had probably been drawn to its sunny, warm appearance.

Sun would've been nice today, too. The morning fog didn't look like it was going to burn off—or maybe it was cloud cover. Hard to tell. A flat gray sky covered the forest and grassland in a monochromatic blur.

I continued searching for Kelly, noting that just like at a nonmagical event, the visitors had trashed the place. Shrub and grass were now flat as concrete. Plastic bags and wrappers... papers and strings and food scraps... a boot, a shoe, a hat... two hats... a teddy bear missing its limbs...

Disgusted with the mess, I shook my head and stroked Random's ears. "I'm going to have to get out of the car," I told him. "I can't see enough from here." I cracked the windows for him and stepped outside. The staff drew too much power to go unnoticed, so I left it on the seat.

Aha—yes. With only open air between us and my boots touching the earth, I was suddenly able to see Kelly walking up the hill. Like me, she was using a spell to hide herself. But what was she doing? She was walking in a straight line directly toward—

The yellow tent.

Interesting. Kelly and Trudy?

She paused, looked around, bent over, touched the tent—

The roar of an engine and popping gravel drew my attention to the spot on the side of the road next to me where a black SUV was pulling over. Darius was behind the wheel, an irritated look on his face. He was making no effort to arrive quietly—in fact, from his speed and the way he braked to a stop in the gravel, I decided he was being intentionally loud. If he'd had a siren, he would've had it on.

He got out of the SUV, the many pieces of silver on his black leather jacket glinting in the weak sunlight, and slammed the door with both hands. "Alma, what in Shadow are you doing here?" he asked—loudly—tugging his coat down. "Don't answer that. You can help me get rid of the *trash*." The hostile scan he gave the field included both the garbage and the people remaining there.

I looked back at the yellow tent. Demon's balls. No sign of Kelly. I turned to Darius. "Either you scared her away, or she's inside. I need to go look."

"Who?"

"K—"

I heard the rumble of a motorcycle, a roar, then the fading sound of its engine heading to Silverpool.

Kelly was gone.

"She's got the visual hiding spell down pat," I said, "but not so much the sound thing."

Darius frowned at the highway where I was staring. "Who?"

"Kelly. Raynor's girlfriend."

His mouth opened, and he turned on me. "You're spying on our boss's girlfriend?"

I let the pronoun stand without arguing, although I didn't think of Raynor as my boss so much as a... a... *client*.

"She's been sneaking around, acting very suspicious," I said.

"Don't you think Raynor would notice if his girlfriend was going around murdering people?"

"I'm not saying she murdered anyone," I said. "But there's something not Bright about her."

"Welcome to the human race." Darius opened the back door of the SUV and pulled out a pair of gloves and a large black plastic garbage bag. "Even the best ones don't pick up after themselves. You should see my sister's apartment. But these creepy ones who think demons are fun—they're the worst. Look at this place."

I watched him put on the gloves and shake the bag open. "You're... picking up garbage?" I asked.

"Just anything with a magical residue."

"That could be everything here," I said.

He gave me a tight, bitter smile. "Nice, isn't it? Years of schooling, working, sucking up—and now this."

"Don't do it. Tell them the Flints should do it. Timms is here with some, he must have—"

"No. I can't afford to complain right now. They're testing us. I refuse to give them the satisfaction."

"Us?" I asked.

"Me and Raynor. Timms seems nice, but underneath he's the same as all the other Emeralds, jockeying for power and status." He kicked the vehicle door closed and looked over at mine. "I just noticed your dog is in the car. You're just going to leave him in there by himself? He doesn't look like he's cool with that."

My spell hiding the Jeep had worn off. "It was only for a minute."

"That's not safe. It gets too hot. Even with the window cracked."

"I-I—" The life-support spells I'd set up in the car for my day as a cat were still functioning, but it would take too long to explain. He was a good guy to care about my dog.

I looked over at the yellow tent. With Darius there, I couldn't approach it without making Trudy suspicious. So far as she knew, we'd never met. Maybe I could return as a cat.

"I was going to sneak around and spy," I said, "but now I can't do that. Your silver jacket kind of draws attention, you know?"

"Don't you dare. If Raynor and I aren't allowed to investigate, you certainly aren't. You should be home even if the murderer doesn't seem to be hunting down cat-shifting witches," Darius said. "Timms is one of those controlling types. If I hadn't dated one of his Flints last year, I wouldn't know a Shadowed thing. But Timms found out she'd talked to me and sent her back to San Francisco."

I hadn't realized Darius had a love life, but this wasn't the time to pry or tease, although I was really, really tempted. "What did she tell you?"

"They're pinning Lionel's death on the cat lady. She had one of his books."

"*Temptations*," I said.

He frowned at me. "That's the one. How do you— Ah. Birdie shouldn't have told you, but of course she would."

"But then who killed Joanna?"

"They're looking for an accomplice," he said.

I looked over at the tent, then back to Darius, my eyebrows raised.

"What?" he said, pursing his lips.

"Kelly was just near the tent of a witch I saw at the meeting in Berkeley. I told Raynor about her. Maybe they're working together."

His scowl deepened. "Who's working together? Raynor and Kelly?"

"No, Kelly and Trudy, the witch from Berkeley."

"So you *are* accusing Raynor's girlfriend of being a murderer."

"I'm just asking," I said.

"Oh, that's OK then. He won't mind. Just asking."

His sarcasm only made me more determined to convince him. "I saw her at the wellspring, Darius. She was alone."

"And you know that because..."

I lifted my chin at him. "I saw her."

"Because you were there too. And I'm pretty sure you weren't there with a Protectorate escort either."

Darius and I had a history. I came to him with my ideas, he rejected them, I eventually convinced him I was right, he admitted he was wrong, I forgave him, we moved on. This time we were still in the rejection phase. But it was worth getting him to see my point, because he was smart, powerful, fair, and still employed by the Protectorate.

I'd try a different tack. "There are three books," I said. "Did you hear about them? A trilogy for witches about possession?"

"Trilogy? I heard there were two books. *Temptations* and the other one, the how-to, *Instructions*. They think whoever killed Joanna has it now."

He only knew about two. Should I tell him more? If I argued about the existence of a third book, he'd want to know why I was so sure, which would lead to him figuring out I had it—and I didn't feel like having the Protectorate take it away from me or ask me how I got it, especially after two people were murdered. "Mm," I said.

"Timms sent the Flint away because she told me about the missing book," he said. "She called me, crying. She hadn't realized he would be so angry."

Darius and I had been partners, and I'd failed him. Even now, years later, I had the urge to make it up to him. "I know something. I don't want you to ask me how I know, but I want you to know it."

He looked at me. A truth scan began to wash over me, then abruptly stopped. Sighing, he looked up at the sky. "You want me to trust you."

"Yes."

"If they really want to learn whatever it is you tell me, they'll be able to get it out of me," he said. "And trace it to you. You know that."

I hesitated. Well, if the Protectorate found out I had the first book, they'd also find out how I got it—honestly—and couldn't punish me. Well, they could try, but I'd have a good case.

"There's a curse," I said. "It falls on whoever has both books at the same time."

His nostrils flared, showing his internal struggle to not ask me more questions. "So you think a curse killed Joanna? Because she had both books?"

"I don't know. I'm trying to figure that out."

"Demon's balls," Darius muttered. "It could've killed Lionel too. Did he know about it? He must've. That's just the sort of thing he'd know."

I shrugged.

Darius shook out the garbage bag again and nodded at my Jeep, where Random's head, pink tongue flapping, was sticking out the window. "Go home. This isn't our case," he said. "If there is a curse that killed Lionel, who was more powerful than any witch I've ever known, including all the Emeralds at the Protectorate, it's stronger than you and me. It was obviously too strong for the bookstore cat lady."

"But *not* knowing could be more dangerous than knowing," I said. "There's a witch I told Raynor about—Trudy—in the yellow tent. Do you know if he questioned her?"

"Wait a minute, I thought this was about a curse."

"Do you know if he found the witches I told him about?" I asked.

"I know he scanned every witch in a ten-mile radius," Darius said. "And it worked. No possessions. The solstice is over, Alma. The boundary spells held. Go home."

"It's not just the solstice. Two witches are dead," I said.

"Which you just said is linked to a curse, not a crime," he said. "And Timms is working on the case personally." He sounded pleased about it now.

"But he might not know about the curse. It might be important."

Of course it was important, but telling him would put me under the microscope—how did I get the book, how did

I know to read the pages under the starlight, who are these gnomes living in my yard, why would Lionel give me the book of all people? The secret of my mother—and demon mother—would be exposed, ruining me or worse.

Maybe I shouldn't have risked telling Darius about the curse, but he'd gotten sarcastic about my ideas and I'd wanted to show off.

My ego was always getting me into trouble.

"Timms should figure things out on his own," he said. "If he solves the case, he leaves, and that's good. But if he doesn't solve the case... That's good too. You know what I'm saying?"

It was exactly what Raynor had said. "You want him to look bad so you can get back to San Francisco," I said.

"Well, now look at that," he said, turning away. "Those Shadowed witches left a petrified gopher on that blanket over there. What's the matter with people?"

❧ 29 ❧

D arius walked up the hill to the far edge of the encampment, his plastic bag flapping at his hip. The silver studs, buckles, and zippers on his jacket drew the gazes of every witch—about twenty or so left—in the camp. They looked up from their folding chairs, blankets, tailgates, and enchanted hammocks. Several quickly stood up, folding their chairs as if the show was over and they wanted to get on the road before the traffic got too bad. A pair of older witches in tie-dyed sweatshirts and beanies stayed where they were, sipping steaming liquid from stainless steel mugs, but I could feel a protective spell rise up around them. Protectorate agents had the authority to detain, question, and even imprison any witch they wanted to, without evidence, for as long as they wanted. Although Darius was alone, he wore a jacket that signified power, status, and threat.

Although the movement in the camp came to a halt, a harpist continued to play a delicate tune from the edge of the forest just beyond my parked Jeep. Random disappeared from the window. I walked around my rear bumper, following the sound of the music, and saw who was playing the harp.

Seth.

He sat on a fallen log, a ridiculously full-sized harp balanced between his knees, strumming the strings. Wood sprites and river fae were flying in the branches over his head, following the rhythm of the notes.

Random had run over to the other side of the Jeep to get closer to Seth, but I couldn't let him out now or he'd draw Darius' attention to my changeling neighbor. I gave Random an apologetic pat through the window and walked over to Seth, wondering why he had to risk his life to annoy me.

I crossed my arms over my chest, pretending not to enjoy the music, which was mystical and beautiful and chilling and delightful, and said nothing while I waited for him to stop.

Finally he rested his hands on the strings and looked up at me. His expression was sad, but he smiled. "I'm not following you, by the way."

I didn't say anything, wondering if I could believe him.

"There are so few days in the year when the fae are at peace with humans," he continued. "They let me get closer than usual. Sometimes I miss the company of my own kind."

"It's beautiful," I said.

In the grove behind him, fairies had moved back a few human paces since I'd approached, but were still dancing even though his music had stopped. The faint tinkle of a bell, barely audible, harmonized with the rustling of the wind.

"There are no lake fae here, but the forest folk can't resist a little harp music." He stroked the harp's frame, drawing my attention to its components—maple, spruce, brass, sheep gut. No wonder the music felt irresistible to me too. It was steeped in magic.

I glanced over my shoulder to check on Darius, relieved

to see he was still on the far end of the field. I turned back to Seth. "Don't stop playing because of me. It's... nice."

He grinned. "More than nice. I could keep you here for hours if I wanted to."

I tensed, afraid he was right. "I thought you wanted me to stay at home."

"Seems witches are being killed for books, not feline transformation abilities," Seth said. "So unless you've got a secret book too..." He looked down at the strings and plucked a note.

If he knew I did indeed just receive the third book of a trilogy that was leaving a trail of dead bodies, he'd get annoyingly protective.

This was going to be a test of Seth's mind-reading abilities. Freezing my thoughts, I avoided reaching for any new magic and took slow, easy breaths, focusing on the fascinating details of the sound's vibration in the air.

"You're not even going to tell me to be careful?" I asked, trying to strike a playful tone.

"You'll always do what you need to do." He looked over at the Jeep. "Besides, Random can protect you, right?"

We both smiled. Random wasn't a guard dog. The best he could do was bark before running away.

"Well," I said, stepping back. If he'd read my mind about *Warnings*, he wasn't going to admit it. "I better get home."

"Might as well," he said. "Kelly left as soon as she saw you were here."

I sighed, embarrassed he'd guessed what had brought me there. "There's something suspicious about her. There's no good reason for her to be here, meeting with demon-groupie witches."

"Maybe she's working for her boyfriend. Love works in mysterious ways."

He was teasing me again. This was familiar and easy to

navigate. "Maybe she killed Lionel and Joanna, and is meeting with her accomplice to exchange the stolen book so they can finally get their wish and invite a demon to possess them here on the boundaries of Silverpool."

Seth's mocking smile faded. "You think that's possible?"

"Don't you?"

He shook his head. "I don't think the pretty motorcycle witch is a murderer, but what do I know? I always see the best in people."

"Even witches?" I asked.

"I admit I have a weakness for the ones who remind me of you." He still wasn't smiling. "She's got a demon mark too, doesn't she? I feel the same urge to climb into her lap."

Was he trying to make me jealous?

I turned away. It was time to join Random in the Jeep and go learn Kelly's secrets on my own.

❧ 30 ❧

The simplest way to learn more about Kelly was to visit her and Raynor at the winery. Random was my pet, not my assistant, so I brought him home before I went to the winery. Kelly had offered me more books, and I'd use the excuse to drop in unannounced.

I rang the doorbell like a normal nonmagical neighbor paying a visit. The winter sky was a clear, bluish black, and the air tasted like woodsmoke and frost. My breath fogged around my head, drawing a thumbnail-sized fairy into my orbit. She was blue-skinned, donned a white bow on her head, and wore a tunic of shimmering silver paper. She resembled a wrapped gift, which was where she'd probably stolen the materials.

Raynor opened the door, holding a glass of wine. He wore a tailored black shirt over black pants, silver-toed cowboy boots, and had the mildly unfocused gaze and relaxed smile of a man after a few drinks.

He was very tall, and I had to look up at him. "Hi, sorry to bother you. Kelly said I could take a few old books you don't want. Is this a bad time?"

I watched his expression carefully to see if her giving me the books was an unwelcome surprise, but he nodded, stepped back, and sipped his wine. "Come on in. She's on the deck with the others."

Touching my necklace to soften the blow of his boundary spell as I crossed the threshold, I followed him into the house. "The others?"

"Timms and his agents." He lifted his wine. "Can I get you a glass? It's a bottle from last year. Not too bad."

I walked behind him, annoyed at my bad timing. Through the glass doors, I could see his guests on the deck. Timms, no slouch, noticed me immediately and waved.

I waved back, forcing a smile. Now I wouldn't be able to poke around as much as I'd hoped.

"I don't want to crash your party," I said. "I only dropped by for the books. I can come back in the morning." Maybe I could talk to Raynor alone, share my fears, tell him what I'd seen, and risk our personal and professional relationship. It wouldn't be easy, but now that I was with him in his own home, it felt like the right thing to do. I had an obligation to tell him his girlfriend was—potentially—bad news.

Kelly left the guests on the deck to join us. "Alma! Fantastic. I didn't think you'd come, or I would've invited you myself. What can we get you? There's an open bottle of red, but I'd love to pop the champagne. Come on, will you join me? Say you'll join me. It's the good stuff."

Her friendliness unbalanced me, in part because it seemed genuine. "I didn't realize you were having a party. I came by for the books, but I can come back…"

Her smile froze. "Books?"

"The ones you didn't want? You said—"

"Oh, of course. I totally forgot. Are you sure you want those old things? I was going to put them in the recycling."

"Yes, I really do. I'm afraid I love that old stuff."

Raynor toasted me with his wineglass. "To the old stuff."

Rolling her eyes, Kelly put an arm around him. "You don't want an atlas of herbal remedies from nineteenth-century Wisconsin any more than I do," she said.

"But I'm not a snob about it with people who do," he said.

With a laugh, Kelly pushed him away and turned to me. "If I was a snob, I apologize. I can be a little too open with my opinions sometimes. But at least I'm honest." She gestured for me to follow her. "Come on, I want to show you what I've been up to. Are you sure you don't want a drink?"

I reconsidered. Timms and his agents were there, but Kelly seemed sociable. I'd have a chance to learn something about her and possibly even the investigation from the Protectorate people. Alcohol loosened even witches' tongues. "All right. Sure, thank you. That sounds nice."

"Champagne? Please say you'll have some." She lowered her voice. "It's from France. Don't tell the locals."

"Sure. Thanks."

She pointed down the hallway. "Meet me in the small room on the left, the one that almost looks like a library. Well, more like a reading room, because it's so small. The trash—I mean, the old texts—are in the garage." She turned and rubbed her hands together. "I'll get us the champagne."

I walked down the hall, my gut tightening. It looked as if she'd pointed at a room I'd been in before, one that had previously contained an impressive blockade of hexes to protect the black-market magical treasures inside. I'd broken through them to explore the collection, looking for clues to the owner's murder. The Protectorate had taken the cabinet with all the objects, but some of the magic might have lingered, and I wasn't eager to reenter the room without powerful magic of my own.

From the doorway, I peeked inside without crossing the

threshold. Yes—the walls were now lined with bookshelves, and old-fashioned leather chairs, swing-arm reading lights, and walnut end tables were placed around the room in an appealing, classic library style. A fireplace—only a gas insert, but it gave off heat—burned from the left wall.

I looked back to confirm I was alone, then put my hand on my necklace and knelt down to the floorboards. That summer, I'd had to pull out the silver nails that were embedded there to bar casual entry. Now, as I brushed my fingers along the pock-marked wood, I felt the shiver of recognition as the wood remembered me. That was an excellent sign. It meant I'd be protected as I entered, not knocked down as a former enemy.

Holding my breath, I got to my feet and stepped inside the room.

Nothing.

Lowering my hand from my necklace, I scanned the shelves for any more residue of the hostile magic that had made me weak and nauseated the last time I'd been there. Over the summer, an enchanted jade gargoyle had struck me unconscious, but I couldn't see him now.

I walked closer to the shelves, feeling a warm connection grow between the bones in my legs and the hardwood floors. Like the timber forming the threshold, the room's interior remembered me as well. I smiled, flattered and relieved. My battle with the hexes in the room had been one of the hardest I'd ever fought, and I felt proud of myself for how well I must've performed for the space to welcome me as a conqueror.

My thoughts turned to Kelly. A weak part of me was tempted to brag to her about my magical powers, but of course I couldn't. It was always better to be underestimated. I reached out to touch one of the old books on the shelf, a volume with a gold spine and Cyrillic text.

My fingertip went through a haze of light, bright air.

I drew back, my breath catching in my chest. I looked back at the doorway to confirm Kelly hadn't returned, then tried again.

My finger went through air again. The book was an illusion.

I swiped my fingers through the other books on the shelf and found the same thing.

Adrenaline rushed through me. She'd stolen the books and risked an enchantment under Raynor's own roof to hide that fact. Kelly had to be impressively criminally ambitious as well as powerful enough to pull it off. What if Raynor came in here and tried to pick up a book? It gave the impression of an appealing reading room.

I put my hand on my necklace and tapped into my power to see the technical underpinnings of her enchantment. A sharp drain on my energy weakened my knees, making me reach out to a shelf for balance. As soon as my skin touched the pine shelving, more power rushed into me, connected with the existing, older spells in the room, and gave me a black-and-white view of the true objects in the room.

The shelves and tables were real, and several of the books. Surprisingly, not only were most of the books an illusion, but also the chairs and lamps, which looked inviting but were actually empty moving boxes.

No, not empty. They contained something unpleasant. Rotten—no, worse than rotten. I walked over, pushed my hand through the false cushion, and lifted the edge of cardboard.

The stench of cat excrement wafted out.

I drew back, my stomach clenching, and at that moment Kelly appeared at the door with two flutes of champagne.

"Is everything all right?" she asked, watching me intently over the rim of one glass.

"I don't know," I said honestly. "I think I need some air."

Her expression turned sympathetic. "Of course. Let's go to the deck." She held out the glass. "Here, this will help."

I was glad to walk away from the box of cat waste and take the drink out of her hand, though I scanned it with my still-enhanced powers before risking a sip. When I walked into the hallway with her, I felt an immediate release of the nasty magic working on my guts.

She continued to watch me, but I thought my reaction pleased her. After all, repulsion was what she'd intended.

Even with my sight and my affinity for the magic in the room, her hex had almost made me vomit. I'd seen the true source of my nausea, but an unsuspecting visitor would merely feel a discomfort and urgent need to go elsewhere before it reached that point.

Impressive. But to play that game in Raynor's own house, a man with the power to hunt demons and manage other witches at high levels in the Protectorate...

Kelly had to be crazy. She'd even told me to meet her there. She'd wanted to test her spells. What kind of person ran unnecessary risks like that?

The kind of witch who was demonprinted yet chose a demon-hunting Protectorate official for her boyfriend, risking constant discovery and therefore interrogation and imprisonment. A motorcyclist. An adrenaline junkie.

But was there more to it than that?

Two witches were dead, and an infamous, precious book was missing. She had to be entwined in it somehow.

For now, I followed her through the house and kitchen to a door leading into the garage.

"The old books are in here," she said, clicking on the light. It was a three-car garage, typical for affluent people who didn't do any manual labor or yard work themselves—clean, spacious, and containing only a few moving boxes, Raynor's car, and her motorcycle. And two little garbage bags near the blue recycling bin.

"You were really going to throw them away?" I made my voice as playful as possible to keep her relaxed. "That would've been a"—I was tempted to say *crime*—"a tragedy."

"Please, take them. Knock yourself out." Smiling, she took a long drink from her glass. "Demon's sake, isn't this good? I love an excuse to have real champagne. How are you feeling now? Better, I bet. A mouthful of this can cure anything."

"It's so weird." I pitched my voice younger, stupider. "I don't know what came over me."

"I told Raynor there's something wrong with that room, but he didn't believe me," she said. "Something left over from the old Protector. You knew him, right? Tristan Rice?"

"Price," I said. "Yes, I knew him."

"I hear he was quite a fox with the ladies."

That was an easy one. "He seemed to have slept with every woman within a ten-mile radius," I said.

She drained her glass and grinned at me. "You too?"

Keeping a smile on my face, I handed her my glass, still mostly full, and walked over to the bags. "I was within the radius, yes." I picked one up, glad it wasn't too heavy to carry with one hand—I wanted to keep a spell-hand free—and nodded toward the driveway. "Do you mind if I leave through here so I don't have to carry them through the house?"

"I don't blame you for wanting to go," she said. "Timms might be the most powerful witch in Northern California now, but he's a bit of a bore. Raynor tried to get him to lighten up with a mock duel, but he just looked horrified."

"A mock duel between Raynor and Timms?" I asked.

"Wouldn't that have been fun? But the big guy acted offended by the idea." She glanced over her shoulder at the door but didn't lower her voice. "I suppose he figured it's not worth the risk of letting Raynor prove he's the stronger witch. The only reason Timms got the job was because New York wanted to knock Raynor down a peg. Everyone knows Raynor could hex the teeth out of him." Her eyes shone with bloodlust.

Well, what I'd seen in the library had made me interpret her enthusiasm as bloodlust. It might have been honest pride.

She hit a button on the wall and one of the garage doors rolled upward. My Jeep was in the driveway beyond.

"Thanks," I said. "I'll come back—"

She set down both glasses on the floor and picked up the second bag. "Don't worry about it. I've got it."

We walked out together into the driveway, lit by flood-lights that had attracted a few small flying fairies, and put the bags in my car. The whole time I was trying to act light and carefree, but deep down my magic senses were raging to scan or blast her. Now that I'd unlocked her illusion in the reading room, I was unraveling her other illusions as well—she wasn't as tall, her voice wasn't as melodious, her smile wasn't as nice —actually, it wasn't nice at all.

But I didn't detect any malice toward me personally. When I turned away from the Jeep to thank her again for the books, she was smiling over at an old, gnarled oak near the tasting-room building, where a pair of white-winged fairies were holding hands.

"I love those lace-winged woodland sprites, don't you?" She gave me a genuine smile. "I can't tell you how nice it is to be able to talk to one of my own kind. Most of the time, I'm so busy pretending I can't see and hear what's *right there*. But of course you know just what I mean."

Unfortunately, I did know. "It can be lonely."

"Exactly. No wonder Raynor took you under his wing. We have each other, but you're all alone."

My cheeks were getting fatigued from holding a smile I didn't feel. "I'm fine," I said. "Well, thanks for the books."

"You're sure you don't want to stay? We could go for a walk around the vineyard. The fairy houses are so cute at night."

I'd decided to tell Raynor about her as soon as possible, but when I did that, I'd have to make sure he was cold sober and that Kelly wasn't able to interrupt or overhear. Her magic was strong and unpredictable, and I had no idea how much control over Raynor she'd already established. The knack she'd shown for illusions of books and furniture could be applied on a deeper, personal level, potentially convincing Raynor she was a sweet, vulnerable woman without a thread of Shadow in her. I'd need to talk to Raynor on neutral ground, away from the winery and her enchantments, when I was certain she was miles away.

"No, but thanks," I said. "I'm not much for parties."

"You're just going to the wrong ones. Don't give up yet. I throw a killer party."

I nodded noncommittally, hoping that wasn't literally true.

Waving goodbye, Kelly went back through the garage. A moment later, the door slid down. I stood next to my Jeep, waiting for it to close all the way, then took a deep, ragged breath.

Maybe I shouldn't wait until the morning to talk to Raynor. If something happened tonight, I'd never forgive myself.

"Hey," said a man's voice. "What's up?"

Across the driveway in front of the tasting room building, Darius stood under an orb of light he held over his head. It was a moonstone.

It wasn't like Darius to use superfluous magic. "Hi," I said, walking over. "Why aren't you at the party with the others?"

He lowered the hand with the moonstone and lifted the other one, which held a bottle of wine, to his lips. "Not feeling it."

I'd never seen Darius drunk before, but he was definitely drunk now. "Are you OK?"

"Come on in. I've got a bottle for you too."

I didn't want a drink, but I'd love his insight, even if it was intoxicated. And he looked like he might need a friend. "Sure, thanks."

He led me into the visitor's building that Tristan had staffed on weekends. Since his death over the summer, it had been closed. A bar was at one end; a large screen for promotional videos hung above it between cabinets of glasses and a chalkboard of the day's specials. Darius had set up five enchanted candles along the bar that brightened the space but were invisible from outside.

He went behind the bar, reached below, and took out a bottle that he promptly uncorked with a tap of the moonstone. Grinning, he held out the bottle. "Cool, right?"

"I'm worried about you." I walked over and leaned against the bar between two of the candles. "Maybe you should ask for a transfer if you're this miserable."

He lifted the bottle, took a swig, and wiped his lips with the back of his hand. "Do I look miserable?" he asked, grinning.

"Yes. You prefer being grumpy. It works for you."

He shook his head and thumped the bottle on the bar. "Ha," he said. "Obviously it wasn't working, or I wouldn't be here."

"This is temporary."

"Protectorship is a lifetime appointment," he said. "Life. Time."

"You're not the Protector, Raynor is."

"My fate is tied to his," Darius said.

"You don't know—"

Darius leaned over and grabbed my arm. "I do know."

I looked down, unnerved by the physical contact. With the touch, I could analyze the energy that poured through him, surging through the moonstone and the linked candles. I tasted his distress, his disorganized thinking, his thwarted ambition, his fear he'd never overcome his troubles.

"I've known for decades my fate would be entwined with his," Darius continued. "A seer in Oakland told my mother when I was a boy. We didn't know Raynor's name then. But when I met him, I knew. As apprentice, as agent, as allies. But linked."

Such prophecies were common, but I was skeptical they were binding. His belief in it was probably more powerful than the actual magic at work, but I'd offend him if I said so.

"That doesn't mean you have to live in Silverpool," I said.

"How do you know? You don't know what it feels like to be… trapped. To have your choices written by some force that never shows itself."

"I know what it feels like," I said. "We all do. It's the human condition. That doesn't mean it's true."

"No, you're different. You're like him. You've got weird powers I don't."

Gently I moved his hand and stepped away from the bar. When he sobered up, he'd regret letting me see him so vulnerable. His confidence had taken a hit, but I might be able to help with that. "Well, weird powers or not," I said, "I need your help. You're the only witch I trust."

As I'd hoped, his gaze sharpened. But he picked up the bottle and had another sip. "So, Raynor was busy?"

I looked over my shoulder and sent out a quick scan to feel for the presence of the Protector of Silverpool. "No, I can't trust him with this." I turned back to Darius. "Only you."

"Seriously?"

I nodded.

He shrugged, set the bottle down, and leaned sideways against the counter. The candle flame illuminated the interest in his eyes. "OK. Shoot."

"I think Kelly is a Shadow-market smuggler. Maybe worse," I said.

He grimaced. "Demon's balls, not that again." He started to turn away.

"Hear me out. I just saw something in the house. It's bad."

"What, just now?"

"Yes."

"Fine. Spill." He made a pouring gesture with his hand, then leaned far to one side, propping his weight on an elbow.

I told him everything I'd seen with the books and repeated seeing her at the wellspring and at the witch campground. He didn't interrupt or argue, and I knew I'd made an impression.

"Maybe I should tell him tonight," I said. "She might be dangerous."

"First of all, not tonight. He's almost as drunk as I am."

Raynor *had* looked pretty loose. "OK, maybe not tonight," I said. "Wait. What do you mean by 'first of all'?"

He tapped his chest. "It should be me. I should be the one. To talk to him."

"But I'm the one who saw her. It'll be more convincing."

Darius shook his head. "Noooooo," he said, slumping onto the opposite elbow. How many bottles of pinot had he had? "He might think you're... You know."

"Persistent?" I asked. "Brilliant?"

He began to lift the bottle to his lips again. "Jealous."

I was too annoyed to respond with the vehemence it deserved. I reached out and held the bottle down so he couldn't drink any more. "Excuse me?"

He frowned. "Don't take it personally—"

"Don't take it personally that I can't talk to a man without feeling hormonal?"

"He's not just any man— Oh, demon's balls." He pushed himself upright.

"Do *you* have a thing for him?" I asked.

"No. I don't. But— Look, you weren't at the Protectorate when he was Director." He spoke more quickly now, as if he'd wanted to talk about it for a long time and had held back. "Sometimes, sometimes I think that's the real reason New York sent him up here. The women—and some of the guys—just found him... distracting. He looks like a movie star. Without magic. It has an effect on people."

"Especially women people," I said.

"And some men. Just not me."

"Well, not me either," I said. "I take your guidance under advisement and will try not to pant, lick, or swoon in his presence when I tell him his girlfriend is a crook."

He reached under the bar and took out a bottle of water. "I'll tell him. Trust me. It needs to be me. Man to man. Dude witch to dude witch."

Maybe he was right. If Darius could imagine I'd be misguided by my gender, so could Raynor, especially with Kelly's influence. I ran my hands over the bar, recalling the feel of the enchantments in the phony library. "It probably would be better to get him away from the house before trying to talk to him. She may have used it to enhance a spell over him."

"Exactly." He leaned his head back, rotated his shoulders, puffed out his breath. "Exactly. Get him alone. In the morning. Got to be smart about this."

"Did you see Trudy at the encampment when you were cleaning up?"

"Who? Oh—the one from Berkeley. Yeah, she was there with her boyfriend. Yellow tent?"

I nodded. "Did you question her?"

"I didn't think you believed in interrogations without

cause."

"Come on," I said. "I don't believe in arrest and imprisonment, but a few casual questions are reasonable."

"Raynor didn't find anything dangerous about them, and neither did I." He unscrewed the water bottle and drank half of it down. "They're young and rude, and I wouldn't trust them with a tarnished nickel, but they weren't casting any summoning spells."

I nodded, thinking about Kelly. Were they all trying to find *Instructions*? What did it have to do with Joanna—had she had it? "It has to be something to do with books."

"You think Kelly's working with them?"

"Maybe," I said.

"I don't see it. Killers? No."

"You never know what people are capable of," I said. "Things get out of hand."

"Lionel never would've let those little nobodies get past the front door if they had murder in mind."

"I'm not saying they killed him. I don't know. But somebody should be questioning them harder."

Darius made a mocking *whoo-hoo* sound. "Listen to you. Witch Friendly isn't so friendly after all."

"Be quiet." I tapped his water bottle. "Drink that. Get some sleep. You can go with me to the campground tomorrow. Maybe we can catch them off guard."

He was still chuckling to himself. "Harder. Question them harder. Bring in the Emeralds!"

I gave him a stern look. "Will you do it?"

Nodding, he tapped the bar with his left hand, and one by one, the candles went out. "If Kelly doesn't kill me first."

"Don't joke—"

But Darius had burst into giggles. I walked out and promised myself I'd never again wish Darius would lighten up, because it was really annoying.

❧ 3 2 ❧

When I got home, I parked in front of the garage and peered into the backyard for any sign of Willy and Olive. It had taken me a week, but I'd finally learned to look before leaping out of the car. Their relationship needed privacy even if it meant I had to use the front door.

At first I didn't see anything but darkness, and I opened the door and stepped out, yawning, planning the next morning when I could face Trudy as a human being, not a cat. With enough redwood beads and my staff, I was confident I could deflect any hexes she might throw at me, especially in Darius' company. His Protectorate status should intimidate her.

Thinking again about Kelly's library illusion—had she sold the books to Joanna, Trudy, or one of the other visiting witches?—I walked over to my back door and scanned the threshold and interior for signs of intrusion before opening it.

A hint of pipe smoke struck my nostrils. I paused with my hand on the doorknob and looked over my shoulder.

The red glow of Willy's pipe hovered near the ground below the redwood tree. Just one pipe. Usually he would greet me if he was outside when I returned home, but not tonight.

I didn't need magical powers to know it was a bad time to chat. Without a word, I went inside and closed the door behind me. Olive wasn't my favorite gnome, but Willy seemed to adore her, and I wanted him to be happy.

Random didn't get up from whatever padded surface he was sleeping on to greet me, which was typical if I was out too late. I kicked off my shoes, yawned again, and peeked out between the curtains at the backyard.

The dot of glowing orange under the tree was still there. It was still alone.

DARIUS CALLED me at dawn the next morning. His voice was rough and hungover. "I can't meet you until eleven," he said. "I'm on boundary spell duty first. I have to do a complete circuit of the town, looking for demon sign. Raynor is convinced they're out there, but Timms says no. He thinks the demon presence here is overblown, that we're wasting our time. I don't know."

I clicked on the lamp near my bed, flinching at the brightness. Random got up from his warm spot at my hip and abandoned me for a soft, dark corner on the rug.

Part of me agreed with Timms that the threat of demons was overblown, but with the solstice only a few days ago and the rising of the wellspring, it seemed reasonable for Raynor to be careful. A few weeks ago, a demon had infiltrated the body of an employee at Cypress Hardware but had fled when I'd confronted it.

I rubbed my eyes, wishing I'd gotten more sleep. "What

has Raynor seen that makes him still worried about a demon threat?"

"He says there aren't as many fae as there should be."

"I saw some at the campground," I said. "And the winery."

"I think Raynor was talking about outside of town," he said. "He thought there should be more."

Seth had commented on the demon presence at the border. "What are you going to do?"

"Raynor wants me to look for demon sign," he said. "I've got to do a manual scan of as much ground as I can cover. I'm starting on the east and moving west as the sun rises."

Demon sign usually involved contact with human beings —an attempted possession—but it could also be a patch of burned grass, an empty fairy house, an overgrown bramble, or a fallen tree. An agent with enough metal could touch the area and determine if the damage was demon made.

"Maybe you could get him to go with you so you could tell him about Kelly away from the winery," I said.

"I tried. He said he can't leave. Timms wants him to stay on site. I don't know why, but he's the boss," he said. "He's going to join me on the vineyard patrol, though, later this morning. We'll walk the perimeter. I'll talk to him about Kelly when we're as far from the house as possible. Maybe she'll still be in bed. It was a late night."

"You haven't seen her this morning yet?"

He snorted. "Yeah, right. It's still dark. She won't be up for hours. Raynor had to get up with Timms, but she doesn't answer to anybody."

That's what worried me. "Are you sure she's still there? You did—"

"I did a scan. Thank Brightness Raynor didn't catch me. My bedroom is off the same hallway as theirs."

"I'll feel better when Raynor knows his girlfriend is up to something."

Darius blew out his breath. "I don't think *he* will, but it has to be done. Well, wish me luck. I'll see you at eleven."

DARIUS CALLED me again just as I was putting on an extra beaded bracelet in preparation for any confrontation with witches at the campground. Or anyone. Leaving the house just kept getting more dangerous.

"Change of plans," Darius said. His voice was so quiet I checked the volume level on my phone.

"Running late?" I asked.

When he didn't speak, my body went cold. I walked over to the kitchen door and picked up my staff, ready to go, ready to fight. "What happened with Kelly?"

"I never saw Kelly," he said. "Raynor fired me before then."

❧ 33 ❧

"**W**hat?" I froze with my staff in midair. "No. He wouldn't. You're his favorite agent. He'd never—"

"I told him what you'd seen. He asked if I believed you. I said yes." Darius' voice got even quieter. "Then he told me not to come back. An agent will return my personal items next week sometime after they've been sufficiently scanned for Shadow influence."

"I don't believe it," I said, my head swimming.

"Thank you very much. I lost my job for saying I believed you," he said.

"No, I mean— I can't— If he was in his right mind, he'd never retaliate like that."

He sighed. "It's an unpleasant reality."

"He must be under a horrible spell to do that to you," I said.

"Sure," Darius said. "A spell called love. Might not be the kind of magic we can do anything about."

Random, sensing my distress, had come over and was

dancing around my feet. I bent over and stroked his head, overwhelmed with guilt.

It was my fault Darius had been fired. It should've been me to talk to Raynor. "Where are you now?"

"Walking back to town. I don't know—about a mile west. Maybe two."

"He left you on the side of the road?" I heard my voice hit an unpleasantly high pitch. "Stay there. I'll come now."

"It's warmer to keep moving," he said. "I'll keep walking. You'll see me."

I put my things in the Jeep, then brought Random over to Seth's house. I didn't know how long I'd be gone. If Darius had really been fired—how could Raynor just sack him like that?—he might need me to drive him back to the Bay Area.

Seth opened the door, holding a book. I eyed it suspiciously, but it seemed to be a dictionary.

"Hi," I said. "Things are getting complicated. Can you watch Random for a while?"

His hair was damp, as if he'd just taken a shower. He looked clean, too. And smelled good. Or maybe that was the fae magic of his house, which was always inviting.

"Are you in danger?" he asked.

"Please don't ask me that." I guided Random into the house. He ran in, then looked back, wanting me to follow. "Why are you holding a dictionary?"

Seth let the pages fall open. Inside was a clump of dried leaves, something ferny, possibly aquatic. "From home. Helps me stay grounded."

Seth had grown up as a human near the lake where his true fairy family lived. I leaned closer to study it, risking a quick touch of magic to identify it. "Lake weed?"

He snapped the book shut with a *thwap*. "I'll take you there sometime. Early summer is the best time. The water's cold, the pike are hungry, loons making a racket. You'd love it."

I met his gaze even though I knew he might see the enthusiasm in my eyes. Visiting his home did spark an interest inside me that had nothing to do with aquatic flora of the Upper Midwest.

Luckily, I had an urgent excuse to run away. I handed him a baggie of dog food. "Thanks for watching him. Really. You're a lifesaver."

As I jogged down the path to my Jeep next door, he called out, "I hope that won't be necessary."

I got in the car and sped off to help Darius. I still owed him for being a terrible partner to him when I was an agent; this was much worse. I drove by Birdie's bookstore, noticed she still had an impressive crowd of customers inside, and drove toward the ocean, braking frequently as I checked the shoulder for Darius. Running him over would be quite the conclusion to our relationship.

Just a quarter mile past the wellspring, I saw him walking on the opposite side and pulled over. Wearing only a gray T-shirt and jeans, which seemed entirely inadequate on a drizzly December day, he jogged over and climbed into the Jeep next to me.

"I'm so sorry," I said.

Frowning, he put the seat belt on. "Not your fault."

"I should've been the one to talk to him."

I thought he was going to argue and reassure me, but he said, "That thought had occurred to me."

Feeling smaller every second, I sank into the seat. "Where can I bring you? San Francisco? Oakland? If he told you not to come back…"

There was a long silence. A light rain continued to fall, but sun peeked through the trees and cast a beam of warm, yellow light across the hillside, creating a rainbow.

Darius said something, but the view outside was making me uneasy, and I didn't hear what he said. The rainbow wasn't breaking any laws of physics, which would mean a witch was involved—given the location of the rain and the sun, it was located just where it should be.

Shaking off my unease, I turned to Darius. "Sorry. Could you repeat that?"

"If you don't mind, a ride would be great," he said. "I'd rather not rely on strangers. The witches who came to Silverpool this week don't have any reason to like me. I've been hassling them every day since they got here."

"I'll drive you, of course," I said. "But you should appeal this. You've been a perfect agent. They must know that."

"Appeal to whom? Timms? He's new. He'll back Raynor."

"New York then," I said.

"They'll agree with whatever Timms says. I'm not important." He pulled down the visor and checked his hair in the window. "I won't miss the rain up here. Did you know it's got twice the annual rainfall of San Francisco? Twice. Two times. That's crazy."

"You're just going to give up?"

He slapped the visor back up. "My sister did. Why not me? Why not learn the tax code like my folks?"

"Because you'd be miserable," I said. "Totally miserable."

"You think?"

"Yes. I do."

We looked at each other for a long moment, me wondering if he'd ever forgive me for ruining his life. But then he licked his fingertip and touched the diamond stud in his left ear. In a flash, the official silver and leather jacket of a Protectorate agent appeared on his torso. The T-shirt had been an illusion.

A mixture of joy and worry struck me. "You kept the jacket!"

He flexed his shoulders. "I always get the ones with built-in camo."

"You're not going to become an accountant!"

"As if," he said. "We're going to search every Shadowed corner of that campground. If there's any evidence to implicate Kelly Tucker, we'll find it."

❄ 34 ❄

I grinned at him, tempted to cheer but knowing that would irritate him. "I'll help you. We'll find it."

"You bet we will." He brought one of the gold chains around his neck to his lips and kissed it. An electric shock of magical promise filled the car.

I started the engine but got distracted by the rainbow again. It wasn't particularly bright, just a pastel shimmer, but something about it...

"If we can't find anything at the campground, there's always the phony library at the house," I said, trying to bring my thoughts back to the immediate task. "If I can get inside again, I might be able to take something as proof. I'd need Timms to witness it, though. I think Raynor must be under her power."

"He's not going to want to admit that," Darius said. "We've got to get a *lot* of proof."

I studied the base of the rainbow where it blended into the misty treetops. Were the colors in the wrong order?

"What's the matter?" Darius asked.

"I'm not sure. Does that rainbow look normal to you?"

He turned to look at it. After a long moment, he shrugged. "Looks fine to me. What are the fairies doing?"

I slapped the steering wheel. "That's it! There aren't any. They love rainbows. There should be some forest fae dancing around at the bottom."

"Demon sign." Darius looked down at my staff resting between the two seats. "Does that thing work out here? I thought it needed to be near your house."

"It's better than nothing. But not as much as I'd like."

"What if somebody has that demon-summoning book, and it had tricks for how to break Protectorate spells around Silverpool, and they've already used it?"

"It would be bad." I put the car in gear and checked the traffic over my shoulder. "Let's go to the campground."

It wasn't far, but it took us longer than usual to get there because I drove slowly to scan the sides of the twisting road for fae. I parked across the highway from the encampment, and we both got out.

"See fairies?" Darius asked.

The edge of the clearing around the witches' tents did have a few forest sprites sitting in the branches, but there weren't as many as when Seth had been there playing the harp. "A few," I said. "There probably isn't a demon too close."

"Just up the hill, Raynor found a nine-foot circle of dead grass," he said, pointing west. "It could've been a bonfire. There was magic there, but any one of these witches could've set it."

Or someone had succeeded in summoning a demon, and it had left its footprint of death on the earth. "I hate the holidays," I mumbled.

Darius smiled. "Right there with you, ex-partner."

I spotted the bright yellow nylon dome immediately. Most of the other tents and trailers from yesterday seemed to have stayed as well. Raynor would have to drive them away physically if they didn't leave on their own in the next day or two. A permanent encampment of witches wasn't a tourist attraction that Silverpool could tolerate.

"Their tent hasn't moved." Darius took out his notebook, wrote something down, clipped his pencil to the notebook, then tucked it all into an inside pocket of his jacket. He might have been fired, but he was still a professional. "I've done a scanning spell. Unless they abandoned it, they're still here."

"You can do one from this far away?" I asked.

He straightened the hem of his jacket, nodding. I could tell he was pleased I was impressed.

"Do you know if they're actually inside it?" I asked.

He turned toward the tent and put his right hand over a silver chain on his left wrist. I felt a wisp of magic slide away from us. "I sense a life force," he said a moment later. "Somebody's in there."

I tightened my hand around the staff. "They might be dangerous. What's our plan?"

He flexed and pushed his shoulders back. The metal in the jacket shone and jingled faintly. "I'll go say hello. You can be my backup. Just in case."

"Look for books," I said. "Ask about them with a truth spell."

"I do know a little bit about how to do this, you know," he said. "I may have been fired, but so were you."

"Yes, yes. You're right, I'm sorry." Stress was making me bossy. "I'll wait here."

Darius only took two steps before I changed my mind.

"You know what," I said, swinging my staff. "I'm going to come with you. I want to cast my own scans."

My experience with Trudy and the books would give me an affinity he didn't have. He accepted my presence with a shrug, and we approached the tent as a pair. As we got closer, I felt the presence of whoever, or whatever, was inside. It didn't seem to be aware of us, although that could've been a trick.

"Let me," Darius said. While I braced myself, he reached out and tapped his finger against the plastic zipper of the flap door.

Nothing.

"Hello!" Darius called out. "Protectorate!"

I tilted my head, detecting a faint roar inside. "Is that an animal?" I asked.

Darius shot me an unimpressed look. "I think it's snoring."

There had been a boundary spell around the tent earlier, but it seemed to have faded. I put my palm on the tent, gave it a jolt of power, and the snoring stopped.

"Hello in there," I said. "Can we talk to you?"

After a faint rustling and the sniff and cough of a human being, the tent door unzipped, revealing the face of the guy sitting with Trudy at the meeting in Berkeley. Brayden.

His bleary eyes widened at the sight of Darius' jacket. "I didn't do anything," he said, scrambling to get out of his sleeping bag. He wore a dark fleece sweatshirt over white-and-green-checked boxers. "Do you think I did something? I didn't do anything. Scan me. Cast a truth spell. Hold on, let me get some pants on."

Before he'd zipped the door shut again, I'd run a scan that told me he was both alone, terrified, and telling the truth as he knew it. I shared a look with Darius, who would've detected the same thing.

Brayden crawled out of the bag and tent and got to his feet on the narrow strip of tarp between us. Shivering, he hunched over, wrapping his arms around himself. "She left."

"Who left?" Darius snapped.

"Aren't you looking for Trudy?" he asked.

"We'll ask the questions," Darius said. Then he paused. "Do you know where Witch Trudy is?"

"I woke up a few hours ago, and her sleeping bag was empty," Brayden said.

"You didn't do anything?" I bent over, peering into the tent. All I saw was clothes and camping equipment, and a quick scan didn't pick up any magic book energy. It could be shielded in a case or velvet bag, however. "Weren't you worried? A witch was killed just up the road a couple of days ago."

"I thought you people got her," he said.

"Why would the Protectorate want Trudy?"

His expression got crafty as he gathered his composure. We'd disarmed him by waking him up, but now he was getting over it. "Who are you?" His scan drifted over me, too light to trigger my defensive spells. His eyebrows rose high on his forehead. "You were in Berkeley."

I tensed. Maybe if I admitted it, he'd be in the mood to tell us more. "How can you tell?"

Stroking a feather-and-copper earring dangling from his left ear, he wrinkled his nose. "Cats are my enemy. Did you know they kill two and a half billion birds every year, just in the United States?"

"You identify with birds?" Darius asked.

"I *am* a bird," he said.

"Shape-shifting into a bird doesn't make you one," I said.

He rolled his eyes. "I don't shift into one. I *am* one."

Darius and I looked at each other. There were many witches who believed in reincarnation, but that didn't seem to be what Brayden was saying.

Darius took me aside and cast a silence bubble around us. "I'll see if I can find her trail. Keep him talking and don't let him leave." He walked around the tent, hands out, his palms facing to the ground like metal detectors.

"You think you're actually a bird," I said, drawing Brayden's attention back to me. "Then why do you look and talk like a human being?"

"You've heard of changelings?" He tried to see what Darius was doing, but my body blocked his view. "I'm like that, except with a bird. Somewhere out there is a bird with my body."

I had no idea if his delusions had any bearing on our investigation, but it might help us find Trudy. "Does your interest in demon possession have something to do with your, um, avian nature?"

"I need to find my true self," he said. Tipping his head back, he lifted his arms in a slow, wide, graceful gesture. Unfurling his wings, apparently. "I might have already passed into the spirit realm. Only a demon can reunite me with my real body."

"But it would be decayed by now." Convinced he was out of touch with reality, I lost interest in him and looked around to find Darius, who had walked down to the road and was investigating the parked vehicles.

"With a demon, its bones will be enough," he said. "But only a demon can find the bones. But I'm not sure I'm dead, because my body would have a human soul. Don't you think that would give it a few decades? I think it would. I can't rest until I find out."

Darius started walking back toward us.

"You could learn to accept the body you've got instead of risking the lives of everyone around you by summoning demons," I said.

"Demons don't hurt anyone," he said. "That's a myth."

I opened my mouth to argue, although I agreed with him more than most since I'd had the unusual experience of having met a nice demon (or demon-like individual) more than once.

Darius touched my shoulder. "A car with her magical fingerprint left a few hours ago."

I turned to Brayden. "What does she drive?"

"A Golf. Why?"

"What color?" Darius asked.

"Yellow." Brayden frowned. "Like the tent. She's a canary, same as me. But—"

A canary. What a bizarre idea. Well, the nonmag weren't the only people to believe fantasies. "We would've noticed it in town," I said, trying to understand how this guy from the Bay Area would rather be a delicate, short-lived bird kept as a pet than a healthy human being with the privileges of youth, masculinity, and magical powers. I hadn't studied psychology, but I thought he could've used a little therapy to work on that.

Darius nodded and took out his phone. "She must've left already. I'll get Raynor, see if we can get—" He grimaced as he remembered he'd been sacked. "Demon's balls. We'll have to deal with it ourselves."

I turned to Brayden. "Does she live in Berkeley? We'll need an address."

"But we came together," Brayden said. "She wouldn't leave without me." But his growing alarm and irritation suggested she would, and had. His girlfriend had used him. Maybe it would make him realize a demon would do far worse.

My phone vibrated in my pocket. I took it out, not leaving Brayden's side in case he'd need to be subdued, and quickly read the screen.

It was from Birdie.

Frank is missing.

✥ 35 ✥

I started running across the campground to my Jeep.

Behind me with Brayden, Darius shouted after me, "Wait, where are you going? We have to search the tent!"

I kept going. "Later! I've got to see Birdie."

He caught up to me just as I was opening the driver's side door. "Hold on, what happened?"

"Frank is gone. The cat. Lionel's cat. And now Trudy—" I got behind the wheel and started the engine. "I bet she's gone to Berkeley. I've got to track her down."

He tapped the roof of the car, making the windows turn as black as a cast-iron frying pan. "Stop. Think. What about me?"

I stared at him, belatedly remembering he was stranded. "Oh. Right. Well, you need a ride. It's perfect."

He reached over me and killed the engine. "I'm going to search that tent. If Trudy has the cat, we'll need an object to track her properly. Maybe she left something behind."

I began to calm down a little. He wasn't going to stop me. He'd help me. "Right, something personal. A belt or a sock or something." Like bloodhounds, Protectorate agents could sometimes follow the magical footprint of a witch if the trail was fresh.

"You'll wait here," he said. It wasn't a question. The windows were still opaque from his spell.

I nodded. "Please hurry."

He slammed the door, leaving me in darkness. While I waited for him to return, I did a few breathing exercises, inhaled the aroma of a sachet of lavender from my garden I kept in the door pocket, and stroked my staff, imagining the hurt I would inflict on anyone who hurt Frank.

Darius announced his return by pounding the roof and returning the windows to their clear state. He climbed in next to me, giving me a look. "You almost stranded me."

"I would've remembered at some point."

"Which point was that? Riovaca? The Richmond Bridge?"

I smiled weakly. "Sorry. I'm mad at myself for not thinking Lionel's cat might be valuable to somebody."

"You spend a lot of time being mad at yourself," he said. "Leave some of that job for the rest of us."

"Will do," I said, pulling out into the road.

Accelerating, I took the sharp turns through the forest at a speed the fairies probably hoped would send me headlong into a redwood or rolling over into the shady understory. I wrapped the staff in the crook of my elbow and gripped the wheel with both hands, drawing on my magic to keep the wheels on the road. A few minutes later, we barreled into Silverpool's business district at seventy miles an hour.

A spell on the brakes helped me stop on the curb next to the store like a helicopter dropping onto a landing pad. Breathing hard, I tumbled out of the Jeep and ran into the store, not waiting for Darius. Birdie was kneeling next to the couch.

I strode over, my hand on my necklace, sending out my magic senses for any traces of the missing cat. "Where did you last see him?"

"Right here," she said, caressing the cushion. "He'd been curled up right here, but some customers were in the store and of course I had to help them find what I could, even though I hardly have any books yet, and then I had to figure out the money thing again, which is working pretty well but they had cash, which was so annoying, and I had to figure out how to make change for a twenty when all I had was nickels and fives—"

"When?" I asked. "Thirty minutes ago? Two hours?"

Birdie started to cry. "That's the thing. I don't know! The customers were here all morning! I don't know which ones took him!"

"We're not sure they did. Maybe he wandered away." I wiped sweat off my upper lip, thinking about the cat. A powerful witch's cat. Visiting witches could've noticed his age, his potential power, and taken him for their undoubtedly unsavory uses. Had they even known he had been one of Lionel's? He might have given off the aura of power.

Giving Birdie a squeeze on the shoulder, I knelt down and put a hand on the cushion. Frank's kitty energy was there —a mixture of mild annoyance, comfort-seeking, sleepiness, indifference—but nothing sinister. At least when he'd last been on the couch, he hadn't been in any serious pain. There hadn't been a struggle.

Dropping to my hands and knees, I closed my eyes and cast out my senses for a trace of him on the floor—or in the air, if somebody had lifted him. His paws had touched here —then here—just walking like any cat—

I crawled across the floor, following the trail to the door.

There, it weakened. Birdie's boundary spell at the

threshold had almost erased the residue of his crossing, but I picked up his trail again on the sidewalk.

I crept along on my hands and knees, periodically stopping to touch my necklace. A few people walking by cast me odd looks, but I gestured at my earlobe, suggesting I'd dropped an earring, and they nodded and walked on.

He'd either walked or been carried to the alley behind the store, which led to the dumpster where Joanna's body had been found. My heart began to pound. Was I going to find his body in the same place?

But the trail didn't go all the way to the dumpster. It turned and stopped at the asphalt facing the building. It vanished there—no, faint, just a trace in the air—

I got to my feet, hands extended before me about knee-high.

The cat had gone into a car. And in my mind's eye, the eye that saw magical fingerprints, shimmering power, and witches' lies, I saw a block of yellow.

Trudy's VW.

A pair of black boots appeared next to me, and I looked up into Darius' face.

"Well?" he asked.

"Trudy has him in the yellow Golf."

He pulled a lacy pink bra out of his pocket. "Shouldn't be too hard to track her. She left this in the tent."

"No T-shirt? An old sock?"

He stiffened. "This was what there was. Underwear is the best to work with."

I shouldn't tease him, especially now. "You're right." I got to my feet, brushing off my hands. "Good find. Do you agree she was here? I picked up the sign of a yellow hatchback."

He pounded the bra between his hands and then formed a cage of his fingers around it. Dropping to one knee, he closed his eyes and sent out his spells. I stepped back, not wanting to contaminate the message.

"Yes. Right here," he said.

Birdie appeared in the alley, wearing every necklace I'd ever given her as well as one she'd made herself. "Did you find anything? Is he OK?" She gave the dumpster a fearful, horrified look.

"He was alive when he left," I said quickly. "We think he's with a witch from Berkeley. We're going to track them down."

"Why would she want him?" Birdie asked. "Do you think she'll hurt him? Is there anything—"

"We'll do everything we can," I said quickly. "We've got to run. I'll keep you posted."

"Text me when—"

I went over and hugged her. "I will. Guard the store. Remember, this is your home now. It's got special power for you." I patted the necklaces around her throat, giving her a warm tap of power and affection through the shared bond.

When we went back inside, Darius and I got in the Jeep, still warm from the magic I'd used to get there at twice its natural speed, and hit the road—this time at a more moderate pace. We wouldn't be able to track her car if we were using too much magic to propel ours.

I drove past Cypress Hardware and turned right at the bridge, flashing a peace sign at the green river fairy who was sitting on the railing.

"Unless you tell me otherwise, I'm going to drive to Berkeley," I told Darius. "If you feel the trail turn off, let me know, but I'm pretty sure that's where she's going."

"Agreed," Darius said. "It's where both she and the cat came from."

"You didn't find any books in the tent? No sign of any?"

"There was a lot of magical residue," he said. "I wouldn't

know if it came from books or something else. They're witches. They had a lot of crap. The dumped dude was worried about finding a ride home."

"If his girlfriend has done something really bad, he'll be getting a ride with one of the agents," I said. "Maybe not to Berkeley, but San Francisco is pretty close. He can take BART home after he's interrogated at Diamond Street."

"He'll probably get out of Silverpool on his own before that happens," Darius said.

"Don't you think Raynor will pick him up?"

"Why would he?"

I risked looking away from the twisty highway. "Didn't you tell—" I cut myself off. No, of course he hadn't told Raynor; he'd been fired.

We had no evidence, just suspicions, and Darius had already lost his job. Whatever use Frank held for Trudy, or how Kelly figured in, was up to us to figure out. Soon—before somebody else died.

Darius pulled on a pair of sunglasses. The bra hung from a thin strap around the rearview mirror—a socially awkward but effective location for using it to guide us. "Steady as she goes," he said, watching it swing above the dashboard.

❧ 36 ❧

As we'd expected, the trail led south on 101, turning off only once at a Novato gas station. The nonmagical toxicity there made it impossible to detect anything about Trudy or Frank, but the trail immediately returned to the highway, and an hour later we were turning off Gillman into the flat streets of northwest Berkeley.

Here the path finally diverged from what would've been the route to Lionel's house.

"Hold on, pull over," Darius said.

The street was crowded, and I had to stop in front of a driveway. Darius got out, walked up the sidewalk a half block, casting search spells with both hands extended, then got back in. "Turn right at the corner. But don't go too fast. She's really close."

I did as he said, my hands sweaty on the wheel. It was difficult for me to do magic while I was driving, especially in a busy city with lots of traffic. At the next intersection, I had to stop for a group of women with two strollers, three toddlers walking alongside, a small fluffy dog, and an older child on a scooter who were crossing the street.

I smiled at the little girl on the scooter. "If this gets violent, bystanders could get hurt," I said, already prepared to feel more guilt. The girl waved, and I waved back.

Darius braced a hand on my arm. "There. Park the car. See her?"

I didn't, but I felt the discomfiting whine of unfamiliar magic somewhere nearby. Shaking off Darius' hand, which was only making me more nervous, I parked near a fire hydrant and hoped there wouldn't be any actual flames over the next few minutes.

"I'll hold her back so you can search the house for the cat," Darius said. "That work for you?"

"Which house?"

"Watch me." Darius jumped out and strode over to an empty driveway.

No—there was a yellow Golf. And then I saw the house —a small, tidy duplex in the same sunny color. It had window boxes, a rose arbor, and a dormant vegetable garden out front. I hadn't seen any of it until Darius had pierced the spell of invisibility. Taking my staff, I got out and hurried after him.

Just below the arbor, Darius flexed his shoulders, shook the metal on the jacket a little, then strode through, blasting the boundary spell with both hands in the air.

I smiled, appreciating his style. He had a lot of frustration to work off.

Behind him, I gripped my staff—weak but not useless— and searched the yard for a sign of Frank. The boundary spells around the property were still active enough to mess with my scans. I'd have to search manually.

Darius punched the air above the first step up to the front door, and a light flashed. Then the door creaked open.

I half expected Frank to saunter through the doorway, but it was Trudy. She ran out, barefoot, wearing only a tank top and shorts, and held some kind of stone in one hand. She pointed it at Darius, frantically muttering something, but he rolled his eyes and knocked it out of her hands with one blow. It fell on the ground—it was green, jade probably, an ugly figure of some kind—and lay still. Outside the property on the sidewalk, I couldn't feel if its magic was engaged.

Darius, however, had the situation under control. Trudy fell to her knees and put her forehead on the sidewalk at his feet, crying and begging for mercy.

He looked over his shoulder at me, his expression contemptuous. Whatever Trudy was, a brilliant fighter she was not. Poor Darius wasn't going to get the match he'd been in the mood for.

I tapped my staff on the concrete under the arbor, pushing a hole through the boundary spell, and stepped into the garden. The jade figurine was faceup in the bark chips, its hideous face trying to threaten me from the ground.

It was a gargoyle I'd seen before at the winery. In its enchanted state, it acted as guard and attack dog, casting spells and curses at trespassers. If Trudy had it, Kelly must've given—or sold—it to her. Afraid it might come to life again, I took one of my emergency velvet bags out of my pocket and scooped up the figurine without touching it. The moment its head landed in the bottom of the bag, it sprang to life and began to kick and punch at the fabric encompassing it. I pulled the drawstring tight and tied it off with the beaded necklace.

Meanwhile, Trudy was still on the ground, begging for mercy, and Darius was frowning at her with annoyance.

"There's no way this girl could've taken Lionel down in his own home," he said to me. "No way."

Trudy looked up with wild, hopeful eyes. "Lionel? Me? Is that what you think I did? No! Of course not! No, scan me, you'll see. Scan me." Propped on her knees, she leaned back, closed her eyes, and held out her arms submissively.

"Where's Frank?" I asked. "The cat. Why'd you take the cat?"

She flinched but held the pose. "I didn't take him."

"Liar!" Darius sent a jolt of power into her body. The violence upset me, but I was too worried about Frank to object—and it was just a wee little shock. I hoped.

"We tracked him to you," I said.

She finally brought her arms down and hugged them around herself. "He *was* here. I'm just saying I didn't take him. He got in the car by himself. I didn't even know he was there until I got gas."

"Where is he now?"

"How would I know? He ran off as soon as I opened the door."

Darius looked at me, still aiming his hands at her. He could hex her without the dramatic gesture, but it warned her to stay still. "I'll hold her here. Go check inside."

I was already walking toward the door. "Give me permission, Trudy," I said as I passed her. Forcing myself over the threshold would take energy I didn't want to spare.

"Please enter, whoever in Brightness you are," Trudy said.

"Thanks." I tapped the staff on the timbers of the door-frame anyway, just in case, then went inside.

"Frank?" I called. "Here, kitty kitty."

There wasn't a cat—I was sure of it, because my highly allergic sinuses felt fine—but there were stacks and stacks of books.

In a pile by the door, dumped hastily there on top of the others, were the ones I'd given Birdie for the store: herb lore, a bird encyclopedia, a witch romance paperback, and the rest. Around the small living room were stacks of other books, arranged more carefully; I walked around and saw they were sorted by topic. Shadow-adjacent hexes, spell craft, more herb lore, animal recipes, stone and mineral science, astronomy, numerology, tarot…

I walked into the next room. A futon, a desk, clothes on the floor. More books. I turned around and found the kitchen, which did have a few books, but it didn't look like she practiced much of the magical lore personally. There weren't the canisters, bottles, jars, and vials I'd expect to see in the kitchen of a witch who was truly interested in the magical sciences.

No—she was a book trader. Probably a thief like my dad. I wondered if she'd gotten into the business on her own or if a family member had pushed her into it.

I shoved aside my curiosity. What mattered now was piecing together what books she'd bought, sold, and stolen; to whom, why, and when.

I picked up as many of Birdie's books as I could carry and went outside. Darius had his arm around Trudy in a way that would look harmlessly friendly to passersby if they couldn't sense the truth spell he was casting into her brain.

"He paid me to put it in the store," she was saying.

"Which book?"

"*Instructions.* The one everybody wanted. *Instructions.* I worked all year to get it."

"You put it in the store? Or is that where you got it?" Darius asked gently. The spell worked better with a soft approach.

"Put. It was a trade. He'd come by and get it later."

"You're sure it was a man?"

"I'm not sure it was a human," she said. "You know how it is."

"How is it, Trudy?" Darius asked.

"You don't know what anybody is in our world," she said. "It's all a lie."

"What did the individual look like?" he asked.

"Like a person. But—I forget. Stop asking me. It hurts to think about."

Darius turned to me, and we shared a frustrated look. She'd been hexed to forget the person, whoever it was. It did narrow the suspect down to somebody with enough power to hold a spell like that over days and then withstand a Protectorate agent's truth spell. Did Kelly have that kind of power? Had Joanna?

"Think harder," Darius said, putting his hand on her cheek. "It's OK to tell me. You're safe now."

But she began to cry. "I didn't kill anyone. I just put the book in the store. That's it. Just the book. In the store."

"What did you get for it?" Darius asked, his tone gentle again. If she calmed down, we could get more out of her, and the method of payment could lead to the suspect.

"Get?"

"You gave him the book," he said. "What did he—or she —give you?"

Trudy began to cry. "I don't know. I don't remember getting anything."

A precious book people had killed for, and she'd given it away for nothing—more than nothing. It might have cost her her freedom. A small fish had been eaten by a bigger one.

"Could it have been a woman?" I asked.

She sniffed. "I guess... I guess it could've been."

"You met with Kelly Tucker," I went on. "Was it her? The Protector's girlfriend?"

Indecision vanishing, she laughed derisively. "No, not her. She's just playing around. You know how rich people are. Just wanting a thrill. The rest of us are fighting to survive."

I tried to hide my disappointment. It would've been so

nice and tidy to blame it all on Kelly. "You're sure she wasn't the one to want *Instructions* from you?"

Trudy's voice was firm. "Positive."

Turning away, I had to admit I'd seen enough. The Protectorate could deal with Trudy—or ignore her. I didn't care. The cat was the priority now. I signaled to Darius, and he followed me to the Jeep, where I put the books in the back.

"We need to follow Frank," I said.

Darius looked torn. "You can't go alone, but we can't just leave this witch here unguarded. She'll bolt. She needs to be questioned at Diamond Street."

"Call in somebody," I said.

He gave me a raised eyebrow. "How quickly you forget."

"They probably haven't heard the news yet about you." I patted his shoulder. "Why would they ever suspect Darius Ironford of breaking the rules?"

He flung a tiny repulsion spell at my hand. "Watch it, Incurable One." A moment later, he flung out his arm and cast the house in an impressive, head-spinning time spell.

Through the arbor, I saw Trudy's eyes widen—slowly, very slowly. "Ohhhhh," she drawled.

"Go inside," Darius called out to her. "Agents will be back later today to talk to you."

From our perspective on the sidewalk, it looked as if she was a modern dancer giving an artistic rendition of a person locked in taffy. To her, inside the bubble of the spell, movements would feel normal. But in real time, she was moving in slow motion.

"It'll be Thursday by the time she gets indoors," I said.

"That's the idea." Darius pulled open the passenger-side door. "All right, let's go. Lionel's house?"

"That's my guess. Let me know if the trail goes cold while I drive there."

We left Trudy, still on her knees, reaching one hand toward the sidewalk. Over the next hour, maybe she'd manage to get to her feet. I pulled out into the road and headed for the old house with the redwood timbers, the residue of too many cats, and Lionel's library of books.

❧ 37 ❧

L ionel's house was about eight blocks away, but we were only halfway there when Darius flung out a hand and told me to pull over.

"I lost the trail," he said.

I had to circle the block before I gave up on finding a parking spot and pulled into a driveway. Darius jumped out and walked along the sidewalk, hand extended with the moonstone to illuminate the ground, shaking his head for a few steps, then stopping. He waved for me to join him.

I jogged over. Frank was stretched out on the sidewalk.

"He's alive," Darius said.

I bent down and lifted the old cat in my arms. He struggled half-heartedly. His journey had drained him.

"Bet you're sorry I took you so far from home," I said, carrying him back to the car. "Well, we'll bring you the rest of the way. You can't get rid of us now."

Darius got into the passenger seat, frowning when I put the cat into his lap. "Is this guy friend or foe?"

Looking into Frank's face, I touched my necklace to

heighten my senses and tried to read the spirit behind the narrowed yellow eyes. "I'm not sure."

Darius spread his fingers around the cat's torso and shook his head. "You're not sure."

Somebody had killed Joanna. If it wasn't Trudy or Kelly, then who?

Or what? *You never know what anything is in our world.*

I got behind the wheel, backed out into the road, and drove the remaining blocks to Lionel's house, glancing every few seconds at Frank. The Protectorate had set up a magical barrier around the front, which was great for us—a reserved parking spot.

An agent was still stationed at the front door, pretending to paint the trim, even though the sun had gone down. We got out of the car, Darius handed Frank to me, and we crossed through the gate into the front yard. In my arms, Frank began to stir. I felt the sizzle of Lionel's magic coming from the house, but it was subdued now. His death and the presence of the Protectorate had overwhelmed what once was. It made me want to rush home and improve my own boundary spells—a foolish urge for a mortal. My magic would end with me. Which was good. Imagine what the world would be like if every witch who'd ever lived had left their magical fingerprints behind?

As soon as the Flint saw the silver jacket, he put down his paintbrush, tapped a zinc plate below the house number—a security lock—and opened the front door for us.

"Good thing you came," I muttered to Darius. By myself, I never would've gotten in.

Darius closed the door behind us and flicked on the lights. In a burst of energy, Frank wriggled out of my arms and jumped to the floor to get away. He was an old cat, though, and I was expecting it. I cast the spell for an invisible wall to slow him down, then grabbed him by the scruff of the neck. I plunked him down in a recliner and held him there.

"Talk to me, Alma," Darius said. "What do you see in him?"

"Wait." I gripped the cat's body until I felt bone under the muscle. Moving my wrist down to push my redwood beads into his fur, I focused my magic on the creature in front of me, inviting—no, demanding—it show its true self.

I felt it then—what I hadn't been able to detect on the night of his apparent murder—the flavor of magic indicating a shape shift. Joanna had given off the same sensation, and now—

I released my grip and took a step back, just in time for a very human, very naked Lionel to come into shape in the chair.

"Demon's—sake," Darius said.

I turned away, lifted a crocheted blanket off the couch, and flung it to Darius to offer the huddled, shivering man. When I turned back around, Lionel had wrapped it around himself and now sat with his gaze locked on me.

Until Trudy had said Frank had been a voluntary stow-away, I hadn't suspected him of being anything other than a cat. The Protectorate had found Lionel's dead body, and Timms had inspected it himself; if the corpse had been enchanted, they should've discovered it. And when I'd introduced the old cat to Willy, he'd said nothing about him being a human in disguise. Even Random's unfriendly reaction had felt natural, given the animosity between the species.

But under Darius' truth spell, Trudy couldn't have been lying about Frank. She hadn't chosen to bring him to Berkeley; he'd used her for a ride. That first morning, he'd chosen me as well, but I hadn't thought he was a witch himself because of the setting. Lionel had identified me in cat shape immediately and would have seen any other witches who came near his house. Which meant the cat had to be him.

Lionel had fooled them all. An old witch with very old, very powerful tricks.

His current human form hadn't completely regained its previous appearance. Changing places with his pet cat seemed to have used up a part of him that he hadn't gotten back. The man sitting here now had the same coloring and features but was soft on the edges, shrunken and distorted.

Lionel closed his amber eyes and slumped back into the chair. "I'm very weak," he whispered. "Leaving was a mistake."

"Why did you choose me?" I asked. But before he could answer, I sneezed. The agents had searched the house for evidence and taken the cats, but the allergy, stronger than their meager spells, remained. I looked around for the container with the magic bean but didn't see it.

Lionel looked at me. "I wasn't myself yet. I was thinking like a cat. You smelled familiar and safe. The other cats were terrified, and I overreacted."

"I took you almost a hundred miles away from your source of power," I said.

"Nearly killed me," Lionel said.

I sneezed again and felt my eyes begin to itch. If I rubbed them—and I really, really wanted to—it would only make it worse.

"There are some mouse bones in the kitchen," Lionel said. "At least, there used to be." He peered around the living room at the shelves of books, half of which were missing, along with most of the knickknacks and wall hangings. The Protectorate often took the excuse to confiscate anything with magic—and like my staff, were reluctant to return it, even after the investigation completed.

His words and expression were that of a considerate host,

but I was smarter now. What if he was exaggerating how tired he was? What if his weakness was an act—both in Silverpool and here now?

I looked at Darius, who was grinning at Lionel like a kid who'd just received a new silver necklace. "I thought you *had* been killed. I cried for you." He laughed. "You… *wizard*. You fooled everyone. For Brightness' sake."

Lionel smiled weakly. "It's nice to see you again, Darius. How's your sister? Your mother and father?"

"Fine, fine." Darius grabbed a stool and sat on it at Lionel's feet. "Who attacked you? Do you remember?"

Lionel held up a hand. "In a moment. I need"—he coughed—"Need to drink something."

"Is there any springwater in the house?" Darius asked. "Beer? You used to love beer."

"Just tap water, please."

My nose began to run. "I'll get it." I pressed the back of my hand against my nose and walked out of the room. First I went to the bathroom to find a tissue while they talked about local craft brews they both liked. Let Darius enjoy his reunion while I dealt with my panicking upper respiratory system.

No tissue in the bathroom, not even toilet paper. Did the Protectorate really think he'd hexed his TP? More likely they'd used it to collect samples from around the house. In the house of an old, powerful witch, even the dust would contain magic residue.

I sneezed again so hard that I bumped into the doorframe.

Oh, for Brightness' sake; I couldn't function with my eyes swollen shut. I went to the kitchen to look for the mouse bones. My gaze traveled over the kitchen counter with its rows of canisters, jars, tins, and bottles. Inside one jar, I saw a collection of tiny bones floating in a cloudy liquid, an unappetizing condiment that I was nevertheless tempted to steal. Too much had been going on that week to hunt for owl pellets of my own.

I grabbed the jar, twisted it open, and fished out a little skull. I shoved it, dripping, into my mouth, and bit down. While my molars ground the bones into shards, I poured a glass of water for Lionel and hurried out to the living room.

Darius was sitting in the stool, watching Lionel with an affectionate expression on his face. My own face was probably distorted with the unappetizing effort of chewing and swallowing a rodent skeleton.

Lionel took the glass from me, nodded his thanks, and gulped it down. Then he closed his eyes, shivering. "How long have I been away?"

"Five days," I said.

He shook his head. "Too long. I had to find a way back. A witch who smelled like home came into the bookstore. I found her car. Every inch we got closer to home was... such a relief."

I inhaled through my magically clear nostrils, feeling relief of my own. Now I could focus.

Darius was overjoyed to see Lionel, but I had no reason to trust him. Nobody seemed to care about the woman in the cat sweatshirt, dying behind a dumpster. Lionel hadn't been killed, but Joanna had. The list of suspects was down to two, and one of them was sitting in front of me, naked.

Every second he was in his house, more strength was returning to his enchanted limbs, his spirit, and his magical well of power. Soon he'd be able to overpower us—if he wanted to.

"So," I said, "who tried to kill you?"

❧ 38 ❧

His pale eyes met mine. "Haven't you guessed?"

Lionel's body had been found the next day—it hadn't been his, but that of a transformed cat. As powerful as Lionel was, the investigator—Timms—should've been able to discover the enchantment.

And the murderer had to have been somebody Lionel knew well enough to invite inside, but who was powerful enough to overpower him.

"It was Timms," I said, angry at myself for not seeing it sooner.

Lionel nodded. "I knew him as Eddie. Met him years ago. One of the first students to come by regularly."

Darius made a noise, then suppressed it.

"He tried to kill you," I said.

"He *did* kill my body," Lionel said. "I switched out with Frank at the last minute."

"Switched?" Darius asked. "What do you mean, switched? Nobody can do that."

Lionel smiled. "It's amazing what you can learn if you live long enough. If a changeling's spirit can borrow a body, why not mine?" Stroking the chain around his neck, he sighed, his smile falling. "It didn't quite work as seamlessly as I'd hoped. It wasn't something I'd been able to practice, you see. It killed poor Frank. I wasn't willing to do that unless my life depended on it. And… I won't be able to keep his cat body in human form for long. Already it… it wants to be Frank again."

"His name really was Frank?" I asked.

He tapped his temple. "It exhausted me, but I managed to put the name in your friend's mind." His face softened. "What a sweet witch she was. Elizabeth is a lovely girl."

"She goes by Birdie." I didn't know if he was trying to win me over by complimenting my friends.

"Poor Frank," Lionel said. "I'd kept him alive long past his time, but I still feel guilty about what I did to him."

I moved closer, playing with the bracelet on my left wrist. "Do you feel guilty about anything else?"

Lionel pursed his lips, glancing at my hands. "Are you going to attack me?"

"What? Of course n—" Darius spun around to look up at me. "What are you doing?"

"Maybe Lionel wanted the third possession book desperately. He's taken Frank's body, so possession interests him. He lives for books. Look around this house. The demon-possession trilogy had been incomplete for decades. He had *Warnings* and *Temptations*, but never *Instructions*." I studied Lionel's face for any flicker of response, but he stared back blankly. "He went to the meeting down the street to strike a deal with the seller. Protectorate agents, watching the meeting, told Timms, who came here to confront him—"

"And killed me?" Lionel scratched his head. "I didn't have the book. Why do that?"

"Maybe you tried to kill him first," I said.

"You're way off base here," Darius said to me. "You don't know Lionel the way I do."

Lionel offered me a half smile. "I think she's annoyed I fooled her all week," he said. "I apologize. I didn't have the power to shift or communicate in any way. Sharing Frank's name was the best I could do."

"I'm not annoyed. I'm suspicious." I turned to Darius. "We still don't know if your old friend here was hungry enough for the third book to kill Joanna in the bookstore for it."

Lionel passed a trembling hand over his eyes. "I'm sorry I couldn't save her. The witch Joanna. I was too weak. She was kind to me, but I was too weak." He lowered his hand and looked up at me.

"You were strong enough to make it back to Berkeley," I said.

"All the witches and all the books at the store gave me strength, but it took a few days," he said.

Could I believe him?

"I never wanted *Instructions*," Lionel continued. "But Timms certainly did. He must've gone to the meeting to find it, maybe buy it. But I was there, and I saw through his disguise. I guess he felt he couldn't let me live after I'd seen him there. I knew what he wanted. What he'd always wanted."

"He could've said he was there for work," I said.

Lionel shook his head. "But he wasn't. A few questions—especially if I'd suggested to my old friends in New York that they ask them—and he'd be exposed. Named and shamed. No more directorship." He lifted the glass and drank the last of the water. "After he attacked me, he took the book he'd loved as a boy, *Temptations*."

"They found that one with Joanna's body," I said. "Maybe

you put it there to confuse people when you killed her for the one you really wanted."

"Why would he do that?" Darius said. "The book was the only reason we linked Joanna with Lionel."

"Why would he care? Everyone thought he was dead." I looked at Lionel, who looked offended but tired.

"I feel dead," he said, closing his eyes. "Could you figure things out without me? I need to take a nap. A few days, at least."

"Lionel wouldn't kill anybody," Darius said to me, angry. "He's the Brightest man I've ever known. Other than my father, of course."

"Thank you, son," Lionel said, not opening his eyes.

I looked back and forth between the two of them, put my hand on my necklace, and directed more energy to my ears. My eyes had been lying to me all week. "That night you were almost killed. Why did you send me away so quickly?" I asked. "What did you think Timms wanted?"

"I wasn't sure," Lionel said, "but I knew I didn't want him to find you with me. He'd been unable to identify you as a cat. It was quite a good shape-shift."

"Thank you," I mumbled, flattered in spite of myself.

"But you'd changed back into yourself, and if he saw that I'd given you that book—and I wanted you to have that book very much, as atonement for your mother—he would've wondered why." Lionel's voice got stronger, his gaze sharper. "It could've led to you and your secrets. The last thing I wanted was for you to experience more suffering because of a witch seeking demonic possession."

"You could've left me alone and not invited me to your house," I said.

"But I had already—" Lionel's lips froze, his words hanging in the air. His eyes bugged.

It took me a moment to realize what had happened: the

genie had locked his voice to prevent him from giving away her secret.

"I understand," I said, and with that, I believed him. He'd paid a price to have me at the house and would have no second chance. The wish was already being fulfilled by a magic greater than his. Timms showing up had been an unwelcome surprise.

"I didn't think he'd actually kill me. I'd thought I could talk him out if it," Lionel said softly. "I can't help myself, always thinking I can dissuade witches from the Shadowed path."

"It's your nature to share your wisdom," Darius said. "That's what you do. It's what you've always done."

Lionel looked at me. "I didn't attack him. Maybe I should have, but I didn't. He'd always been curious about possession. Just like Alma's mother, he wouldn't hear a word against it."

"What a creature of Shadow," Darius said, his voice dripping with disgust. "You invited him into your home. You mentored him. And he tried to kill you."

"Well, I'd like to think he hoped to silence me without taking my life," Lionel said. "I'm very old. He probably thought he could hex my brain, scramble my wits, then take the book that had so much of his essence on it. I really should've destroyed *Temptations* decades ago, but I believe in knowledge, choice, and, obviously, books." He gestured around the room.

"Do you have any idea what secrets are in *Instructions*?" I asked. "What it explains? Any clues to what Timms will be doing, where he'll go?"

"The book probably enhances the setup of a Summoning Circle without being too finicky about the talent of the witch doing the summoning," Lionel said.

"So any novice could use it?" I asked, horrified, thinking of the clumsy witches who had come to Silverpool.

"That's the book's power," Lionel said. "Your best bet is that a bond will take time to establish. Three or five or nine days in his keeping, perhaps, for him to claim the book's power."

"We have to tell Raynor about Timms," Darius said suddenly, reaching for his phone. "He's there with him right now."

"Be careful," Lionel said. "Eddie has killed one and a half witches already. He knows I survived, but he probably thinks he captured me with the other cats that morning."

Darius froze with his phone in midair, then pointed at me. "You have to call Raynor. I'm fired."

"He won't believe me either, not over the phone," I said. "We've got to talk to him in person. He's got to be able to scan me."

Lionel cleared his throat. "If Timms finally gets a demon inside him and manages to hold on to some of his own consciousness," he said, "he'll be stronger than you two and Raynor, even joined together against him."

Darius went over to him. "You're in danger. He'll come here and finish you off. There has to be something we can set up to protect you."

"I will become Frank again as soon as you leave." Lionel cast a tired glance around the room. "If I stay here, I'll be able to spend a few hours now and then in human form. The old magic of the timbers is still here. But this body is still Frank's, and I don't have the power to fight against that all the time."

Darius removed the platinum chain from his neck—the most precious metal he had—and put it in Lionel's palm, closing the old fingers around it. "I'll come back after we've avenged your, uh, near death."

"Be careful." As Lionel adjusted the blanket around his shrunken torso, the platinum chain glittered between his fingers. "He's a lot meaner than he looks."

"Aren't we all," I muttered, opening the door. I hated to leave Lionel alone in the same room where he'd almost been murdered, but the remaining battle would be fought in Silverpool.

Timms knew Lionel was still alive, but he didn't know we suspected him. He'd been in a position to thwart the investigation into Joanna's murder, now had the power to invite a demon into himself and Silverpool, and was probably feeling confident he could get away with it.

The problem was...

He might be right.

❧ 39 ❧

Trying to look as casual as possible, I walked out of Lionel's house behind Darius—who, unlike me, never had trouble looking official. The agent on duty at the door watched us as we passed, casting basic scanning spells at us, but his divided attention suggested he'd become genuinely engrossed with his painting project. He'd set up a shop light to keep working. Getting the window trim tidy had become important to him, which I was sure Lionel would appreciate. Maybe by the end of the year, Lionel would have a new witch to mentor in his library.

When we were both safely in the Jeep, I sped away from the house with its Protectorate guard, hoping the news we'd been there wouldn't reach Silverpool before we did.

"Timms might be summoning a demon right now," I said. "Can you cast some traffic spells to get us out of Berkeley faster? I can't do good ones while I drive."

"Already on it." He tapped the zipper over his chest, and the red light ahead of us turned green. The cars in our way began pulling over or turning onto side streets, and we drove on empty streets for the remaining blocks to the freeway.

Once there, he emptied the lanes we needed to go north. I floored it, pushing a little magic into my headlights. With so few other cars, the eight-lane highway was darker than I'd ever seen it.

"You really think that book will tell him how to summon a demon?" Darius asked.

"He was willing to kill for it, so yes," I said. "He must've lacked the natural talent to do it on his own."

"Quite a talent," he said sourly.

I thought of my mother, who Vera had praised for the same gift, one she thought I'd inherited. "Yeah," I said.

"I just don't get it," he said. "Why, with all the power and prestige he's got, why would he still want a demon possession?"

"Still?" I asked.

He pointed a finger at a slow-moving pickup hauling a mattress in front of us.

"Yeah, still," he said. The pickup suddenly veered out of our way. "The witches I've met who want possession are like those fools camping in Silverpool, who are just looking for anything that makes them feel powerful and important. They're young or small, don't have much power, their families don't have an old name—"

"Like Bellrose."

"Like Bellrose," he continued. "And they think having a dangerous immortal spirit hitching a ride inside will be worth the cost of their own free will."

"Sometimes people want something for so long they forget why they want it," I said. "It just becomes part of them. Their identity is wrapped up in it."

"He never struck me as somebody with much identity at all," he said. "But maybe that's it. You know what nickname the Flints at Diamond Street came up with for him?"

"What?" I asked. All Directors had to pretend not to know what the rank and file called them behind their back.

"Nothing," he replied. "They didn't think he was interesting enough to come up with anything other than Timms."

"He hasn't been there very long."

"One day should be all it takes. It gives you something to do while you wait and see what kind of witch they're going to be. Are they going to insist you call them 'mage'? Bow at the doorway? Kiss their diamond toe ring?"

Even before Raynor had become Director, everyone had called him The Rock behind his back. The resemblance was so close it almost wasn't a nickname so much as a label.

"I wonder what they'll call him if he's got a demon in his brain?" I asked.

"That's my point," he said. "Whatever it is, I bet it won't be Timms."

"Right. He'll finally be *interesting*." I shook my head. "That's a different kind of power. He sure doesn't have that now. Well, he does to me, but only because of the murdering thing."

"We need to get through to Raynor," he said. "He's already turned against me. It's got to be you."

I sped past the cars pulled over before the toll booths for the Richmond Bridge. As I went through the open gate at ninety miles an hour, the device in my car beeped, indicating I'd paid the toll. Having magic didn't mean a witch should get away with stealing.

Smug atop my moral high horse, I thought of Kelly. She was a liar and a thief who was manipulating a more powerful witch to get what she wanted. What else was she capable of doing?

"Do you think there's any chance Kelly is working with Timms?" I asked. "If she's this far into Shadow, why not go all the way?"

Darius flung another spell at the cars in front of us, giving me room to go as fast as the Jeep could go.

"We'll find out," he said.

"Careful with those road-clearing spells on the bridge," I said. "You might throw somebody into the bay."

"You asked me to clear the road. I'm clearing the road."

Flinching as yet another car slowed and swerved toward the railing, I gripped the wheel and drove on. When we reached the other side without hearing any crash or splash behind us, I sighed with relief.

With Darius' magic, we reached Silverpool in under two hours, even with a detour at In-N-Out Burger. My adopted town was dark under a clear, moonless sky. The temperature had dropped without the cloud cover, and a thin layer of ice had formed on the road through the forest. Without Darius casting spells out the passenger window, the Jeep would've slid off the winding road a dozen times.

I turned right at the winery and put it in park at the bottom of the hill. "All right. I'm going to go in there and try to get Raynor to come outside for... I'll think of something."

"Don't leave it to chance," Darius said. "Have a solid plan."

"Fine, fine," I said, patting the wheel. "I'll say I need help with my dog. The fairies are torturing him." Silverpool fairies had an unfortunate history of harming humans' domesticated animals if they were angry about something. Goats would drown in the river, horses would bolt into the road, dogs would bark, whine, or run away.

"It's almost ten at night," Darius said. "Is that believable? Who would bother the Protector of Silverpool with a little problem like that so late?"

"It was Tristan's biggest complaint about the job," I said. "Everyone has a pet or two, and they expected him to protect them, not just humans. Nightfall is the most dangerous time."

"Huh," Darius said. "Something to look forward to if I get my job back. I guess that's a good cover. Urgent but boring."

"Thanks." I closed my eyes and put both hands on my redwood necklace. My head needed to be clear before breaking through the protective spells ahead. Any agitation or aggression in my thoughts might cause the wards to repel me.

Next to me in the passenger seat, Darius zipped up his jacket, which would be protection enough, and muttered a strength spell under his breath.

I made myself think about something good and pure.

Random. His big brown eyes. His joy to see me when I came home.

Then I thought of Birdie, my sweet, honest friend. She'd have a hard time moving on if Joanna's murderer wasn't caught.

And then another good creature popped into my mind: Seth, who wasn't a demon, although the Protectorate said he was. Inhuman he might be, I would do a lot to protect his life—and I had. If Seth had a girlfriend who was lying and stealing behind his back, making him do things he wouldn't do with a clear head, what would I do?

Violent revenge came to mind.

Violent. Revenge. And then I'd drag whatever was left of her witchy self to the Protectorate for interrogation and punishment.

I smiled to myself. So much for my Incurable Inability to kill.

A split second later, I realized I hadn't felt the same bloody zeal for Raynor's sake, even though his condition was real and immediate.

Well. That was interesting. It was almost as if I cared more about the changeling than the demonprinted human I worked for.

"Are you having second thoughts?" Darius asked next to me.

I patted the wheel, bringing myself back to the present. "Just getting ready. You ready?"

"Ready."

I drove up the hill.

❧ 40 ❧

I parked the Jeep with its nose facing downhill so I could leave in a hurry. Darius got out and strode around the parking area, scanning the arbor to the garden, the tasting-room entrance, the garage doors.

"Any demon sign?" I asked, realizing what he was looking for.

"No," he said. "Do you see fae?"

I looked around. "No, but there's no moon, and it's cold. They're probably resting after the solstice parties."

Darius held two hands out toward the middle garage door. "Or he already ate them."

"Don't say that." I watched him press his palms together, then extend them out again.

The silver jacket he wore gave him a key to the house's defenses. The garage door creaked, then rose, showing an empty spot between Raynor's sports car and Kelly's motorcycle.

"My SUV is gone," Darius said. "It might already be too late."

A shiver ran down between my shoulder blades. It was

bad enough Timms was a murderer, but to know he'd spent five decades seeking the possession of a demon in his own body and might have achieved his dream today…

Maybe he'd already walked between the vines, consuming the families of fae in their little houses, fueling the unnatural union of their two entities, demon and human.

I shivered again and pulled on my magic to see farther through the darkness. There. I saw a few tiny lights in the fairy houses under the dormant rosebushes—just a few, but they were there.

Momentarily relieved, I walked to the front door. Darius moved behind one of the potted citrus trees along the path to the tasting-room building. When I couldn't sense him anymore, I brought my redwood pendant to my lips, kissed it for good luck, and rang the doorbell.

A Flint named Max answered the door. He'd been a trainee at Diamond Street at the same time I had, and I'd been seeing him around Silverpool the past few days. He was probably the one they'd sent out for coffee at Joanna's murder scene.

"Good evening, Agent Max," I said. "I'm here to see the Protector."

He gave me a skeptical head-to-toe scan. "Why?"

We'd never been friends, not even before my inglorious departure from the office. "It's regarding the mental and physical health of my canine familiar," I said. "The fae are causing trouble."

"Your dog?" He frowned. "It's late."

"And getting later." I crossed my arms over my chest. Maybe the dog excuse hadn't been a good one. I hadn't expected to see a Flint from the city. Like Darius, he didn't know enough about Silverpool to realize how common a problem it was. "He won't be happy to hear you obstructed the witch he trusts most to inform him about the detailed supernatural threats in Silverpool—as they occur, not during the comfortable, lazy daytime hours of nonmagical civilians."

Giving up on being tough, Max nodded his head and took a step back. "Won't you come in, Witch Bellrose?"

I smiled and accepted the invitation, inwardly patting myself on the back. So much of life was just faking it.

But he wouldn't let me walk past the bronze eagle statue on a marble pedestal—an enchanted guardian—next to the coatrack. "Wait here, please. I'll tell the Protector you're here."

Every moment was too long, but I nodded and moved to one side to hide behind the eagle. If Kelly saw me, she'd interfere. After several long, agonizing minutes, Raynor finally appeared in the hallway.

"What's wrong?" he asked.

"Hey, um—" I looked past him. "Can we talk in private?"

He promptly cast a scanning spell over me and frowned. "You're in a state of anxious distress. Why?"

Before I answered, I needed to know his state of mind, how much power Kelly had over him. It would be best if I could get him out of the house.

"Will you come for a walk with me?" I asked. "I want to show you something in the vineyard." I would draw his attention to the fairy houses, then comment on how aggressive they could be, even with my affinity for communicating with them, and ask him to help protect my dog by coming to my house. I'd implore him as a fellow demon-printed witch of even greater power than me. In my house, I'd be able to wash away any enchantments Kelly had on him.

Anyway, that was my plan.

"No," he said. He had dark circles under his eyes, but he didn't look sleepy—instead, he seemed excessively alert.

Smiling and vibrating with nervous energy. A little sweaty. "I'm busy."

"Please, Ray—"

He held up his hand and looked to one side. "Have you seen Kelly? She was with me a second ago. We were watching TV."

I looked past him. Luckily, we were still alone. "Just a short walk outside—please? You can come right back." Hopefully, with the fresh air, he'd regain some of his thinking.

"I need Kelly." He wiped the sheen off his upper lip. "Do you know where she is?"

"Raynor," I said, pitching my voice lower and sharper. "Listen to me. I need you to come on a walk with me. There's something you have to—"

"Kelly can see fae just like us," he said. "Do you realize what a relief it is to be with somebody who understands?"

"Yes, but—"

"I've never felt like this before," he said. "I didn't realize life could be so important. So… much."

I hoped an amnesia spell was part of the enchantment Kelly had put on him, because he was going to be really, really embarrassed in the future if he could remember how he was acting right now. "We need to talk about Director Timms," I said. "Edward Timms. Do you know where he is?"

"He's the Director, not me," Raynor said. "That's good. I wouldn't be able to spend as much time with Kelly if I was still the Director."

I looked past him. Kelly was still out of sight. "Please will you go for a walk with me? It's really important. Remember how I don't say that unless it's true? You trust me, right?"

"Of course," he said, smiling at me with more affection than I'd ever seen before. His natural reserve was missing. "You're like me and Kelly. We can see what others can't."

Maybe that attitude might work in my favor. "I've seen something in Timms. It's not good. It's bad. You need to be—"

His gaze sharpened. "Bad?"

Perhaps I'd have to shock him to break through the enchantment. "I have reason to believe Timms is the killer," I said. "Walk with me and I'll show you—"

"What? What are you talking about?"

"Lionel is alive," I said. "He told me it was Timms who tried to kill—"

"No," he breathed. He lifted his hand and turned the face of a heavy gold watch toward me. "You just want me to be Director again so you can get me away from Kelly."

A small cloud of power was forming around his watch. Eyeing it warily, I continued. "This has nothing to do with Kelly, who is wonderful and wise," I said, trying to speak his crazy language. "Timms wants a demon possession for himself. Has for years. He killed Joanna. He killed—tried to kill—Lionel. He's close. He might already—"

A white bolt of magic shot out from Raynor's arm and came at my face. With an involuntary yelp, I flung up my arm and blocked the hex. Small fragments of magic dug into me and crawled up toward my head, but my necklace neutralized it.

"You want me to go back to San Francisco," Raynor said. "I want to be with Kelly. She's my life. She's everything. She's —" He cut himself off and turned around.

Kelly came running down the hallway, a warm smile on her face. "Alma, how great to see you again."

"She's here," Raynor breathed. "You're here. Where did you go?"

"Even the demonprinted need to use the little girl's room sometimes," she said, capturing his face in her hands and going up on tiptoe to kiss him. "Why don't you invite Alma inside? We never got to enjoy that glass of champagne. I'm sure I have another bottle around here someplace."

"I'll go get it." Raynor kissed her hard on the mouth and strode away. If he remembered I was standing there or what I'd told him about Timms, he made no sign of it.

I'd failed. As long as Raynor was in the house, I couldn't reach him. He was in too deep with Kelly to be able to help us with Timms.

"I'll have to skip the drink," I told Kelly. "I came by to get help with my dog. The fae are bothering him again. But it wasn't fair of me to drag him away from home this late. I'll talk to him later."

"The fae aren't afraid to harass you in your own home?" she asked.

"Well, you know how they are," I said. "Wild and free and all that."

"But you have the Print," she said. "Show that to them. They'll be sure to stay away after that."

"I don't want them to stay away. They're fairies, and I'm living in their forest."

"Didn't you say they're hurting your familiar?"

"Yes, but—"

"I'll come over myself," she said. "I'll show them—"

"No," I said. "No. I enjoy their company. And I don't want any other witch to act on my property."

She smiled approvingly. "Quite right," she said with a bow. "Well then, I wish you luck. I don't think Raynor will be much use tonight. As you may have noticed, he's gotten into the wine again. If this continues, I think he's going to need a sobriety enchantment to help him break the habit. If it comes to that, will you help me? Interventions can be so, so difficult."

So, *that* was going to be her excuse for his behavior. "Of course," I said. "I guess it's hard with all this wine around."

"Very hard." She walked over to the door and opened it. "Good luck with your cat."

"Dog," I said.

"Of course."

I stepped out and she closed it behind me. Waves of boundary spells shimmered before my eyes, pushing me off the step and into the driveway.

Darius stepped out from behind a lemon tree. "You're alone."

"We're on our own. He's too far gone."

"Kelly?"

"He's wrapped around her finger like a platinum ring that's a few sizes too small," I said. "Let's get out of here."

⚝ 41 ⚝

We got in the Jeep, and I drove us down the hill. Although I was tempted, I resisted the urge to cast a bubble of defensive magic around the Jeep. I didn't want to make Kelly suspicious; I'd wait until we were safely over the vineyard property line.

"Did they buy the dog excuse?" he asked.

"I'm not sure." As soon as I turned onto the road, I flung up a slowing spell behind me. Blocking visibility might make someone drive off the road into the river. "She was worried about me noticing Raynor was hexed. Said he was drinking too much."

Darius cursed her under his breath. "She's going to suffer for what she's doing to him."

"I think Raynor will make sure of it," I said.

"How can we just leave him there like that? He'll hate us."

I drove onto the bridge, looking around for the river fairy. When I didn't see him immediately, I braked in the middle and touched my necklace, pulling some power to aid my senses, but it seemed empty. No green river fairy, no tree fairies shimmering in the branches.

"We have to get Timms," I said. "Raynor will underst—" I noticed a flash of light in my rearview mirror.

"What?"

"Not good." I hit the gas. "I think it's Kelly."

Darius twisted around in his seat to look. "Go faster. She's on the motorcycle."

"I can't outrun that thing, even with your help. Not with a witch at the wheel."

"Bikes don't have steering wheels."

"You know what I mean!"

I had planned on driving toward the campground to look for Timms out at the outskirts of town, but I first had to shake Kelly from my tail. To look as if I had been telling the truth about my poor dog, I took the turn for home. My slowing spell seemed to be working to keep her from catching up.

"We can't get stuck at your house," Darius said. "It's a dead end. She won't let us out."

With Seth's help, I would, but I didn't say that to Darius. It didn't matter, anyway; I had other plans.

"Not going home," I said, twisting the wheel again. Her solo headlight was slowly getting larger in the rearview mirror. I wanted to make sure she could see me make the last turn toward my house—

I cast a mirroring spell behind me—

I turned hard in the opposite direction and killed the headlights. Leaning over the wheel to see the road in the dark, I slowly made my way up a one-lane road to a vacation rental house's driveway. Then I turned off the engine and began to pull a cloaking spell around the Jeep, but Darius was already setting it up, a nice reminder of what a partner could do for you. I leaned back in my seat, catching my breath, wiping my sweaty hands on my jeans. I hoped my trick had worked.

"Why do you think she's following me?" I asked.

Darius finished the spell and found a bottle of water in the door. "I don't know. To kill you?" He uncapped it and took a sip.

I let my head thud against the window. Sometimes it could be so exhausting just staying alive. "Would she really risk the Protectorate coming after her for murder?"

"We don't know if she was working with Lionel," he said. "Maybe she's already killed a witch this week."

"What's one more?" I asked weakly.

"Exactly."

The roar of the motorcycle didn't come. Like us, Kelly could've used cloaking spells to hide her movements, so I didn't restart the car right away. I hoped she'd gone to my house, but she might be waiting right behind us.

Sitting in the darkness, I thought about the other, bigger enemy and where he might be. If Timms—an Emerald witch with all the agent bodyguards, magical amulets, and training of his high position—was already possessed by a demon, we might have a hard time escaping with our lives.

If Timms had the demon inside him, he'd begin eating the fairies and taking down the town's boundary spells. If he did that, other demons, already gathered for the solstice, would rush into Silverpool and consume the weaker fae. Stronger fairies from miles around—gnomes or even goblins —would sense the massacre, rush to Silverpool, and use their unpredictable power against the demons. Humans could die in the cross fire, just as they had in years past before the Protectors were installed near wellsprings.

"We should check each of the spots where Raynor saw demon sign," I said.

"There were three serious ones," he said. "Miles apart."

"Where was the one with the circle of dead grass?"

"Out west. Past the campground a mile or so."

"That's the one," I said.

"How do you know?"

"I don't. Total guess."

"Comforting," he said.

"But a Circle of Summoning would look like that."

"All the sites of demon sign were circular in shape," he said.

"I feel good about the dead grass."

Darius was quiet for a few seconds. "I trust you," he said finally.

The generosity of his statement, given our rocky history, brought me to the edge of tears. It was just what I'd said to Birdie. I cleared my throat, knowing he'd hate my crying. "I trust you too," I said.

"Then my vote is to go now. She'll figure out your trick soon enough. Let's be long gone when that happens, get a head start."

I took his advice and began driving through the narrow, hilly back roads, taking a circuitous route past other witches' houses that would make it harder to follow. Finally I came out on Main Street a mile away, just past the dark and sleepy business district.

"Do you sense her out there?" I asked, looking back and forth.

Darius held out his hands, then flinched and drew back.

"What?" I asked, alarmed.

"Something's out there that shouldn't be."

"Don't say that," I said. "I mean, you have to say that, but I wish you didn't have to."

"Are you panicking on me?"

"It's just... he's the Director! If he gets a demon inside him who's powerful enough to cloak itself, then Timms can do all kinds of horrible things and people won't believe it's him. We'll tell them, but he'll be stronger than we are. We'll end up in some Protectorate jail in Death Valley. Dying slowly. It's like the planet Mercury. Did you know it hit a hundred and thirty-four degrees Fahrenheit? That's like, what, fifty degrees Celsius—?"

"Fifty-seven," he said. "But the summer average is a bit below that."

My voice rose. "A bit? A *bit*?"

Darius put a hand on my shoulder, and calm energy, as airy and sweet as whipped cream, flowed into me. After a few moments, my panic drained away and I was able to take a breath that reached the bottom of my chest.

"Thank you," I said quietly.

He released my shoulder. "We can do this. We were trained for it."

"I have an Incurable Inability to kill."

"But I don't," he said. "Let's go."

❧ 42 ❧

I t was closing in on midnight, an unlucky time to be fighting Shadow. Brightness had gone to bed for the day, leaving the morally unfettered spirits more flexibility to roam the earth, sea, and sky. I drove us west through Silverpool, pitch-black under heavy cloud cover, toward the ocean.

"What do you think he'll do if he realizes we're onto him?" Darius asked. He was going through the pockets of his jacket, taking out amulets, stones, velvet bags, pocket knives, chains, handcuffs. "What should we be prepared for?"

I gazed down the center of the road lit by the Jeep's headlights. To either side of the road, the delicate lights of forest fairies bobbed in the tree branches. Without the clouds, such tiny lanterns wouldn't be visible, even to me.

It had been three nights since Timms had finally acquired the book *Instructions*. Lionel had said there might be a delay before it would work for him—three days being the least.

There could be other benefits to tonight, too—the position of the moon, the cloud cover, the tide. Vera had said I hadn't needed so many crutches to summon a demon, and neither had my human mother—but Timms did, or believed he did, which was the same thing.

Darius thrust a hand out, pointing ahead. "Careful. Deer."

I braked just in time. The doe bounded away, disappearing into the blackness of the forest. Heart pounding, I let out my breath and continued. "I've never seen it so—"

Of course. That was it.

"So what?" Darius asked. "So dark?"

"Yes. I bet we're looking for fire." I nodded, feeling confident. "Timms will need fire for his Summoning." That's what I would do, and apparently I had a *gift*.

"OK. I've got a seashell in one of these pockets somewhere," he said, unzipping one over his chest. "It can spray water if I get the spell right."

I thought about the Circle I'd used in Armstrong Woods to call Vera. "The fire might not be the source of power, just the summoning stage. If the demon is already there, it won't do any good to put it out."

"If the demon is already there, what in Shadow are we going to do? Stab him?"

The standard procedure for eliminating a demon threat was to drive a silver weapon—knife, dagger, stake—into the human host's chest. "If you have to," I said.

"He's a Director of the Protectorate."

I glanced at the trees, comforted to see a few more fairy lights. "So? I thought you said you could kill."

Darius unfolded his blade and held it up. "What if we're wrong? What if he isn't actually possessed yet, I stab him, and there isn't any evidence of demon decay?" In the event of a violent death caused by silver, a demon's spirit would burn up the host body. "What if he's just Timms, except dead with my knife in his chest? New York might look critically upon me for that course of action."

"Raynor already fired you," I said. "Unless you save him and the rest of this town, you won't have a chance to prove your case and your career is over anyway."

"But I won't have to live in the Mojave Desert," he said.

"No, because if Timms gets that demon inside him and finds out you know his secret, you'll be dead," I said. "And so will I."

Darius took out a second knife, this one from his boot—long and deadly. "Right. I'm counting on you to hire me one of those good witch lawyers your father uses to get away with crimes. When they put me on trial at Diamond Street. Deal?"

"De— Look!" I pointed at the glow of a fire in the distance.

"That's the witch campground," he said.

I patted the wheel, telling myself to calm down. "Right. They have campfires."

"The burned grass is another mile or so in the forest."

We drove on, past the witches in tents and campers. I heard the music of guitars, flutes, drums, and saw figures dancing. Only some were human. Just beyond the glow of the bonfire, a few fairies had gathered to enjoy the party.

I told Darius, who agreed it was a good sign but got out a third knife, which he tested on a strand of my hair before offering to me.

"No, thanks," I said. "Stabbing isn't my thing."

"You could try slicing."

I shuddered. The idea of tearing into their flesh and drawing blood was... impossible. "Remember my Incurable—"

"There!" He pointed at another glow up ahead, flickering between the trees. "That's it."

I'd prepared a shielding spell for my headlights and cast it now. Darius did a similar enchantment over the sound of the engine. When we were level with the ring of fire, about twenty feet from the road, I pulled over next to a black Protectorate SUV. Timms hadn't even bothered to hide it.

I turned off the engine and peered between the trees at a figure standing inside a ring of fire. Arms outstretched—with a book in one hand—he didn't seem to mind the heat. It was indeed Timms, and he was wearing the same everyday business clothes he always did. Khakis, button-down shirt.

"Huh," I said.

Darius, with his knife in one hand and the door handle in the other, paused to look at me. "What?"

"I thought he'd put on a more interesting outfit for the big moment," I said. "A robe or a cape or something. At least a hat. He is barefoot, though."

He didn't answer, probably because he thought I was crazy. "Ready?"

I wasn't nuts, but I was very, very nervous. My hand was sweating around the staff I'd picked up from the back seat. "Ready."

We climbed out and walked toward the fire. There were no fairy lights here, no dancing, no music. Cold wind snaked down a gap between my neck and my jacket.

I shivered.

My staff was vibrating with energy, recognizing the magic in the Summoning Circle. If he hadn't yet called the demon, we could extinguish the fire, distract him, and with our combined forces, subdue him, even though he was an Emerald with decades of experience and Darius and I were only recently trained and young—

Inside the Circle, Timms turned around, lowered his arms, and looked at us. Then he snapped his fingers, and every flame was extinguished at once.

I heard Darius suck in his breath.

"Oh no," I whispered, beginning to shake.

I tried to see Darius, but it was too dark. Timms, or whoever he was now, was moving closer. I lifted my staff, pulling from its power, and imagined a ball of cool, bright light that I could throw around the possessed figure before us. Demon hunters would finish the job with a silver blade, but we were taught several ways to slow and detain the suspected enemy so that we could get close enough. An orb of neutralizing magic would deprive the demon of its spiritual energy for a few seconds, long enough to let Darius get closer.

Without hesitating, I flung it out into the darkness where I heard the crunch of approaching footsteps. Darius, anticipating my strategy, crept forward with his knife.

But Timms knocked us both down before we'd drawn a second breath. He didn't pause to speak or finish the job—he strode on as if he hadn't even noticed we were there. We were insignificant to him.

I scrambled to my feet, staff in hand, and aimed it at the departing figure. Another orb of light floated out from its tip, but it was weaker, smaller—not enough. I'd used the bulk of my power on the first shot.

Darius ran after him, but it was too dark. He tripped over something, grunted, fell. By the time we were both running toward the road, the SUV was roaring to life and backing out into the highway. A moment later, its wheels screeched and it was gone.

Toward Silverpool.

❧ 43 ☙

Darius and I got in the Jeep and raced after him. I concentrated on going as fast as possible on the dark and twisting road while Darius cast spells to light the way and keep us from rolling over. We went over a sharp rise, then a sharp turn, swerved around another deer, its eyes reflecting the Jeep's headlights, and then we were speeding toward the witches' campground.

"I can't see him," I said, wishing I could do more magic while I was driving, but it took too much concentration to control the car. There were figures moving around the campground, silhouetted by the fires, and I didn't want to risk running anyone over.

"I've got a trace on him," Darius said. "He's on the road, just up ahead. He's— Wait. Feel that?"

Something seemed wrong to me too. I braked and looked more closely at the campground. The witches weren't singing and dancing like they'd been before; they were screaming and waving for help.

I pulled over, my tires squealing in the gravel. "The boundary spells," I said. "Where were they?"

Darius jumped out of the car. "They *were* at the top of that hill back there," he shouted back at me. "Brightness save us."

I got out with my staff and turned to see a witch in a white puffy coat running toward me. Wild blond hair was whipping around her terrified face.

"Something's happening!" she cried. "There's smoke, bad smoke!"

I held up my staff and sent an illumination spell across the open field. There was smoke, but not where the campfires were. It was in the trees. Something was consuming the fae.

"It happened so fast," I whispered.

Darius ran over to me with a silver knife in his hand. It glowed pink and vibrated slightly. "Demon sign," he said, panting. "I have to take a stand here. They're attacking now."

A hot wind roared down from the road and pushed the blond witch over onto her knees. She curled into a ball and screamed, "Help me, help me!"

I looked at her, then at Darius. The demon inside Timms was on his way into town, but it had already blasted through the boundary spell, allowing more of its kind to enter.

Darius pushed the open air over the witch's head, clapped his hands, and mouthed a series of silent words under his breath. The witch stopped screaming, then looked up at him with awe. A second later she was curled around his feet.

"Stay with me," she said. "Don't leave."

A male witch with long, dark hair cast a spell into the darkness. One of the tents flew up and hung in the air, ten feet above the ground, then flipped upside down and burst into flames.

Darius lifted his seashell and aimed a jet of water at the tent, reducing the blaze and knocking it to the ground. Then he turned to me and said, "I have to fight here. I can't leave them alone. You go. You get Timms."

I understood. It was his training, his oath, his job. Being fired didn't change that. I felt the same pull, but I couldn't give in to it. "I will," I said. "I'll get him."

He ran toward the tent, still holding the seashell in the air with one hand while a silver knife glinted in the other. The blond witch ran after him as if his presence, even in the midst of demon battle, was safer than running away.

"I'll come back," I called after him. He didn't hear me, but I hoped he knew I would. With his silver jacket, he should be protected from any possession himself, but he might not be able to fight so many Shadow spirits on his own while saving the lives of the dozen or so humans and the countless fairies nearby.

I'd just have to be quick. I'd come back, and I'd bring help.

Once again I got in the Jeep and floored it. I didn't have Darius' magic to assist me this time, but I was angry. Until now, a demon invasion into Silverpool had been an abstract concept I'd discounted as overblown by the Protectorate; they wanted power, so they'd exaggerated the demon threat.

But that wind…

It had been hot and evil. I had confronted demons before, but the energy roaring through the broken boundary spell was more Shadowed than anything I'd ever felt before—and so fast. I was terrified for Silverpool. But of all the Protectorate agents I knew, Darius was the best witch for the job. I just had to make sure his fight was worth it.

I took a turn past a redwood that had grown so big they'd had to redirect the road around it, painting a wavy yellow line to curve around its girth. When I reached the straight-away, a motorcycle zipped past me, heading the opposite direction. I glimpsed the white fairing and Kelly's pale helmet.

She'd followed me. And then, a moment later, a car followed *her*.

I couldn't see him, but I felt Raynor's magical fingerprint as he sped past. His powers were directed at the woman on the motorcycle, and he was making no effort to hide his magic. He was crazed. Wherever Kelly was going, he was going too.

Shaking my head, I hoped I found Timms before they realized they'd just passed me. Maybe they'd stop and help Darius—

No, I couldn't count on that happening.

I was moments away from the wellspring, which I thought would be Timms' destination. If I was wrong about him heading there, I didn't know what I would do. At the winery, he'd be able to call upon Protectorate agents like Max the Flint—who wouldn't know he'd been possessed by a demon—and wield the absolute power of a local Director. Those of us who knew what he was would be silenced or killed, and he'd return to San Francisco without anyone suspecting him of anything at all. Just an unusually boring witch who had climbed the ranks of power through hard work but who was utterly forgettable.

Until they suddenly discovered he was much more interesting than they'd thought. People would be drawn to him, impressed and charmed. Other demons had become CEOs and senators—how high could Timms go?

I turned off the road and parked near the ravine that led to the wellspring.

Yes, there—the black SUV was parked on the left. I jumped out with my staff, prepared to fight the hiding enchantments around the wellspring, but discovering they were gone. Instead of brambles and overgrown bushes, now there was a paved walkway leading from where the SUV was parked down a gentle slope through the redwoods to the flooded ravine below. The wellspring was around a curve in the creek bed.

Did Timms know I was following, or was he too busy with his immediate task?

I hurried down the path, casting protective spells around me, scanning the area. The fairies in the trees seemed to be smoking. Their small dots of light were now gray, hazy, and motionless.

As Timms had moved past, he'd consumed them like a whale eating krill. The energy force of multiple fairies was necessary to maintain the possession. The unnatural effort would drain both human and demon, especially at the start. That's why he'd come to the wellspring: concentrated healing power for both of them. Large numbers of fairies for the demon and wellspring water for the human.

Hearing the rumble of a motorcycle on the road, I broke into a jog. From up ahead I heard splashing and the sound of a man's voice singing opera.

Another engine—a car—followed the motorcycle. Lights reflected off the trees, then went dark.

Both Kelly and Raynor had caught up to me.

❧ 44 ❧

I had to stop Timms before they stopped me.

I turned the bend in the path and saw the wellspring lit up like a hotel hot tub. Standing in the middle of it was Timms in his button-down shirt and khakis, playing with the water with childish glee, splashing and smacking the surface.

Recently I'd exorcised a demon from a local girl, an act which I hadn't known I'd be able to do until I'd done it. With that accomplishment in mind, I lifted my staff, put my hand on my necklace, and prepared to do the same to whatever creature was inside Timms.

But Timms wasn't a teenage sales associate at the local big-box store; he was an Emerald witch with decades of experience. He glanced up from his splashing and blasted my feet out from under me with... with nothing that I could see. It just happened. One moment I was aiming my staff, the next I was sliding into the water at high speed. I lost my grip on the carved wood and tumbled under the cold, murky water in my boots and jeans and heavy coat. Magical hands pulled at me when I tried to rise, then pushed me over after I managed to get one breath.

Was this going to be how I died? I'd run right into it. The wellspring didn't hold the same healing powers for me as it did for others—I could easily drown here.

I kicked off the rocky bottom and broke my head above the water. Timms stood a few feet away. No longer splashing or laughing like a child, he stood with his arms over his chest, regarding me with paternal disapproval.

"I'm going to need your help with this one, Protector," Timms said. "I've been watching her. I'm afraid my suspicions were true. She's been exploiting the wellspring."

I looked behind me and saw Kelly and Raynor standing on the bank. Raynor didn't seem to be paying Timms any attention, but Kelly was. She grabbed Raynor's arm and pointed at me in the water.

"Listen to the Director, honey," she said. "He needs your help with Alma."

Raynor gave Kelly a beatific smile, then looked reluctantly over at me. "Alma?"

"You're going to capture her," Kelly repeated. "For the Director."

Raynor's smile didn't falter. "Sure," he said, lifting a finger and pointing it at me.

I dove under the water. The wellspring's magic would deflect any spells—at least I hoped it would. Under the surface, the water was bright and clear, giving me a clear view of Timms' wet khakis and loafers standing on the pebbled bottom.

So many witches forgot about their feet. I hoped a possessed one wouldn't be any better.

As my head ached with holding my breath, I cast out a spell at the gap between the floating fabric of his pants and his exposed ankles, directing it through the skin, under his personal protective spells, into his flesh and muscle, bone and blood.

Although a demon possessed him, Timms was still dependent upon the body. Chest aching, I shot a barbed spell at him, not able to tell it what to do in particular, just wanting to break his concentration.

Then I cast a quick blinding spell to pop above the water, sucked in a breath—sparks flew around me—and went back down again.

Timms' legs had changed. My spell had broken through somehow. Now he had the calves of a child. Then a horse, a woman, a child again. The past lives of the demon were on display. Then he was a man again, this time with black pants. And then...

To stop myself from floating to the surface, I grabbed a stick wedged between some stones on the bottom of the pool.

As I watched, my lungs burning, the fabric of a white wedding dress appeared in the water before me. The legs were a woman's legs, and the toenails were adorned with a French pedicure.

How many demons did I know that had just posed as a bride? That had a tendency to linger near Silverpool?

I let go of the stick, shot to the surface, and gasped for breath. "Vera?"

Timms—or was it my father's former bride?—ignored me. Above the surface he looked just like the magical bureaucrat he always had.

I turned and saw Raynor was thankfully obsessed with Kelly again, kissing her cheek and stroking her hair, my criminal presence in the forbidden wellspring forgotten. Kelly however, was trying to get him to attack me.

"I've sensed her here before," Kelly told him. "What

other laws has she broken? We don't want her here in Silver-pool. Stop kissing— Listen to me. Ray— Please."

I turned back to Timms. "Vera? It's me, Alma." I took a step closer, searching his face for any flicker of recognition. "Poppy's daughter. Remember Poppy? And Malcolm. Malcolm was my dad. You loved him. Vera? Please."

Timms stared blankly for a moment. Then he hunched over and scooped wellspring water into his cupped hands, drank it, rubbed his face in it, did it again.

Behind me, Raynor was telling Kelly how lovely her hair was in the glow of the wellspring, and she was telling him to shut up.

I saw my redwood staff floating in the water and grabbed it. Casting my senses into the magic of the wood and the water around me, I tried again to break through Timms' dominant human consciousness. "Vera. Vera Vanders. It's me. Alma. Please. Alma Bellrose. You—"

You gave birth to me, I thought.

But no. She hadn't. That was my real mother, Poppy Almasi. The one Lionel had told me about. She was my mother.

"Now, Raynor," Kelly said. "Strike her down so we can be together."

I glanced over my shoulder, alarmed to see Kelly's latest argument had gotten through to him and he was now turning to me.

Shivering with cold and panic, I began to walk backward toward the bank. Since drinking from the pool, Timms had become more serious, more terrifying. He gave me a nasty, subdued smile and touched a gold chain around his neck. A hum of power began to encircle his head.

"Vera!" I shouted. "It's me, Alma. Please! Please help me! The man you're inside of is about to kill me."

Timms struck my right shoulder with a current of energy

at the same time Raynor struck the surface of the water beside me. It bounced off and hit my hair; dried by magic, it immediately caught on fire.

I dropped under the water to extinguish the blaze, watching Timms' legs for signs of another attack.

The wedding dress was still there. Now I recognized the details of the unusual dress Vera Vanders, my—my mother— had chosen. The Grecian toga styling, almost angelic...

Using my staff as leverage, I rose to the surface again, sucked in a breath, and cried out, "Mother. Please help me. Please." I began to cry. *"Mommy."*

I'd never called her that before. I'd sworn to myself I never would. But...

Things changed.

Timms tilted his head, lowered his arms, and gave me a tender smile. "Hello, darling. It's so nice to see you again. Should you really be swimming outside in December?"

✣ 45 ✣

My relief faded fast. The nauseating sound of sizzling magic made me spin around to see Raynor aiming a silver knife at me. Before I could react, his hex struck me in the chest and knocked me into the water again.

I lost my vision for a moment as the cold pool swallowed me whole. My waterlogged clothes dragged my stunned body to the rocky bottom where the stick I'd held earlier poked me in the back of the head.

The surface above me flashed with green light, then white. I focused on holding my breath until my head cleared.

No wonder Raynor had been the most famous demon hunter of his generation. That was the most devastating hex I'd ever experienced. I was pretty sure my name was Alma Bellrose, but a few strong words could've convinced me otherwise. Was I dead? My lungs hurt from holding my breath, so I hoped that meant I was still alive.

A woman's arm reached down and lifted me up. Above the surface, it was Timms' face who smiled at me. "Poor honey, let's get you out of the water."

I sagged against her-him and looked over at Raynor, flinching when I saw he was still pointing his finger at me. Kelly was hanging on his jacket, pinching his cheeks, trying to get him to move, but he appeared to be frozen solid.

"Don't worry about the big handsome one," Vera-Timms said. "His mind was scrambled."

"Was or is?" I asked, alarmed to think Raynor's enchantment might be permanent.

"We'll see," Vera-Timms said.

I splashed through the water over to the bank and climbed out. Timms' voice changed from making gentle, nurturing noises to a grunt and a curse. He'd subdued Vera's control over his mind.

"Raynor, she— Strike her!" Timms rasped.

I scrambled away from the pool and shot a quick look at Raynor. His limbs were moving again, and he'd turned his head to look at Kelly.

"Hello, sweetheart," he said.

Kelly put her hand on his cheek and slapped it. "Not me, buddy. The witch over there. Alma. Get Alma."

Ignoring her command, he continued to smile at her. "You're so beautiful," he said. "I can't stop looking at you."

"You have to!" She slapped him again. "Look at—"

An invisible force lifted Kelly from the ground, pulling her away from Raynor. He reached for her, but she was just out of range.

Kicking and punching the air, Kelly craned her neck around to gape at me. "Are you doing this?"

I looked at Vera-Timms, now standing on the bank next to me. The business casual clothing was dry, clean, and perfectly pressed. Had Timms fought off Vera's mind control? "Director?" I asked.

"It's me, honey," Vera-Timms said. "I think it's safer for

the woman to be out of reach right now, don't you think? The big one has a strong enchantment over him."

I nodded. "It's coming from her, the one in the air."

"I don't think so," Vera-Timms said. "It seems to be coming from inside this man. Timms. That is, me."

Ah, that's why the hex over Raynor had been so sudden, so strong. That might make Raynor feel better later to know a Protectorate Emerald, his boss, had been the one with enough power to take over his mind—and not his girlfriend.

Raynor continued to reach for Kelly, still dangling just above him.

"Free him," I said. "Break it now."

"You don't think it's romantic?" Vera-Timms asked. "He'd die for her."

"That's not romance, that's horror," I said. "Break it!"

"If you're sure, but—" Vera-Timms shuddered. I looked at Raynor, who continued to gaze lovingly at Kelly.

"But what?" I asked.

Vera-Timms stumbled over to me and gripped my shoulder. "Give me a little of your strength, would you, hon? He's fighting—" The fingers dug in to the bone.

"I'm trying," I said as needling pain shot down my spine.

"I've... waited... too... long," Vera-Timms said, the voice low and male again. "No! I'm not— This isn't how— This isn't what—"

The sharp pain in my shoulder began to burn. I put my hand over Vera-Timms, closed my eyes, and imagined the woman I'd met in San Francisco as my father's future bride. She'd been kind to me, and I'd liked her, not knowing who or what she was.

"Hang on, Mom," I said.

Vera-Timms' eyes widened. The fingers loosened on my shoulder. The face looking at me was kind again.

"If I break that spell on your friend," Vera-Timms said in

a soft voice, "I'll only have a few minutes left. I'm… weak. Even with… the water. Even with the fairies."

Alarmed, I looked at Raynor. If I told Vera to free him, she might be too weak to control Timms afterward.

I had no choice. Raynor was being tortured. "Do it," I said.

Vera-Timms reached out for me. "Give me your strength again."

I accepted her embrace, trusting her not to give me over to Timms.

A moment later, Raynor shouted. "What in Brightness have you done to me?" He spun around, addressing everyone in sight.

Timms' body leaned against mine. The clothes were wet again, the hair damp and straggly.

"Are you OK?" I whispered.

"Are you sleeping enough?" the male voice asked.

"Sure," I said. "Of course."

"Don't lie to your mother."

I smiled but felt like crying. "Now I need you to turn yourself in," I said. "Tell Raynor you killed Joanna Morrow. They'll get the rest out of him later."

"She's not the only one he killed," Vera-Timms said, making a face. "I remember others."

"They'll learn about them all," I said. "But first Raynor needs to get silver cuffs on you."

Raynor was now aiming a hex at Kelly. "You did this to me. Payback time, darling," he said.

"Raynor, wait!" I guided Vera-Timms across the muddy bank to him. "The Director has something to tell you."

"I am a very bad man," Vera-Timms said. "I'm the one who pickled your brains. You should punish me, not her."

"Tell him about the murder," I said.

"I killed people too," Vera-Timms said. "And just a few

minutes ago, I devoured fifty-two delicious fairy spirits. Their light will never shine again."

Raynor looked between Vera-Timms, Kelly, and me, not sure who to yell at first. "What?"

"Director Timms is responsible for the murder of Joanna Morrow," I said. "He's confessing."

"What did he say about my brains?" Raynor asked.

"It's true," I said. "Timms also cast the love charm that made you crazy about Kelly. I guess he knew it would keep you out of his way."

"He was enchanted with me before that," Kelly said. "I don't need magic to make a man desire me."

"Were you working with him?" I asked her. "You and Timms? He'd kill, you'd steal?"

She flapped her arms and kicked the air in outrage. "I had no idea he was killing people. Besides, I always work alone." Then she looked down at Raynor with a worried smile. "Not that I've been working on *anything* at the moment. I'm with you because I love you. It has nothing to do with you being relocated to Silverpool during the solstice."

Maybe Kelly had loved Raynor, but I thought she'd loved the access to illegal trading in Silverpool more. "I think you should stop talking," I told her.

"Why did Timms—" Raynor began.

Under my arm, Timms' body began to spasm, suggesting a battle for his mind and body was raging.

"Cuff him, for Brightness' sake," I said. "He's dangerous. Ask questions later."

Raynor looked happy to hurt somebody, even the man who'd been his boss—or especially him—and within three seconds he'd wrapped silver handcuffs around Timms' wrists and locked them behind his back.

Or *her* back. Was Vera still in there?

"Where's Darius?" Raynor asked, looking around.

I suddenly remembered the demon assault at the campground. "We've got to go help him," I said quickly. "Timms broke the boundary near the campground."

"Oh dear," Vera-Timms said. "Be careful."

Raynor's face twisted in outrage. "Be careful? What——"

"We will. Goodbye," I said.

"Mother," she said.

I hesitated. "Mother."

"Or Mommy," she added.

I wrapped my arms around myself, suddenly aware of how cold and wet I was. "Maybe next time," I said, my teeth chattering.

Timms collapsed face-first in the bank. I felt a soft, balmy wind pass through me, warming my bones and spirit.

She was gone.

❧ 46 ❧

With Vera gone, Kelly Tucker fell from her enchanted prison in the air and landed behind Raynor in the mud. She jumped up and began to run, but the thorny branch of one of the blackberry bushes whipped out and wrapped around both her legs.

Raynor, who had spelled the blackberry, spun to face me. "You're going to explain this," he said, his hands up for battle.

Timms groaned at his feet and struggled to get up but was too weak without the use of his arms.

"First we have to help Darius," I said. "The town is being invaded from the west."

"We can't do that until we deal with these two." Raynor put his boot on Timms' back and pressed him into the ground. A visible bolt of energy sizzled down his leg and surrounded Timms in a blinding white light. It must've been painful, because he began whimpering.

"Raynor, no. We can put him in the car," I said.

"Flight risk," Raynor said. Another bolt of energy, a scream—and then silence. Timms was still.

"It's a Protectorate vehicle," I said. "Prepped for prisoners. Neither one of them will be able to get out. Let's go." At that very moment, Darius could be surrounded by possessed witches coming at him like zombies at the end of the world.

Leaving Timms motionless on the ground, Raynor turned to Kelly and began walking slowly toward her. "And *you*," he said.

Sprawled on the ground, she kicked at the brambles wrapped around her legs. "I love you. Baby, I love you. You know that! So much. I love you so—"

He held up one hand and formed a claw, fingernails pointing up. "You. Hexed. Me."

"I didn't! That was him! The Director!"

"You knew," he said. "You must've known."

"No!" She flung slicing spells at the branches, but they bounced off. "Love is mysterious. Anything can happen. The heart—"

He lifted his other hand and formed a second claw. "You allowed it to happen."

"How could I stop him?" she cried. "He's an Emerald. He's like you! I'm just—"

"Don't." Raynor brought his hands together, fingertips touching, then lifted his arms. Kelly rose from the ground. The branches fell away, but invisible bars kept her in a crouching position. He'd used the remainder of the spell Timms had put her in. "Alma, I need you to put her in the car. I don't trust myself."

I rushed over, digging my staff into the earth for the extra strength. "Got it." I found the fringe of his magic in the air and eased myself into it, taking it over for myself. "Now get Timms. We have to hurry. He broke the boundary spell on the highway. Demons are flooding into town. There's smoke everywhere. Everywhere. Darius is trying— He's waiting—"

"It's OK, Alma," Raynor said, interrupting my panic. "We're going."

We dragged the prisoners up the steep, wooded bank to the cars. With the demon's power gone, the Protectorate enchantments had returned. I was grateful Kelly wasn't putting up a fight, which would've made her harder to control. She sat cross-legged in her invisible cage and cried, which I think was for Raynor's benefit. She had to know she was lucky he hadn't blasted her head off. I was feeling like crying myself.

The Protectorate SUV that Timms had driven to the wellspring was designed to hold witch captives: black velvet seats in the back, copper buckles on the velvet seat belts, silver trim around the windows, and boundary spells between seats. After Raynor unlocked the door for me, I tugged Kelly inside like a balloon, pulled the seat belt over her lap, then broke my hold on the spell.

Raynor dropped Timms, still unconscious, into the seat next to Kelly. To hold him upright, Raynor slung a steel chain around his chest and under his arms, then attached it behind the headrest with an iron padlock.

The SUV's engine turned on.

"You drive," Raynor said to me. "I'll keep an eye on these two."

Reluctantly, I got behind the wheel. Driving the Protectorate SUVs had never been my favorite job because they were so huge; it always felt like maneuvering an aircraft carrier. But my attitude soon changed when I slipped my staff under the seat and felt something hard and smooth. It wasn't metal or stone, but it—leather, paper, ink—sizzled against my fingers.

Glancing at Raynor, whose attention was on the prisoners on the back, I lifted the book and slid it under my shirt with the poise of a former child thief. Heart pounding, I began to drive.

The Protectorate loved to hoard things. It was in their nature. Sooner or later, a curious Flint or Emerald would want to experiment with *Instructions*, and the infamous book would go missing. Another demon would be summoned. Perhaps another child would grow up motherless.

I'd make sure that didn't happen.

Kelly continued to cry until Raynor suggested she'd be happier on the roof. In my rearview mirror, Timms looked pale as death, and I wondered if he'd survive.

I was getting extra familiar with the road between the wellspring and the campground. Hyperventilating about Darius, I took the twists and turns at full speed. When I pulled over next to one of the visiting witch's cars, the campground was in upheaval: oversized campfires illuminated clouds of smoke in gray, green, and pink. Between them, witches flung spells against invisible assailants.

The moment I'd parked, Raynor and I jumped out of the SUV. I wiggled around, wedging the book under the waistband of my jeans.

"Do you see him?" I waved my staff at the field, the surrounding forest, the road, even up at the sky, trying to enhance my vision. The smoke was everywhere, but especially in the forest where the fae gathered.

Raynor took a narrow copper pipe I'd never seen before out of his jacket. The ends had been crimped shut, probably to hold an enhancing substance of some kind—iron filings, aluminum foil, gemstones. He held it out and pointed it at the field, rolling it between his fingers, and a pale blue light glowed around his hand.

It seemed to work better than my staff had. "That way," Raynor said. "He's doing all right now, but he'll need help in... three minutes, I'd say." He lowered the wand and looked at the road. "Where do you think Timms broke the boundary?"

I pointed west. "Top of the hill. We were chasing him. He didn't have time to go off the road."

"I'll close the gap. That should draw the demons back out. They don't want to be trapped." He kicked the SUV's rear tire. Light shimmered along the bumpers, locking the prisoners inside. "You help Darius."

"Right." I was terrified of him leaving us but knew he had to. "Good luck."

Tapping into my own magic, I ran in the direction Raynor had pointed, unable to see more than several feet ahead. The book was large enough to be awkward on my hip, but not so large to prevent me from running. The campfires provided light, but everything was shrouded by smoke and defensive hiding spells. All demons would consume the fairies for their spiritual energy, but some would try to possess human beings—especially if they'd been invited. The witches who had come here, so curious about Shadow, had no idea what danger they were in.

It was annoying to have to defend the lives of witches who had brought death to Silverpool, but it was the only way to stop the mayhem.

As I moved through the smoke, I saw a group of witch campers, a dozen at most, had gathered in a large ring around the yellow tent.

And inside the Circle stood Darius with another man.

❧ 47 ❧

I ran faster, tapping into my magic to fight. Darius looked all right now, but I couldn't see what was happening under the surface. Was a possession already underway?

I realized suddenly how quiet it was. There was smoke and blinding flames, but none of the crackling and popping of a natural wood fire. The wind, too, was silent.

One of the bonfires illuminated the faces of the witches forming the Circle. Their expressions were suspicious and afraid, but not deranged. One lifted a pewter cup and shook it at me, but her neighbor, an older bald man, pushed her hand down.

"She's with him," he said.

"What are you doing?" I demanded.

"Shielding them," the bald man said. "We didn't know what else to do. He's trying to help Brayden."

Inside the Circle, Darius was holding the man who I now saw was Trudy's hapless boyfriend. His mouth was wide with terror.

"Let me in," I told the bald man, holding up my staff.

After a pause, he nodded and released the hand of his neighbor.

Pulse racing, I stepped over the boundary. All at once, the sound of a man's screams split my ears. I felt the Shadow surrounding Brayden. Darius was trying to expel the demon, but they were locked in a stalemate. Brayden, mouth and eyes wide, was trying to lift his hands, but Darius stopped him.

"I'm here," I said.

Darius shot me a relieved but frustrated look. "Help me hold his arms. He keeps trying to hit himself in the face."

"He's trying to hit the demon," I said.

"Yeah, well, not working," Darius said.

"Give me his hand," I said, reaching out.

Darius gripped one of Brayden's wrists and thrust it at me, but it kept flopping and flailing. I grabbed his hand, pressed it against my staff, and felt a blast of sticky, hot darkness climb into my heart.

"He's... possessed," I gasped. Then I gritted my teeth, closed my eyes, and reached deep into my well of power for the feel of a clean, transparent magic that would repel the Shadow.

Brayden stopped screaming. Panting, he managed to swing his head around and look at me. "What did you— Ah!" He let out another scream.

I tried again, this time intentionally remembering the other demons I'd exorcised. There had only been two, actually, and one of those times I'd had Raynor's help, but I knew what it felt like, and I was motivated.

The thread of sticky Shadow was clinging to Brayden's mouth, of all places. I sensed the demon between his open teeth, clinging to the flecks of spit and terror.

I had a strange impulse which at first I dismissed as

repulsive. But it was always best to go with the subconscious when fighting a demon at midnight under a moonless sky.

And so I kissed him.

"Alma?" Darius asked.

I didn't linger. Just the press of my lips against Brayden's was enough to snap the hold the unnatural spirit had inside his body. And when the demon, expelled from its host, tried to dig its hot, nasty talons into me, I blew it away from me as if it were dandelion fluff.

Easy.

"Open the Circle," I shouted. "The demon departs."

The witches hesitated, but Darius pushed through. Then all nine witches dropped their hands and dropped to one knee, and a hot wind blasted out like a mushroom cloud. Brayden fell to the ground and curled up in a ball.

"Look! They're leaving," Darius said.

All across the campground, the smoke was forming an iridescent river about chest high and moving toward Raynor.

"He's closing the boundary," I said. "He said they'd rush to get out so they wouldn't be trapped."

Darius wiped his forehead. "For Brightness' sake, he better make sure he lets them all out. That one nearly got me."

"I'm sorry it took so long to get back," I said.

"Got Timms?"

"In the SUV," I said.

He nodded. "Kelly?"

"With him," I said.

"Good," Darius said, swaying on his feet. "Excuse me." He sank to his knees, then collapsed on the ground next to Brayden.

❦ 48 ❦

I sat on the ground next to Darius, making sure he was breathing steadily while I waited for Raynor to return.

The other witches, realizing they'd escaped death and disaster, but that the Protector was about to return and make their lives miserable in a different way, began rushing for their campers, cars, and trucks to leave before he got back.

I didn't try to stop them. In fact, I was tempted to join them. Already exhausted, I was dreading the inevitable trip to San Francisco to be interrogated at Diamond Street about what had happened *this* time in Silverpool. Dawn was only a few hours away. When would I sleep? It could be days before the Protectorate was satisfied and let me go home.

They'd want to know about Timms. I'd tell them he'd dreamed of being possessed by a demon so he could be more interesting. How he'd gone to the meeting in Berkeley to pay Trudy, a book trader on the Shadow market, for *Instructions*, the infamous third book of the possession trilogy.

They would ask "Why had he killed Lionel, then, if he'd already found the book he wanted?" Some Emerald witch would probably hold me in the air with a nasty spell that made me feel nauseated, just to confirm I was telling the truth.

I'd tell them Lionel had seen through his disguise, as he'd seen through mine, and Timms couldn't risk having him tell others about his plans to be possessed by a demon.

Lionel, however, had narrowly avoided death by trading his spirit with that of his old cat, Frank, and Timms had killed his body but not his mind. The next morning, Timms discovered the corpse was a decoy, so he had all the cats rounded up and put into cages. To avoid capture, Lionel snuggled up to me, and I brought him to Silverpool.

Timms then proceeded with his plan to get *Instructions* from Trudy in Silverpool during the solstice. Amid crowds of witches and magical chaos, Timms believed the trade could be made more safely than anywhere near San Francisco—and as a new Director, he had an official reason to be there.

The interrogator would stop me there and demand to know how I knew what Timms believed. Had he ever spoken to me?

I would have to say no, but his behavior strongly suggested it. Why else had he come to Silverpool when he had an important murder investigation going on hours away in Berkeley? A famously powerful witch, Raynor, was already in Silverpool to deal with the annual threat. Timms had just arrived in San Francisco, and it just didn't make sense he'd come to Silverpool right away unless he had other motives.

The Emerald interrogator would point out how another witch had been killed. I'd point out Joanna Morrow—I'd mention her name so they didn't forget it—was a human being with a curiosity for demon possession and a fondness for cats, and her murderer deserved to be punished. Lionel had survived Timms' evil actions, but Joanna hadn't.

The interrogator would insist Joanna wasn't entirely

Bright herself, that she'd collected many books on possession. Her car was loaded with Shadowed texts. How could I be sure a demon hadn't killed her?

Stupid questions like those were one reason I didn't miss working for the Protectorate. I'd explain that Trudy had arranged for Timms to pick up *Instructions* from an unmarked shelf in Birdie's bookstore—a perfect hiding place for a magic book—but that Joanna had found it. When Timms came to collect the book, Joanna confronted him, and he killed her.

I wouldn't tell them about the curse, because then they'd learn I had *Warnings* and take it from me. But for a brief period, just before killing Joanna, Timms had owned books two and three at the same time—sealing his fate.

Or maybe it had been me and Darius who had made sure of that.

Anyway, they would tell me about the theory that Joanna had killed Lionel and taken a different book, *Temptations* (which wasn't a romance novel), later found near her corpse.

I'd tell them that obviously Timms had stolen that book from Lionel and planted it near her to implicate her, not him, in his murder.

The Protectorate interrogators would believe me, because Lionel would back me up, but they'd pretend they didn't just to hold on to me longer and show off their authority.

It would all be a huge waste of time and effort. And poor Raynor—how humiliating for him to admit Timms had used his girlfriend as an enchantment hex to neutralize him. When the Protectorate learned about that, they'd never let him be Director again. He might even lose his job as Protector. Darius, his fate tied to Raynor, would also find his career coming to a halt. He might end up joining his sister Rochelle at the family accounting business, hating life forever.

As I imagined this unhappy ending, still waiting for

Raynor to return from closing up the boundary spell at the outskirts of Silverpool, I looked down at Darius' unconscious body. Brayden, his nose pressing into the mud, looked even worse than Darius—but at least he deserved it. He and Trudy had wanted demon possession enough to bring havoc upon themselves and others.

"It's not right," I said aloud.

"Totally agree," Seth said.

I turned, surprised though I shouldn't have been, to see him sitting at my side. He handed me a cup of something hot.

"Spearmint tea," he said.

I smiled and took it. "Thank you." It was made with springwater, but I didn't mind.

"I can help you if you let me," he said.

"I was surprised you didn't intervene earlier."

"Raynor's girlfriend did come by on her motorcycle, but I sent her back to the winery," he said. "She didn't mean any harm. Lonely, mostly."

"Lonely?" I asked with a snort. She'd allowed Raynor's mind to be taken from him.

"Like so many of us."

I bumped my arm against his and sipped the tea. "True enough."

"Speaking of which, your gnome friend is bummed about his wife going back to the old country."

I choked on the tea. "What? No, his wife is dead. Olive is…"

"His wife. Gone again," Seth said. "Mr. Willow did his best, but she wasn't buying it. California couldn't compete with the homeland, wherever that is. He wants to stay here, she wants to stay there. It's a stalemate."

"I don't believe it," I said. "He sings songs about his dead wife that go on for hours."

"As you know, death isn't always what it seems."

I thought about that. "Joanna really is dead. That's real."

"I am sorry about your cat sister." He put an arm around me.

I hesitated, then sank against him, grateful for the comfort. He was strong, warm, and smelled like men's cologne and cinnamon rolls.

A long sigh escaped me. What could be better than that?

"Let me bring you home," he said, brushing the hair off my forehead.

I smiled and closed my eyes, enjoying the idea of just disappearing from my troubles. Raynor would be back any minute. "Just like that?"

"Nobody has to remember you were here," he whispered in my ear.

I laughed. "Right."

"I'm sure Raynor would love to forget a few things," he said.

I drew back and looked at him. "You're serious."

"Of course, sweetheart. Your role can easily be forgotten. Darius and Raynor will be happy to take all the credit."

"And I don't have to go to San Francisco tonight? Because I was just in Berkeley a few hours ago, and I'm tired. I don't want to deal with those stupid witches tonight."

Seth pulled me close and pressed his warm, soft lips against mine.

"Done," he whispered.

EPILOGUE

Two weeks later, I was helping Birdie in the bookstore.

"Put it over there," she said, pointing at the empty wall behind me.

I gave the heavy bookshelf a kick. "It weighs more than you and me put together," I said. "Do I look like I could lift that much? I'm not Raynor."

"Use your magic. I noticed you've got a new tattoo on your arm. That means you're getting stronger," Birdie said.

I tugged the sleeve of my sweater down to my wrist. After the night of Timms' capture, I'd discovered a new black ring on my arm, leaving me with five arcs, like tree rings, under my bracelets. The cold weather had made it easy to hide them, but come summer, I'd have to devise a spell to cover them more consistently.

"They don't give me the power to lift hundreds of pounds," I said. "In fact, they don't give me power at all—"

Birdie waved aside all my claims of weakness. "Ask Seth to come over. I bet he could do all kinds of amazing things, lifting and moving and wiggling and pushing and all that stuff." She winked.

I stepped away from the shelf. "You've got the wrong idea about—about so many things."

"Do I?" She pushed aside one of the many boxes of books Darius and a few other agents had brought up from Trudy's house in Berkeley. Reassigned to his former job in San Francisco, Darius hadn't stayed in Silverpool any longer than the fifteen minutes it had taken to drop off the books and leave again.

Raynor, restored as Director, had made a deal with the young Shadow-market book dealer: give all her books to Birdie and she could walk away with only a warning. Keep them, and she'd be sunbathing in Death Valley with Edward Timms.

Birdie suddenly had twenty times her original inventory. And although the winter solstice tourists were gone, the rumors about the holiday demon mayhem had drawn new curious witches to town every weekend—and they, with little else to do in Silverpool, were coming to the most welcoming store in town.

Birdie, who didn't even need the money, was making a killing. Used books in the witch world carried a higher price tag than new, sometimes much higher.

Much, much higher.

"Do you think I spent too much on these walnut book-shelves?" Birdie asked, stroking the beautifully aged wood of a low shelf in front of the window. She'd arranged a display of metalworking books on top facing the sidewalk.

I was glad she'd dropped the Seth conversation. "Not at all. It's powerful timber. It'll pay for itself within the month," I said. "I feel the urge to buy the books you put on it, and I don't even like the metal arts."

"You're more into crunchy, earthy stuff," she said.

Why did the word *crunchy* always get associated with hearth magic? I hadn't eaten granola in years. "I like magic that's mysterious, powerful, and warm," I said.

"Like Seth." She grinned.

This was getting difficult to avoid talking about. I'd been trying for weeks to keep... *it*... a secret. I dipped into my new redwood bead necklace and used my enhanced strength to drag the heavy bookshelf to the wall.

"You can't fool me," Birdie said. "The cat's out of the bag."

"Speaking of cats in bags," I said, "Frank's former kitty family is back home at their house in Berkeley. That witch who gave you all these books—"

"The one who took Frank?"

"Trudy didn't know she'd taken Frank," I said. "He hitched a ride."

"But she was bad, right?"

I shrugged. There but for the grace of Brightness... I might've ended up in Trudy's place. Like me, she'd had parents who'd taught her the Shadowed business of thieving and fencing illicit goods. "Trudy's making amends. She found all the cats Timms had locked up, nurtured them back to health, and returned them to Lionel. She's thinking about starting a magical cat rescue with her boyfriend."

Brayden had stood by her as long as she swore off demons. His one taste of possession had cured him of his curiosity.

"I thought Frank—Lionel—has to live as a cat most of the time now," she said.

The old witch had never fully recovered from Timms' attack. "He's got help at the house," I said. "Darius' sister Rochelle has moved in. In exchange for... her guardian-ship... she gets the property when he passes on."

"I hope she likes cats," Birdie said.

I smiled. "She likes them more than accounting." Darius had been right about his sister; she'd started missing the Protectorate a week after giving notice. When Raynor regained his Directorship, he'd rehired her. Rochelle had to put up with her brother being smug about it, but she'd already started redecorating the big house. "Lionel spends most of his days as Frank, sitting in the sun. He says he's never been happier. Witches chasing demon possession don't realize how good cats have it, he said, or they'd just do that instead."

"I wish I could shape-shift into a cat," she said. "Why didn't you tell me before you could do that? It's so cool."

"You didn't know anything about magic or witches," I said. "And then... I don't know. I can be a little overprotective of my privacy sometimes."

Birdie laughed and punched me in the shoulder. With her increased magical powers, her fist landed with a painful sizzle on my bicep. "No kidding."

"Sorry," I said.

"We're friends, right?"

She paused and stared at me, and I realized she was seriously asking.

"Of course," I said.

"Then why do you keep hiding things from me?"

"I really am sorry I didn't tell you about shifting—"

"Hello," Birdie said, hitting me again. "That's not what I'm talking about."

I rubbed the sore spot on my arm, feeling my face redden, avoiding her gaze.

"When did you two start getting it on?" she continued.

"Hey, watch your language."

She lifted her arm to hit me again, but I darted out of range. "The best friend needs to hear the good stuff, not just the bad," she said, chasing after me.

I ran across the store and put the couch between us. "It isn't what you think," I said, short of breath.

"It's exactly what I think." She strode after me with her hand raised, prepared to hex me with—

"You're not going to use a truth spell on me!" I cried.

"Like Shadow I'm not." She flung the spell at me.

I dropped behind the couch, laughing but terrified. I was *not* ready to talk about Seth with her or anyone. Whatever was going on was too new, too strange, and too...

Magical.

She blasted another spell above my head. Sparks of magic rained down on me like snow.

I cast a protective shield around myself, but it was her store, and my barrier was relatively weak. At best it would buy me a few minutes. "I promise I'll tell you about it when I'm ready," I called out.

The truth spell was in my hair, sneaking past my defenses.

"Promise?" Birdie asked.

"Promise," I said with a sigh, feeling the binding power of her magic twist around my heart and tongue. I sat panting on the floor behind the couch for a long moment.

Finally she said, "OK. Just so you understand how it works. You tell me the good stuff, I tell you the good stuff, but because at the moment I don't have anything juicy like that to keep me going, so you've got a responsibility to spill, understand?"

"Understand," I said.

"For a while I thought you were going to hook up with Raynor because, well, obviously, look at him, but then he showed up with that girlfriend," she said.

I peeked out from behind the couch. "Can I come out now?"

She waved at me to rise—the boss of her domain, a witch

in her home. "What happened to her, anyway? The hot motorcycle chick?"

"They broke up." I'd happily made a promise to Raynor not to share with anyone how utterly he'd been enchanted with Kelly Tucker. With Raynor regaining his power as Director, she'd managed to keep her demonprint a secret from the Protectorate, but only under the Emerald-binding condition that she leave California and never come back. I was surprised Raynor hadn't done worse to her, but… love was filled with mysteries.

"I'm surprised," Birdie said. "He was crazy about her."

I shrugged.

"You're keeping secrets from me again," she said.

"Not my own."

"I guess that's all right," she said, "as long as you don't make a habit out of it."

I thought of a few deep secrets I still had—why Cypress Hardware always had exactly what the customers wanted, how I'd hidden an infamous magic book and jade gargoyle in my filing cabinet, how I felt about my demon mother, what Seth had said to me late last night under the stars.

"I promise to share what I can," I said, "when I'm ready."

Birdie came around the couch with her arms extended. Thinking she was going to hug me, I dropped my defenses—and then she punched me again.

"You better," she said.

ABOUT THE AUTHOR

GRETCHEN GALWAY is a *USA Today* bestselling author who writes mystery, fantasy, and romance. Raised in the American Midwest, she now lives in in Sonoma County, California.

For more information:
www.gretchengalway.com
gretchen@gretchengalway.com

Made in the USA
Middletown, DE
25 February 2021

34228807R10198